OVER THE THRESHOLD

She breathed an abbreviated sigh. Finally, she would be able to loosen her laces—except she didn't have a single stitch of clothes here.

Oh, my goodness! She couldn't get out of the overly tight laces with nothing to wear. She pivoted and slammed into Sterling's chest. "I have to go home."

"Mary, you are home." He wrapped one arm around her and reached behind her to unlock the door.

"I don't have any clothes here. I need just a few things."

"No, you don't. Not tonight." He scooped her up with one arm under her knees and one arm behind her shoulders.

Alarmed, she clutched his shoulders while her head spun from a lack of oxygen. "I can't stay in this dress any longer."

"Good." Sterling kicked the door shut behind him.

Oh! He meant to . . . they would . . . consummate their marriage. Oh, heavens. In all the anxiety of the day she had tried only to get through each minute as it came. She hadn't really thought about the wedding night. "It's still light out."

"You prefer the dark?" He grinned down at her.

She was mesmerized by his deep dimples and the amusement in his eyes. "Yes, no. I don't know."

He carried her still, but they hadn't moved to the stairs. They would need a bed, wouldn't they? Lord, she didn't even have anything to sleep in.

—From *Silver and Satin* by Karen L. King

BOOK YOUR PLACE ON OUR WEBSITE AND MAKE THE READING CONNECTION!

We've created a customized website just for our very special readers, where you can get the inside scoop on everything that's going on with Zebra, Pinnacle and Kensington books.

When you come online, you'll have the exciting opportunity to:

- View covers of upcoming books
- Read sample chapters
- Learn about our future publishing schedule (listed by publication month *and author*)
- Find out when your favorite authors will be visiting a city near you
- Search for and order backlist books from our online catalog
- Check out author bios and background information
- Send e-mail to your favorite authors
- Meet the Kensington staff online
- Join us in weekly chats with authors, readers and other guests
- Get writing guidelines
- AND MUCH MORE!

Visit our website at
http://www.kensingtonbooks.com

Going to the Chapel

Caroline Clemmons

Yvonne Jocks

Karen L. King

ZEBRA BOOKS
Kensington Publishing Corp.
http://www.kensingtonbooks.com

ZEBRA BOOKS are published by

Kensington Publishing Corp.
850 Third Avenue
New York, NY 10022

All Kensington titles, imprints and distributed lines are available at special quantity discounts for bulk purchases for sales
promotion, premiums, fund-raising, educational or institu-
tional use.

Special book excerpts or customized printings can also be created to fit specific needs. For details, write or phone the office
of the Kensington Special Sales Manager: Kensington Publishing Corp., 850 Third Avenue, New York, NY 10022. Attn.
Special Sales Department. Phone: 1-800-221-2647.

Zebra and the Z logo Reg. U.S. Pat. & TM Off.

First Printing: June 2004
10 9 8 7 6 5 4 3 2 1

Printed in the United States of America

CONTENTS

Happy is the Bride

Caroline Clemmons

Thanks to Sandy Tucker Crowley, Jeanmarie Hamilton, and the Rosebuds from Yellow Rose RWA—especially Geri Foster and Bea Smith.
Thanks to everyone who shared their wedding horror stories—truth is always stranger than fiction.

One

Texas Hill Country
June 8, 1885

Beth Pendleton stared at her cousin Rachel. "I'm *not* an old maid."

"Beth, face the truth. You're pretty"—Rachel wrinkled her nose—"if a man likes the tall, skinny, blond sort, but for heaven's sake, you're twenty-eight years old and not married. Besides, everyone in town thinks you're jinxed."

Her cousin's smug arrogance gave Beth an almost irresistible urge to choke Rachel. Why had Beth given in to her mother's insistence that she pay a call on her cousin? Guilt, of course. It had been weeks since she'd visited Rachel. That and Beth's desire to please her mother, an increasingly difficult task.

To appear calm when her emotions churned inside her, Beth smoothed a knife pleat in her new navy and gray faille skirt. Her mother had ordered the spring walking suit for her, copied from a Paris original by her mother's favorite couturier, Mr. Henrí of Galveston. It was a bit warm for early June in central Texas, but Beth knew how much the latest fashions meant to her mother, so she wore it.

Beth took a deep breath. "It's true I've had bad luck with the men Daddy chose, but I'll find the right man on my own some day and we'll marry."

He'd certainly be a nicer man than Rachel's doltish husband, Ben Bigelow. And the Bigelow children! Heaven help her, any children Beth and her husband had definitely would be better behaved than Rachel's screaming horde.

Rachel shook her head, but the bun on the top remained firm, coiled tight as a wagon spring. "Who in Ransom Crossing is going to propose to you? The men who aren't afraid of Uncle Howard are afraid of the bad luck that falls on any fiancé of yours. Look at the disasters that happen when you plan a wedding."

Beth shuddered at the memory of her past fiascoes. "Those troubles were beyond my control. No one could possibly blame me." Though it scorched her ears, Beth had heard the gossip about her bringing bad luck to any prospective groom. It hurt beyond words, but she'd die before she'd let any of the gossips know.

Rachel displayed the smug smile married women reserved for the single women they pitied. Beth hated that smile.

Rachel held up three sausagelike fingers. "Three engagements, three failed weddings. Sorry, Cousin Beth, you'll never get another chance. You may have the latest Paris fashions, but you'll never have what I have."

"I could marry if I really wanted to." Beth inwardly recoiled at her hasty statement. Why had she said such an absurd thing? She didn't have a single prospect. Besides, to hear her cousin, if the town were full of unwed men, then her father or her bad luck would scare them away.

Rachel adjusted her considerable bosom that threatened to burst out of the bright green poplin dress and then smoothed her hands down her girth. "Ben says I'm *all* woman and that's why we have six kids."

She giggled. "No one wants to marry an old maid who's jinxed. It doesn't mean spit that you're the only child of the wealthiest man in town. Men want a real woman with some meat on her bones. Besides, everyone around here calls you the Ice Queen."

Ice Queen? Beth had heard this before, and the crude label made her want to stamp her foot or throw something in childish temper. As usual, she forced her emotions under strict control, lifted her chin and gave Rachel an icy glare. The fact that her actions lived up to the accusation only angered her more.

But she wasn't an Ice Queen. She was warm, loving, and sought to be kind. Except, no one had taken the time to notice that. They were too busy whispering behind her back and making fun of her.

"I told you I'm not an old maid yet and I'm not jinxed. And the fact that I don't flirt with every man I meet doesn't mean I'm cold. I'll marry soon, you'll see." Beth appraised her rotund cousin's figure. "When I do, will you be able to wear your attendant's dress? That dress was made three years ago, and you've had two more children since then."

"Of course I can still wear that dress. My Ben says I'm a perfect size, exactly right for cuddling." Rachel's narrow-set brown eyes glinted with malice. "But I'll bet you that new bolt of cream silk your mama ordered from New York that come the end of June, you'll still be unwed."

Up to her ears in insults and injustice, Beth couldn't stand this any longer. The past years of embarrassment and ridicule exploded inside her like a Fourth of July firecracker. "I'll take that bet. When I win, you have to give me . . . that new quilt you won at the church picnic."

Mercy sakes, what had she said? Anger must have melted her brain. She wanted to call back the words, but it was too late. The gauntlet had been thrown and accepted.

Needing to get away before Rachel noticed her shaking hands, Beth straightened her bonnet, then gathered her reticule and parasol. "Now, I must be on my way. Do come see me when you can get away."

Never would be soon enough, even if Rachel was her only cousin. In fact, other than her parents, Rachel was her only living relative.

Beth wanted to slam the door and run to the buggy, drive away, and hide somewhere. But she couldn't. Instead, Beth pushed down her emotions and glided as she had learned in Boston at the Meriweather School for Young Ladies of Good Families. She climbed onto the seat and cracked the whip in the air over the backs of the horses.

The perfectly matched bays took off with a jerk, and she set the whip back in its holder to concentrate on the reins. Ben Bigelow's large apple orchard whizzed by her view. The buggy bounced over the rutted road. Determined to stop the ridicule she'd tolerated for years, Beth tightened her grip and clenched her jaw. She'd show Rachel. She'd show everyone in Ransom Crossing.

Darned if she'd let her fat cousin Rachel win that insulting bet.

Darned if she wanted to remain the laughingstock of the whole county.

Darned if she knew why she shouldn't have her heart's desire—a family with children. Lots of children, with a kind man who'd be both a loving husband and a good father.

To her surprise, a man's face appeared in her mind. Why not him? No reason at all. The answer had popped into her mind like a miracle, a heavenly sign. And if there was anything Beth needed right now, it was divine intervention.

Instead of taking the road to town, Beth guided the rig west with hardly a thought to her actions. When she realized the course she'd chosen, she decided her instincts were on target. She'd go see Mason Whittaker, the friend she turned to in every crisis.

He was the one person she relied on to offer her solace. Mason knew her innermost thoughts and the embarrassment she suffered. Of all the people she knew, he was her one true friend.

Beth had never been to his new home before because he no longer lived with his parents and it wouldn't be proper for her to visit him without a chaperone, but desperation emboldened her. Mason had told her about the house he was building on the acreage his father had deeded over to him. Hadn't he told her every boundary of his land and every turn of the road? She'd heard him give directions often enough that surely she could find the place.

A large tree split by lightning caught her eye, and she turned the horses in that direction. The trail narrowed and the ruts deepened. A frisson of fear skittered down her spine, and she pressed her lips together. Had she made the wrong turn? She'd been upset and might have missed the way.

In her indecision, Beth slowed the team as she rounded a corner. Suddenly, Mason's ranch buildings appeared in view, laid out in an efficient group on a hill overlooking the river. Beth sighed with relief and guided the team up the dusty road to the front door. His new house sat fresh and neat, snuggled into a grove of ancient trees. A rock-lined walk led to the long front porch.

Though not a large place, she thought it probably had five or six rooms. He'd painted it a soft green—her favorite color. White paint on the eaves, porch railing, and around the windows glistened in the sun, and dark green shutters at the windows added to the pleasing appearance.

Beth stopped the team and climbed down from the buggy. What if Mason wasn't home? He could be on the range or at his parents' home a mile away, and she had no idea where to look. She sighed in relief when Mason appeared at the barn door, then hurried toward her as fast as his limp allowed.

Beth pretended to stare at the house while she waited, knowing Mason hated anyone watching the labored gait due to his crushed limb.

Did she dare do as she planned?

From the corner of her eye she observed his progress. Tall and powerful except for the leg he'd smashed under a wagon wheel at thirteen, he cut a rough but handsome figure in denim work trousers and chambray shirt with rolled-up sleeves. He'd been her best friend since childhood; she could tell him anything without fear of censure, so she confided all her secrets to him.

He frowned as he stopped in front of her. "Beth?" He looked at the buggy. "Are you all alone? Is something wrong?"

Before she could change her mind, she took a deep breath. "Mason, will you marry me?"

Three Weeks Later
June 29, 1885

"What a glorious morning." Beth threw back the covers and hurried to the window. Sunshine poured into her room. Thank goodness. Blue sky overhead promised perfect weather. "Nothing can spoil *this* wedding day."

She pushed down the giddy laughter that tickled her stomach. Dare she hope the perfect wedding she'd always dreamed of would occur today? Heat traveled up her throat to her face when she thought of her life as Mason's wife. Slowly she pressed her hands down the front of her nightgown, and her nipples tightened in response.

What would it feel like tonight when he made her his wife in fact as well as name? When they became one would it hurt or would her heart explode with love and joy? She trusted Mason and knew he'd never hurt her. That meant there would be joy.

She touched her cheek where he'd kissed her last night right in front of her parents. They hadn't been alone a minute since he'd agreed to marry her, but she recognized the longing in his eyes. She hugged her arms, yearning for a real kiss from him, one where his lips settled over hers.

Elated she'd soon know that pleasure, she washed

quickly and put away her nightgown. To go with her mood and the sunny day, she pulled on her yellow silk morning dress and perfectly matched slippers. She brushed her hair and wove a yellow ribbon into the braid she curled into a neat coronet.

When she had completed her morning toilette, she added a few last things to the open trunk at the foot of her bed. Tomorrow, she'd awake no longer a maiden, but in her new home with her husband. She took one last look around the room. She had lived here a long time. She said goodbye to childhood and hello to her new life as woman and wife.

Ignoring the butterflies fluttering in her belly, she turned and headed for the stairs.

Her father's booming voice floated up to her and drew her to a halt. "Louise, I tell you Whittaker doesn't deserve our girl. We sent her to the best finishing school money could buy. I expected her to marry a wealthy businessman. Dammit, Whittaker's not only a hayseed cowpuncher, he's a cripple. Only time he's been out of the county is on cattle drives. What kind of match is that?"

"Shhhhh, Howard. Bethany will hear." Her mother's voice sounded peevish, as usual. "You know very well this is probably her last chance. We'd better pray Mason actually shows up at the church."

Beth sighed and ran lightly down the thickly carpeted stairs. Clearly even her mother doubted she'd be married today, or that she'd ever marry. Her mother held little hope for her only child.

"With her training and upbringing she should marry a society leader, perhaps someone with a future in politics, not that cowboy. He's not good enough for *our* girl." Her father sat tall and regal with the newspaper at his elbow.

Hiding the sting of her parents' words, Beth glided into the breakfast room and kissed her father's cheek beside the silver tingeing his dark sideburns. "Good morning. Mason's almost thirty, Daddy. He's hardly a boy."

Crossing behind her father, she kissed the air near her mother's cheek, then slid into her chair and spread her napkin across her lap. "According to folks in town, I'm an old maid, a jinxed spinster, and not a girl at all. You'd best be grateful to Mason for taking me off your hands."

Even from her own lips, the mean-spirited labels sliced through her heart. Old maid. Spinster. Did no one realize the cruelty of those words or how utterly hopeless they sounded?

Her father regarded her as if he'd not seen her when she kissed him. His brown eyes were not unkind, yet she stiffened under his gaze, bracing herself for the censure certain to come.

He didn't disappoint her. "We didn't send you to that exclusive finishing school so you could marry a common cowpuncher." He already wore his suit, his dark hair brushed neatly, ready for his day at the bank he owned three blocks away in Ransom Crossing.

"Mason owns the ranch, Daddy, and it's three thousand acres joining his parents' land of even more acres which he will inherit some day. Besides, the men you chose were city men, but they were hardly suitable."

The humiliation of those engagements washed over her. She wondered how she had endured so much embarrassment in the past few years. Once more she wondered how her parents could have thought any of those men would make a good husband. And she wanted to kick herself for letting her parents push her into accepting their proposals.

Her father had the grace to look uncomfortable. "Don't remind me of those bounders, even though each came with good recommendations. My usual judgment might have erred there—"

Beth interrupted her father. "Yes, as it has with Mason. He's a kind man who would never let me down." She couldn't resist adding, "And he certainly won't run afoul of the law."

Beulah, their housekeeper, brought in a plate of fluffy scrambled eggs and a rack of toast and set them in front of her. "You eat up, honey. This is gonna be a busy day." She poured Beth a cup of tea.

Beth stabbed her fork into the eggs with determination. She refused to let her parents or anything else spoil her mood. "The sun is shining, and it's going to be a wonderful wedding."

"Hmph." Beth's father scowled at his plate.

Mrs. Pendleton appeared regal this morning in a pale blue gown the color of her eyes and her strawberry blond hair swept into a neat chignon. She patted Beth's hand.

"Now, dear, don't get your hopes up too high." The pity and unspoken criticism in her mother's voice sliced into Beth's heart.

Didn't anyone but her believe she'd marry today? That tonight she'd lie in the arms of her new husband? That some day she'd have children and live happily ever after?

Beth pulled her hand away from her mother's. "Mama, Mason *will* be at the church, and the wedding *will* happen."

Her father peered over his spectacles. "Let's hope so. You'd better get married this time." He looked down at his paper and muttered, "Probably *is* your last chance."

Beulah put her hands on her hips. "Y'all leave Miss Beth alone so she can eat without getting the jitters. She's gonna be the prettiest bride this town ever seen."

Finally, one other person who believed Beth would be wed today. Beth smiled her thanks, and Beulah went back to the kitchen.

"Don't eat too much, dear, or your dress might be tight. After all, we've had it for several years."

"Mama, I know precisely how long we've had the dress." As usual, Beth's sarcasm was wasted on her mother.

"It's just like you to be thoughtless and agree to wed that boy with only three weeks' notice. There's been too much to do. As soon as you've eaten, we need to hurry to the chapel. The buckets of flowers and other supplies are already loaded on the buckboard."

"I'll hurry." Beth dug into her food, thankful for the fact that Mason would never leave her at the altar. But after being jilted three times in as many years, a tiny seed of doubt swelled deep inside her. She prayed that nothing would keep Mason from meeting her at the chapel.

Dear God, help me. I couldn't take the humiliation of another wedding gone wrong and cancelled.

Tomorrow morning she would be mistress in her own home, subject only to sweet Mason's directives—but no more than he would be to hers. Then the folks in town would be forced to admit she wasn't jinxed. It might take a couple of children to convince them she wasn't cold, but surely her marriage to Mason would put an end to the constant gossip about her. That thought cheered her. Today was indeed a special day.

Two

Mason forked straw from the loft onto the wagon. The sun shone brightly overhead, but he thought rain clouds gathered low on the southwest horizon. He figured the church grounds needed the coarse stem roughage spread to prevent buggies from sticking and help keep folks' feet dry if it rained before the wedding.

His ranch hand, Rowdy Vines, worked beside him. "Boss, you sure this marriage is what you want?"

"Yep, dead level positive." Mason had loved Beth for as long as he could remember, but had never told anyone. He thought of her eyes when he looked at a perfect spring bluebonnet. Her hair matched honey, or maybe cornsilk. He couldn't decide, but it didn't matter. He loved her, and after tonight she'd be his forever. Nothing could please him more.

Thinking about her made him grow hard and his denim britches fit too tight. Dang, he wanted Beth so much he had trouble sleeping nights, but he wanted more from her than her body. He loved talking to her, wanted to spend his life at her side. Until now she'd had little love in her life, but he planned to protect her and shower her with the love and devotion she deserved.

For years he'd dreamed of building his future with

her as his partner. She was the woman he wanted as mother to his children, and he hoped their future held a couple of blond, blue-eyed girls like her and a boy or two to carry on the ranch. With or without children, they'd have a grand life together.

Mason knew how hard her parents were on her, always wanting her to be a society leader, sending her to that fancy school when she wanted to stay home, never saying anything nice no matter how she tried to please them. The Pendletons had never consulted Beth to ask what she wanted. He'd see Beth had anything she desired that was within his power to give her.

Though Beth and he had been friends since he was eight and she was seven, she'd never given him any indication she returned his affection other than to tell him she thought of him as her brother and best friend. That was, until her proposal three weeks ago.

Wait. He stopped and scratched his head. Come to think of it, she hadn't said a word about love. No matter, she must love him or she wouldn't have asked him to marry her.

Mason wiped his brow with his bandana. "All I have to do is tolerate the endless details Mrs. Pendleton insists on and make it through today. Come nightfall, Beth'll be my wife, and we can live out here without anyone interfering."

Mason didn't know what, but since he'd announced his engagement, something had bothered Rowdy. Now the lanky older man mumbled something under his breath.

"What was that?" Mason leaned forward to hear.

Rowdy stopped and leaned on his pitchfork. "Sorry, boss, I didn't mean you to hear that."

"Not sure I heard right. Say it again."

Rowdy took a deep breath before he spoke. "You know folks say she's jinxed?"

Yeah, Mason knew and he hated it, but he counted to ten and reined in his anger. Losing his temper seventeen years ago had landed him in the fight that resulted in his smashed leg. Since then, he'd tried to control his fury and succeeded—except in one area. Hearing things against Beth always riled him. He'd done his share of brawling in vain attempts to silence the talk. Folks loved to gossip, and evidently that included his hired hand.

Mason vowed nothing would spoil his wedding day, so he counted to ten a second time and went back to forking. "Don't believe that superstitious nonsense. Good or bad, each of us makes his own luck."

He tossed another forkful of straw, and his knee gave way. Standing on the edge of the loft, he grabbed for the roof support as he lost his balance. His hand barely missed the post, and he flew off the edge.

"Boss? Boss? You okay?"

Mason opened his eyes and wiped the moisture from his face. "Did you throw water on me?"

"Didn't know what else to do." Rowdy leaned over him. "Hit your head on the side of the wagon. Knocked yourself plumb out. Good thing you landed on the straw."

"So you drenched me?" Mason sat up and held his shirt from his body. Hot as it was, the cooling effect of the water wasn't bad.

"Couldn't wake you up. Scared me something awful, so I fetched the water bucket and doused you. Then you come to."

"Thanks." Mason struggled up, conscious of an aching head and soaked clothes.

Rowdy leveled a knowing look at Mason. "See, I told you. The jinx done started."

"*There's no jinx!* I fell because this damned leg gave way. It's done that for seventeen years."

Mason explored the lump high on his forehead. What a damn fool thing to happen on his wedding day. Maybe he could comb his hair differently to hide the lump and the bruise sure to follow.

"Gee, boss, I don't know." Rowdy stared up at the loft and back to the wagon. "You ain't never fell outta the loft before. I think it's 'cause of the jinx."

"Told you there's no jinx. Get in the wagon." Mason hadn't meant to snap at Rowdy, but—with or without counting to ten—that kind of talk about Beth heated his temper. "This is enough straw. Let's get on over to the chapel."

Beth paused with a fern stem in her hand and scanned the small sanctuary. Though she would have preferred using the larger church in town, she admitted a fondness for this little chapel near the Medina River. The white frame building stood at the edge of a small clearing by a steep slope. Six steps led up to the small porch at the front, but the rear of the building suspended into space and rested on high rock pillars.

On the hillside nearby was the small cemetery where some of Beth's kin were buried. Her mother's father had died twenty years ago of a stroke; his wife had died ten years later in the same influenza epidemic that had taken Rachel's mother and younger brother. Rachel's father had been thrown from a horse and struck his head against a stone five years ago. Beth knew there were plots marked off for her own parents when their time came, but she hoped that wouldn't be for many decades.

Beth's mother and father had wed in this chapel almost thirty years ago, and Mrs. Pendleton had insisted Beth wed here. Since then, the town had moved the other direction. Time had passed the chapel by, and now it stood a half mile from any other buildings.

In spite of the short notice, Beth's mother had forged ahead with plans for an elaborate wedding and reception. Mrs. Pendleton hired a local man to shine the windows and clean the chapel, which saw little use nowadays. On the lectern hung a white silk cloth on which Beth had embroidered linked wedding rings flanked by turtledoves in silver and gold thread. A half dozen candles in a brass holder flanked each side of the altar.

"Bethany, you're doing that all wrong. The vases need to be fuller." Beth's mother pushed her out of the way. "If I want a thing done right, I have to do it myself."

Beth sighed and watched her mother stuff more greenery and flowers into the already full urn at one side of the altar lectern. Beth had liked it best the way she'd arranged it, graceful instead of overblown, but she supposed her mother knew best.

"If you'd given me more time, I could have brought in a consultant from Austin to decorate the church and our home and arrange the flowers. As it is, I have to do everything myself. You're so inconsiderate."

The unjust accusation hurt Beth. "Beulah and I are helping, Mother. And we cut all the greenery and flowers for you." Yesterday Beulah and Beth had cut flowers from the Pendleton garden and those of friends, plus ventured into the woods for ferns and other greenery. They'd woven garlands from part of the greenery on lengths of wire. "Besides, we could have hired someone local to do this."

Her mother rewarded her with a glare. "And leave all this to chance? I think not. No, it's a considerable burden to me on such a busy day, but I'll make certain the chapel looks properly decked out for a Pendleton wedding."

Beth picked up a white silk ribbon and tied it on the end of a pew.

"Not like that, dear. Must I do everything? We want them fuller." Mrs. Pendleton tugged the bow, then left it looking exactly as Beth had tied it. "There, doesn't that look better?"

Beth bit her tongue to stop the angry retort that sprang into her mind. She wanted this day to end. Once she'd thought this big wedding with her perfect dress was important. Now she just wanted the ceremony and reception behind her. She longed to be at Mason's home—no, Mason's and her home—where they could relax and enjoy each other's company away from constant criticism or unfair gossip.

Beulah tapped her foot. "Mrs. Pendleton, if you're gonna redo everything me and Beth does, then we might as well leave you here and go home. I gots them cakes to frost and all."

Beth's mother struck what Beth thought of as her martyred pose. "Does no one appreciate that I'm trying to uphold our position in society? The people in this town look to the Pendletons to set the standard of good taste. It's my duty to present the most gracious and elegant decorations possible with such short notice."

Beulah rolled her eyes and picked up a length of ribbon.

Beth didn't argue, but she suspected the people in town didn't give a fig about the decorations. They already thought she and her parents were snobs. Those who attended the wedding would come in hopes of seeing Beth jilted again and her parents embarrassed. This time, the naysayers would be disappointed. Mason would show up, and the wedding would proceed without a hitch.

"Good thing it's sunny. If it rains, do you think the river might reach the chapel grounds?" Beth walked to the window and peeked out. She'd seen a heavy rain turn the Medina River into a boiling brown torrent with few crossing places. Today, the river looked peaceful, reflecting the deep blue of the sky.

"Don't you worry, missy. The river ain't never come up this high. I reckon the folks what built this was just cautious." Beulah tied another ribbon. "Just like rich folks to donate land for a church where no one can't do nothing else with it."

Mrs. Pendleton put her hands on her hips and glared. "Beulah, you know very well my father donated the land for this chapel. He was a generous civic leader and helped found the town."

When Mrs. Pendleton would have touched the bow, Beulah glared, and Mrs. Pendleton went back to her flowers.

"Yes'm, Mr. Ransom did at that." Beulah picked up another ribbon.

Beth had the impression Beulah hadn't liked Beth's Grandfather Ransom. Recalling tales she'd heard of her mother's father, she reckoned no one had cause to like the man. Beth's mother had never said a word against Grandfather Ransom, of course, and talked as if she thought he hung the moon and stars.

Others in town had less glowing things to say about him. He'd died when Beth was only eight, but she remembered him as a mean-spirited, cold, pompous man who sought the public eye and one who did not tolerate children. Not even his own grandchildren. He was said to have been relentless in forcing others to his will. Perhaps that explained why her mother couldn't show affection and why she thought appearances were so important.

Beth returned to the pews and tied more bows. When she had finished one side of the wide aisle and Beulah completed the bench ends of the other side, they stood at the back of the chapel and admired the effect. She had to give her mother credit; the chapel looked beautiful—just as lovely as it had when she was to have wed George Denby and her mother brought in that expensive wedding consultant.

George was the only of her three fiancés with whom she had actually gotten close to the ceremony, though news of his injury came early in the day long before Beth had donned her wedding finery.

Beth's father had insisted he should arrange a suitable marriage for her, and three times he had pushed her into an engagement. For a different reason each time, three weddings had been cancelled. In spite of the embarrassment, she had been relieved when each ceremony was called off. She shuddered to think of the horrible life she would have had with any of those men, though she supposed George was nice enough.

Her reprieves came through no fault of her own,

but she still had to live with the pain and embarrassment of being jilted. Everyone in town talked about the snobbish, rich girl no one wanted to marry. After the second cancellation, talk of her being a jinx spread. To this day, she heard the whispers when she went into town for church or shopping—as if she were to blame for the shortcomings of the men chosen for her.

It hurt, but she never showed that pain in public. Public humiliation at the hands of three men had hurt her, and the gossip that followed hurt more. Each cancelled ceremony had whittled away at her confidence. But Beth thanked God none of those weddings had occurred, because now she could wed a man she admired and who understood her.

A large vase rocked and snapped Beth from her reverie. Mrs. Pendleton caught it before it fell.

"Mother, those two urns look as if they might turn over easily. If they fall, they'll soak someone in the front pew."

"They're exactly as I planned, so be careful not to brush against them. You see how the effect is visible even from the back pew? I'll warn Rachel since she'll be standing near one." Her mother joined them at the back of the chapel. "All we lack are the garlands."

"I'll get the stepladder." Beth picked up two empty buckets and headed for the buckboard. At the top of the steps, she saw a wagon approach. Her heart skipped a beat when she recognized the driver. "Oh, look, Mason's here."

Mrs. Pendleton rushed to the door and tugged on Beth's arm. "Hurry, back inside. He's not supposed to see you on your wedding day. It's bad luck, and you've had all of that I can stand."

"Nonsense, Mother. Surely you don't believe that sort of thing. It would be rude not to greet him now that we've seen him."

Besides, she wanted to see him. Wanted it a great deal. She needed him to reassure her he hadn't changed his mind. Beth descended the steps and set her paraphernalia in the buckboard.

When the wagon drew alongside, Mason grinned at her before he climbed down, and his smile set her mind at ease. He wore denim pants and a gray-checked shirt with sleeves rolled against the summer heat, and straw and mire stuck to his work boots.

"Hello, Mason. Hello, Mr. Vines. It's lucky for us you came. We need help with the garlands inside."

Rowdy Vines tipped his hat. "Happy to oblige, ma'am." He hopped down and took the stepladder toward the chapel.

Mason stood in front of Beth, staring as if he hadn't seen her in months instead of only yesterday. His warm gray eyes searched her as if he memorized each part of her.

She smiled up at him. He was the handsomest man she knew and the kindest. "We decorated the chapel with flowers and such." What a silly thing to say when he knew why they were here. Suddenly, she felt shy and awkward as a schoolgirl with her first beau.

Mrs. Pendleton stood with hands on her hips at the top of the steps. "You're not supposed to see the bride on the wedding day. You should have known we'd be here and stayed away."

Mason paid her no mind except to remove his hat respectfully. "Already see Beth, so I might as well talk to her, ma'am." He resumed gazing at Beth. "You look pretty as the sunshine this morning."

"Mason, you're hurt." When he'd removed his hat, she'd spotted a large bruise on a raised lump. Beth pushed his hair from his forehead. "Oh, there's a break in the skin." She didn't believe in the jinx, but this worried her. Did she bring bad luck to any fiancé? No, surely not.

"Aw, I fell, but it's nothing. You know how my leg acts crazy sometimes." He nodded toward the wagon. "We're gonna spread this straw so if it rains people won't get so muddy or the buggies stuck."

Mrs. Pendleton threw up her hands and went into the building with Rowdy. Beth was glad to see them go so she could talk with Mason alone.

"That's real thoughtful of you, Mason." Beth could count on Mason to think of others before himself. She thanked her lucky stars she'd be wed to such a kind man. "I sure hope it won't rain. You know, 'Happy is the bride the sun shines on'?"

He flashed that cocky grin that signaled he teased. "Afraid of bad luck?"

Three

Beth realized she wasn't afraid of bad luck anymore. She shook her head. "Not with you. I know you'd never let me down."

"No, I never will. I promise you that." Mason took Beth's hand and tucked it in the crook of his arm. "Let's take a stroll by the river."

She looked back at the chapel, knew she should help her mother, and weighed her mother's irritability against her own desire to walk with Mason. He put his hand over hers, and that contact swayed her. Instead of the comfort his touch used to arouse, currents of lightning shot through her.

Why would an engagement make a difference between her and a friend of more than twenty years?

All she knew was that since she'd proposed to Mason, her reaction to him had changed. His presence incited escalating odd sensations, and she had the most scandalous thoughts. She questioned whether he had the same thoughts, and the heat of a blush reached her cheeks.

There hadn't been time for proper courting. He'd called on her, but other than the day she proposed to him, they'd had no time alone. Her parents accompanied her to his home and that of his parents. When he called on her, one of her parents remained in the room. A hasty kiss on the cheek was all he'd given her, but his soulful looks let her know he wanted more.

Her breath hitched, and she struggled to keep her eyes averted for fear he might read her mind. Her mother said a lady never had thoughts of the flesh, yet Beth couldn't stop dwelling on it. Would he be scandalized? Right now she wondered how his lips tasted.

Mason guided her under the back edge of the building between two of the stone columns and pulled her into his arms. "Forgive me, Beth, I can't wait for this any longer."

Strawberry jam.

He tasted sweet as the jam she'd given him last week. She melted against him, and he deepened the kiss. His tongue traced the line of her lips, and she opened to his invasion. She gasped, but his tongue probed against hers and created a pool of warmth low in her abdomen. Her knees threatened to give way, and she clung to him.

Surprised at the giddiness his action evoked, she soon matched his thrusts with her own tongue. Dear heaven, the thoughts that aroused. A pulsing, aching heat built in her private place. Much more of this and she'd burst into flame.

One of his hands caressed her breast, and new tingles shot through her. He broke contact with her lips to murmur between kisses to her neck, "I can hardly wait to view these beauties tonight."

She looked up at him. "V-view them?" She whispered, "You mean see, um, see me without clothes on?"

He smiled. "Yes, that's what I mean. Not a stitch on either one of us, just like God made us."

"Is that proper?" Panic seized her. Right now she wanted to give Adam back his rib.

But then Mason moved his hand across her nipple, those tingles changed to jolts of pleasure, and she reconsidered. Maybe this man-woman thing wouldn't be too bad, in spite of what her mother said.

Mason's other hand cupped her bottom and tucked her into him. She sensed a hard bulge pressing against her as he resumed their kiss. It must be his man thing, and she worried at the size of it. How could that fit inside her?

Breathless, she broke the kiss. He pulled her to him and cradled her head against his chest. She slid her arms around his waist and savored his embrace. In spite of her worries about tonight, in his arms she knew peace.

He kissed her temple. "Can't tell you how much I've needed this. I've dreamed of us alone in our own home tonight."

That's when they'd come together. But Mason wouldn't do anything to hurt her. She trusted him.

"I look forward to it, too. We make a fine couple, and we'll have a good life together." She raised her head and asked the question that had worried her since she'd proposed to him.

"Mason, you're not sorry you said yes, are you?" She knew he'd never go back on a promise, but it worried her that he might regret that he'd agreed to wed her.

He brushed his lips against hers in a soft, sweet kiss. "I'm only sorry we've wasted years when we should have been together. We belong with one another."

"I'm relieved you feel that way." She sighed and nuzzled into him. "In spite of all the talk, I'm feeling very lucky right now."

"Not nearly as lucky as me. I've wanted this as long as I can remember."

Thunderstruck, she looked up at him. He wanted her? "Mason, you never said. Why didn't you tell me long ago?"

"I couldn't. You were so all-fired set on pleasing your folks by going to that fancy school up north. Then when you came back, well, I thought you were too fine a lady for the likes of me."

Did Mason think her a snob? The suggestion created a ball of worry in her. "How could you think such a thing? If—if I gave you that idea from anything I said or did, then I apologize. There's no finer man anywhere than you, Mason."

He pulled her back to his chest, and she heard him exhale, a great whoosh of breath, as if he'd been holding in the air. "I thought you deserved a whole man, someone not hampered by a limp."

She pushed away from him with her hands rested on his chest. "Mason Whittaker, don't ever let me hear you say another word against yourself. I'm real sorry about your leg because I know it pains you, but that doesn't make you less of a man. In fact, you've achieved success in spite of being slowed by it, so that makes you twice the man of anyone else I know."

He pushed a stray curl from her face. "You always championed me. Guess that's one reason why I love you."

He loved her.

She didn't know what to say. Mason Whittaker actually said he loved her. She should answer him. But how? Instead, she clung to him, pressed herself against him, and held on.

Dear Lord, and she'd asked him to marry her because of a bet. She should tell him, confess right now. But she knew his temper and his hard-shelled pride. If he found out, that pride of his would drive him away. She couldn't bear another cancelled wedding. More, she couldn't bear losing Mason as her best friend and their future together.

Now she was forced to face the question of whether she loved Mason as a man or just as a friend? She hadn't considered that. She'd been so determined to show her cousin Rachel and stop the laughter and humiliation that she hadn't stopped to consider the consequences for Mason.

How selfish she'd been. The knowledge made her ashamed of her hasty proposal. Then she remembered that when she decided to find her own groom, she hadn't considered anyone but Mason.

Did she love him?

Mrs. Pendleton's shrill voice saved Beth from answering Mason.

"Bethaneeeeee. Where are you?"

"Oh, dear, we'd better go around by the wagons. Mother sounds upset with me." She loathed breaking contact with him, but stepped away. "Soon I'll be out of yelling distance, even for her." She laughed, wishing it were funny instead of sad.

Nothing she did would ever please her mother. Heaven knew she'd tried for twenty-eight years. She couldn't remember one time when her mother had a kind word for her, not even one.

Mason grabbed her hand. "Knowing my temper, I can't promise I'll never yell at you, but I give you my word I'll try not to."

"You haven't yelled at me yet. And I'll try hard to be the best wife in the world, the kind you deserve."

Mason loved her.

Why hadn't she seen that? He'd always been so thoughtful of her every wish, listened to her secrets, took up for her against anyone who said hurtful things to her.

"One more." He swept her to him in a fervent embrace.

Beth slid her arms around his neck. Who would have dreamed kissing Mason would render her into a melting puddle? But it did, and she wanted to continue for a long time.

She wanted him to touch her breast again. Did that make her wanton? Her mother insisted only harlots enjoyed the things that went on between men and women.

Someone coughed. "Boss?"

Mason and Beth jumped. She knew her face reddened at being caught in Mason's arms.

Rowdy pretended to look away. "Mrs. Pendleton made me come fetch you two back up there right away. She seems all het up, and I reckon you'd better hurry along before she has a spell or something."

"Thanks, tell her we're on our way." Mason took Beth's hand and smiled. "In a few hours, no one can interrupt us."

His words gave Beth hope. They rounded the corner pillar and climbed the slope to the front of the chapel.

At the buckboard, Mason held her hand and looked into her eyes. "Guess Rowdy and me better get this straw spread. I'm expected at my folks later this morning."

Mrs. Pendleton tapped her foot. "Straw's not necessary, but if you've nothing better to do, I suppose it won't hurt."

Rowdy helped Mrs. Pendleton and Beulah climb onto the buckboard. Beulah took the reins, but smiled at Beth and Mason and waited patiently.

Mrs. Pendleton snapped open her parasol. "Bethany, we don't have time to dally all day."

Beth sighed, wishing as she had many times that her mother was a kinder, more patient person. No matter, soon she and Mason would answer only to each other. Mason still held her hand, and she squeezed his fingers before she pulled free. "I have to go."

Mason pecked her on the cheek. "Yeah, I know, but it won't be long until we're wed." He helped her up and stepped back. "See you later."

Beth waved. "In a few hours." She thought ahead to tonight when they'd come together and knew she blushed.

His eyes darkened. Plainly, his feelings matched hers. She recalled his words about seeing her naked and wondered how her body would look to him. Would she disappoint him?

Beth hoped not. All her life she'd disappointed her parents, though she tried hard to please them. She had no intention of disappointing her husband. Would being a good wife be as impossible as being a good daughter?

Mason watched the women until they made the bend in the road. Then he grabbed his pitchfork. The sun still shone and the stifling heat slowed them, but he and Rowdy spread straw in low spots where no

grass grew and at the base of the steps so folks alight-
ing from buggies could step on it instead of damp
ground.

Mason wondered why his soon-to-be mother-in-law
was so impossible to please. How had Beth endured
constant criticism without becoming hard and cyni-
cal? He didn't know, but somehow she had. He knew
his bride helped many less fortunate citizens in the
community, and she tried to be kind to everyone.
Thank goodness she'd finally be his wife.

When they'd finished, Mason looked inside the
chapel. Unwilling to enter with dirty boots, he stood
in the doorway. He visualized Beth and him standing
at the altar. The day he'd secretly dreamed of for years
had finally become reality. Damned if he wasn't the
luckiest man in the state.

Rowdy climbed the steps and stood beside him.
"Looks purty, don't it, boss? Reckon if you're determined to go through with this, there ain't a more
fitting place."

Mason ignored Rowdy's remark as he carefully descended the stairs. He sure wasn't looking to break his
leg like George Denby had. "Wait until you see it this
evening with the candles lit and the prettiest woman
in all of Texas standing next to me."

Rowdy followed. "She's a looker all right and seems
nice to boot, but danged if that mother of hers isn't a
snipey old biddy. Couldn't please her with a blessing."

"Yeah, but the lucky thing is that Beth isn't turned
like either of her parents." And Mason could hardly
wait to get her in his bed. From the way she had re-
sponded just now, she would be a willing lover, not
anything like the cold Ice Queen the gossips had labeled her.

Secretly, he'd suspected that all along. He knew for certain that she was a warm and compassionate woman who loved children and longed for a home of her own. Each time she had been promised to someone else had been hell for him. He'd fought with himself each time, told himself over and over that the man chosen for her would be a better husband than he ever could be. After all, he had this bum leg and lived on a ranch away from town and all the niceties she was accustomed to.

The relief he had experienced as each wedding fell through sawed at his conscience. He had rejoiced in his heart that Beth wouldn't spend the night in bed with another man who had made her his woman. But every one of those occasions had torn a little piece of Mason's heart away that she hadn't stood up to her parents and chosen him. He knew how the Pendletons deviled her, nagged until they bent her to their will. Just once, he wished she'd stand up to them and speak her own mind.

Mason smiled. She had in a way, by asking him to marry her. Darned if that didn't stick in her pompous parents' craw. But they'd given reluctant permission because they believed the gossip that had grown with each cancelled wedding. He'd have thought the parents of such a wonderful woman would have more faith in her.

"If it don't rain, you're gonna be mad as hell we went to all this trouble." Rowdy tossed his fork into the wagon.

Mason peered at the horizon. "Those clouds building in the southwest haven't turned threatening, but the ache in my leg never lies. It's gonna rain." He laid his pitchfork next to Rowdy's.

"Well, then I believe it. 'Pears to me that leg of yours is better than any barometer for predicting a change in the weather."

When he'd climbed up on the wagon seat, Mason rubbed his temples. "Dang, my head's pounding like a sonofabitch."

"Reckon you shouldn't a been in the sun like this so soon after banging your head."

"Likely not." Mason handed the reins to Rowdy. "Maybe you'd better drive. Drop me at my folks' place, then you can take the wagon back to the ranch."

"Sure thing, boss. Your ma's sure to have something to soothe that lump. It's gonna worry folks, though."

Four

Mason clenched his jaw to prevent saying harsh words to Rowdy. Danged if a lump on the head was anything to worry anyone. Why did folks believe that jinx business?

"Hate that the furniture hasn't arrived." He hadn't fully furnished his house, but he had a new brass bed and a big kitchen stove and a table with four chairs. Beth had helped him order more furniture, but it hadn't arrived yet. He couldn't get his mind off Beth and him in that big bed.

Rowdy nodded. "Nice she helped pick out the things, though. Women set a big store by choosing their own things."

It had pleased Mason for Beth and him to pick out their furnishings together. "Yeah, both sets of parents tried to put in their two cents."

Rowdy laughed. "Reckon her mama wanted to do all the choosing. She's a hard woman to please."

"You got that right. She wanted the fanciest stuff available. But we stuck to our guns and got what we wanted, practical things that would please a body after a hard day. Of course, we picked some things just for the heck of it." This marriage was a partnership as far as he was concerned, and he wanted Beth to speak her mind about decisions.

The ride to his parents' ranch took thirty minutes, and Mason thought his head might burst before he arrived. When Rowdy stopped the wagon, several buggies stood in the yard.

"My kin are here, at least some of them are." Mason climbed down from the wagon.

"See you at the church, boss . . . maybe, if you ain't too jinxed to show up."

Ignoring his ranch hand's doubt, Mason waved and went inside. Soon as he got in the door and hung his hat on a peg, his mother spotted the lump on his head.

"What happened, son?"

Usually he hated her fussing, but this time he hoped she had something for the ache. He touched the lump. At least the swelling had decreased.

"Fell and hit my head. You know anything that'll help?"

His mother pushed him into a chair. "I'll get my ointment."

He heard laughter coming from his father's billiard room at the back of the house. Mason rose and wandered that way. The laughter grew louder as he drew closer.

In the gaming room, Grandpa Whittaker sat in a leather wing chair by the fireplace. Mason's father and cousin Beau played billiards. From the sound of their voices and the near-empty bottle on the bar nearby, Mason thought they'd already started celebrating even though it wasn't yet noon.

Beau looked up and saluted. "Hey, cuz. I put five dollars on you in town."

"What?" Surely Mason had misunderstood.

Beau offered his cocky grin. "You know. Everyone's betting you won't show up for the wedding or that if you come, you'll call it off before you say 'I do.' I said you'd go through with it."

Damn. His own kin betting on him. Lucky for Beau he'd bet the right odds. Mason hoped the idiots in town lost their shirts betting he'd fall prey to a jinx or desert Beth. How could people believe that superstitious bunk?

Grandpa shook his head. "I don't know. That girl's jinxed. Look what happened to Fred Mahoney last year."

Mason fought his temper. He hated this kind of talk, and if they weren't his relatives, he'd start swinging.

"Grandpa, have you forgotten Mahoney was a crook and a bigamist? The U.S. Marshal arrested him because he embezzled from a couple of banks back in Iowa and had at least two wives there, not because of anything to do with Beth."

Grandpa took a sip from the glass he held. "What about George Denby three years ago?" He pointed a bony finger Mason's way. "You can't explain that away so easily."

"Yes, I can. He broke his leg falling off his horse. He'd spent the night drinking and never could ride worth a damn. Then later he took off with that woman hired to nurse him. Heard they're married and living in Denison."

"Beth didn't look that sad to see him go." Mason's father leveled a glare at him. "Mark my word, son, that girl's cold as ice. You'll be sorry if you marry her."

Mason wasn't about to tell anyone of the heated response Beth had shown him. Danged if she hadn't caught on to kissing real fast. He thought back to holding her in his arms this morning. Her fervor had almost matched his.

A cold woman wouldn't have shown the passion Beth had, and he could hardly wait until they were alone tonight at his ranch. He planned to make good on his promise that they'd both be naked as God made them, and he visualized soft lantern light spilling across the bed. He grew hard as a fence post thinking about it. Dang, if he didn't stop thinking along these lines, he'd embarrass himself.

Mason smiled and kept his knowledge of his bride's ardent nature to himself. "She hides her feelings, Pa, except to me. You know how snobby her parents are. They're always yammering at her and criticizing everything she does."

Mason knew it hurt Beth when folks hereabouts called her snooty and cold or made fun because she'd been jilted so often, but she hid it from everyone else. He figured he was the only one in the county, besides maybe her housekeeper, Beulah, who'd ever seen her cry.

Grandpa frowned and scratched his chin. "Who was that one in between Fred and George—the one who ran off with them actors that come through here?"

Beau said, "Oh, yeah, Leon Tilton was his name, had him a law office. Took off with that blond with the long curls."

Grandpa shook his head. "No, that actress was a redhead and a real looker. I ain't likely to forget her."

Beau laughed. "Not her, Grandpa—him. Tilton turned into a Nancy Boy and took up with the tall blond man what wore that fancy velvet cape."

Grandpa sat up straighter. "Well, I'll be damned." He grabbed his drink and swigged a couple of gulps. "You mean Tilton was so upset at marrying the Ice Queen that he turned to another man? Don't that beat all? Still, I can't believe a fella would choose another fella over a looker like that redhead. Lordy, she had a tiny waist, but did you see the size of her—"

"*None of that matters.*" Mason had heard more than enough speculation. "Her father picked those men, not Beth." He pointed a thumb at his chest. "*She chose me*, and by damn, I want all this rough talk about her to stop. Is that clear?"

His kin all looked at the floor and mumbled.

His mother came in carrying a jar. "Here you are, son. Let's put some ointment on that bruise."

She pushed his hair back off his forehead and spread on the vile-smelling goo she used for most everything, but it eased the stinging pain.

He saw his father and grandfather exchange looks before his father spoke. "How'd you get hurt?"

"Blasted leg gave way. Fell out of the barn loft onto the wagon. Lucky for me the damned bed was full of straw."

As usual when he or his father cussed, his mother pretended to be shocked. "Mason Whittaker, you watch your language." She put the lid on her ointment and left the room.

His father and grandfather exchanged another meaningful look. Mason couldn't believe what he saw. Bad enough Grandpa believed that claptrap gossip, but Papa actually looked worried, as if he believed in the jinx nonsense, too.

Papa shook his head. "Son, this doesn't look good.

You never fell out of a hayloft in your life before today."

Mason closed his eyes and counted to ten. He kept reminding himself that if he could get through today without hitting anyone, he'd have Beth all to himself in their home. That was likely to stop some of the gossip, and they'd be on the ranch and wouldn't have to listen to the rest.

Life with her promised to fulfill his dreams, and he'd do his damndest to make Beth happy. She'd be the mother of his children, his partner for life. All he had to do was hold on to his temper a few more hours. He exhaled, opened his eyes, and faced the other men in the room.

Beau shook his head. "It's clear the jinx has started, cuz. Reckon what'll happen next?"

As soon as they returned to the Pendleton home, Beulah started cooking the wedding cake frosting and giving orders to Emma, the daily girl. Beth mixed the lemonade punch, then helped her mother and father rearrange the already perfect drawing and dining rooms.

Though he tolerated more from his wife than anyone else, Mr. Pendleton lost what little patience he possessed. "Louise, this is the third time we've moved the sofa. Be certain where you want it this time, because I'm not moving it again."

"Oh, all right. Leave it there." Mrs. Pendleton cast an admiring gaze around the room. "Lovely. Now, I must bring the dress out of the airing closet so Beulah can press it."

Mr. Pendleton patted Beth's shoulder. "It looks quite

impressive, doesn't it? I hope that cowpuncher will provide you with a drawing room to match this someday."

"Mmm." Beth couldn't tell her father she'd never felt comfortable in this ornate room. She remembered visiting Mason's home over the years, but especially when his family invited hers as a get-better-acquainted gesture two weeks ago. Even on that occasion, when his mother must have wanted everything perfect, their home made visitors feel welcome and invited them to linger. How nice that must be.

"Can you cook?"

Beth had let her mind drift, and her father's question startled her. "What?"

Her father was a handsome man, impressive with his military bearing and well-tailored wardrobe. Beth knew he loved her mother, for the only person to whom he ever displayed the slightest affection was his wife. Not that he criticized Beth constantly as her mother did, but he let her know his expectations and how she failed to meet them. In twenty-eight years, or at least as many of those as she remembered, he had never once told Beth she pleased him.

Now he looked at her, examining her in that way of his that made her think he looked for flaws. "I asked if you can cook. I don't suppose that cowboy will hire you any servants."

"He hired a girl to help me in the house, but she won't start until Monday." Beth stood straight and poised. "However, at the Meriweather School for Young Ladies of Good Families, I learned many skills needed to run a household. Others, such as cooking and cleaning, Beulah has taught me. I believe I'll make Mason a good wife. Certainly I intend to make every effort to please him and make him proud of me."

Before her father could answer, a scream split the air. Beulah rushed from the kitchen and followed Beth and Mr. Pendleton up the stairs and into the guest room where Beth's dress had been stored since last year's cancelled wedding. The door to the airing room stood open, and Beth's mother half reclined on a couch.

Mr. Pendleton halted in front of his wife. "Louise, are you all right? What on earth caused you to shriek like a banshee?"

Mrs. Pendleton stared at the dress she'd thrown to the floor. "It's ruined. The wonderful, expensive dress Mr. Henrí made is ruined, and there's no time to fix it."

Five

"Mother, what's wrong? The dress looks all right to me." Beth bent and gathered the folds of silk and satin, then spread it across the bed. "If some of the pearls or beads have fallen off, I can sew them back. Mr. Henrí even left me a spool of thread. Oh, my stars . . ."

Apparently a mouse had nibbled away at the dress. A spot above the ruching and several inches up displayed the results of tiny teeth. Knowing the cost of the dress, Beth figured the mouse might as well have eaten pure gold dust.

Mrs. Pendleton fanned herself with her handkerchief. "What will we do? Everyone knows Mr. Henrí came from Galveston to make this dress and Rachel's. Oh, that awful Hazel Weldon will spread this over half the state." She put her face in her hands and sobbed.

For once Mr. Pendleton looked at a loss for words, but he patted his wife's shoulder while Beulah and Beth examined the dress.

"Mother, it looks as if it's only this one place. Oh, dear, it's right in front." Now that she finally had a reliable groom, she had no intention of letting a small rodent cheat her of her wedding splendor. She'd find a way to repair the dress.

Beulah measured the hole with her hand. "You cut this out and hem it, this dress be too short in front. If you seam it up so it don't show, it'll be so tight you can't walk a step."

"True. We need something to cover the holes." Beth searched the train. "If we remove one of the train ruffles to tack onto the front, the cut stitches would leave a mark in the satin. I think the same is true of the flowers at the shoulder."

Mrs. Pendleton sobbed and pulled out her handkerchief. "We'll never match that satin. It's imported from Paris. Mr. Henrí's seamstresses spent hours and hours embroidering with the beads." She looked up long enough to make a point. "They're pearls and Austrian crystals, you know, and ever so expensive."

An idea occurred to Beth. "What if I take Grandmother's hanky—the one I intended to carry—and make a little waterfall of it here over the nibbles?"

Beulah nodded. "You could do it; you're sure enough good with a needle. I'll get your sewing box and your grandmother's handkerchief."

Beulah left, and Mr. Pendleton made his escape. Beth examined the dress to make certain the mouse hadn't any friends at work in another area. A few dozen loose beads rolled across the floor, freed by the hungry rodent's gnawing. Above the damage, thousands of beads formed butterflies that flitted among silk cord and beaded flowers on the skirt.

The bodice and long train appeared undamaged. Beth loved this elegant dress, and she knew it displayed her figure to advantage. The dress had taken weeks for the couturier's staff to complete, and Beth thought it the prettiest dress she'd ever seen. It displayed her neck and shoulders much as a ball gown would. Determined Mason would be impressed when he saw her walk down the aisle, she'd fix the holes.

Had she lost her mind? Mason knew her innermost thoughts; she didn't have to impress him. He'd been her rock through good times and bad, and she didn't have to put up a front for him. Though she wanted him to be proud of her, he'd always accepted her as he found her.

Except, now she knew he loved her. That changed everything.

Mason helped his cousin up from the floor. "Sorry, Beau, shouldn't have lost my temper, but you know I get riled when folks talk against Beth."

"Damn, you haven't hit me since we were kids." Beau rubbed his jaw.

Mr. Whittaker shook his head. "Mason, how many times have I told you to control that temper? That's what got you injured years ago. Dammit, you're a smart man. I'd think you would have learned from that horrible experience."

Mason examined his knuckles and his cousin's jaw. "I know, Papa, I tried. Counted to ten, like you said I should. Even counted a second time. I swung before I could stop myself."

His father sank onto a chair. "Son, you've made me proud, building up your share of the ranch like you have. You work hard and have a shrewd head for business. I don't understand how you can be all that and then lose your temper like you do."

Embarrassment flooded Mason. He'd had the same argument with himself for years. "It's only when someone talks against Beth that it happens. Don't know what comes over me, but I see red and start swinging."

"Son, this is a serious problem. A married man can't be brawling like you and that Rasmussen boy did the day you were hurt so bad." Mr. Whittaker pounded his fist into the other hand. "That's what comes of losing control of your temper."

"Don't you think I remember that every day of my life?" Mason looked down at his crooked leg. "I wish I'd never heard of Alfred Rasmussen. You can be damn sure Alfred wishes to hell he'd never heard of me."

Beau rubbed at his jaw. "He moved to Galveston, didn't he?"

"Yeah, thought the salt air might be good for his injury. Folks here never did take to him or his family." Mason closed his eyes, and the nightmare appeared of the fight he and Alfred had seventeen years ago. Alfred was larger, but Mason angrier. He was winning, too, until they rolled under a wagon. Alfred's arm and Mason's leg were crushed.

Beau rubbed his jaw and stared at Mason. "You know, I remember now why you lit into him. He called Beth a bad name. Tore her new dress trying to kiss her. She ran crying to you with him chasing her."

"I-I don't remember that part." But he did. Lord, he'd never forget the sight of twelve-year-old Beth holding her torn dress up as she tore across the school yard after school with that bully Alfred running after her. Mason had sent her straight home while he tackled Alfred.

Mason had never told anyone what started the fight, but he'd forgotten his cousin and others would have seen. Mason hadn't wanted Beth associated with that awful memory. She represented everything good to him. He didn't want her tainted by the accident that destroyed a part of his life.

"Damn. Think this calls for another drink." Beau headed for the bar.

Mason pushed the acrid memories away. He grabbed Beau's arm and steered him toward the kitchen. "Food will be better. You need to keep up your strength for the wedding." He'd bring back some food for his grandfather, who looked as if he were sinking in his chair with each drink. The old man could hold a lot of liquor, though, so probably he wouldn't even show the effects of the alcohol when he walked or talked.

"You're going through with it, then." Mr. Whittaker followed Mason and Beau.

"No reason not to. She's the one I've always wanted."

"Hell, son, why didn't you ask her, then? Why let her get mixed up with those three worthless no accounts instead of speaking up?"

Mason wished he could explain it. He couldn't admit to his father that he didn't feel worthy of a woman like Beth. "She always said I was her best friend and like a brother. What can a man say to that?"

Mr. Whittaker shook his head. "Being friends is a good start, but thinking of you as a brother? Damn, that's hard to fight, but you sure as hell should have tried."

"Yeah. Maybe, but I don't know if I ever would have asked her before. Soon as I finished my house and got settled, I reckon I would have. Now I don't have to because she saved me the trouble."

He pushed Beau onto a chair at the table. Looked like his mother had set out food to feed several times as many kin as were expected. He lifted the kitchen towels laid across the food to keep out flies and sliced off a piece of ham. He laid the ham on Beau's plate.

Beau looked up, and his mouth dropped open. "You mean she asked you? Well, I'll be damned. You never told me that."

His mother set a cup of coffee in front of Beau. "Just shows she finally came to her senses. She never seemed like her pompous parents, and I always liked Beth. Now I know why." She raised on tiptoe and kissed Mason on the cheek. "Not a finer man in the county, unless it's your daddy."

Beau pouted. "What about me, Aunt Millie?"

Mrs. Whittaker patted Beau's shoulder. "You're drunk, Beau, but when you're sober you're a wonderful man. Now, eat something and drink your coffee before your folks arrive and see you in this sorry state." She peered at his face. "What happened to your jaw?"

Mason looked at the floor.

Beau smiled innocently. "I fell down."

She patted his shoulder. "No wonder, dear, you've had far too much to drink." Mrs. Whittaker turned and shook her finger at her husband and son. "Don't let him have any more liquor."

Mr. Whittaker filled his plate. "Son, you'd better look after your grandfather. He's already three sheets to the wind."

"You sit down and eat, Mason." Mrs. Whittaker threw her dishtowel on the table. "Lawsy, I'll be glad to have a daughter-in-law. I'm tired of being stuck with a house full of men and no women but Josephina and me to show a lick of sense." She bustled out of the room.

Beau looked at Mason and burped. "Reckon when Beth's feelings toward you changed?"

Mason wondered the same thing. He'd known all these years that he loved Beth. When had she realized she loved him as a man and not merely as a friend? Whenever it was, he was damn glad she had because now his dreams were coming true. His own ranch, a new house and barn, and the woman of his dreams to live there with him. What could be better?

Thinking his cousin could use more coffee, Mason crossed the kitchen and reached for the pot as Josephina rushed by. The back of his hand pushed onto the stove, and he jumped. The coffeepot fell, and the scalding brew hit his leg on the way to the floor.

"Yeow!" He rushed for the water dipper and slung water on his britches where the coffee had spattered. When he turned around, the others in the room stared.

Josephina crossed herself. "*Madre de Dios*, it is true. Señorita Beth brings a curse."

"Nonsense, Josephina." The cold water had taken the heat from the coffee if not from the cook's words, and Mason set to cleaning up the spill. "We make our own luck, and Beth Pendleton is not jinxed. In fact, marrying her will be lucky for me."

"I beg your pardon, Señor Mason. Of course, you are right. She is a lovely young lady." Josephina took the towel from him. "Please, I will make more coffee and clean the floor. You must see to your burn."

Mason looked at his hand, then down at his soaked britches. "Reckon Mama will want to douse me with that awful-smelling goo if she sees me. I'll change and be back to eat."

When he returned, Beau appeared somewhat restored by his food and strong coffee. Mason's grandfather also sat at the table and didn't look as if he'd had a drink in days.

Mason fished out the gold band he'd bought Beth in Medina. He opened the box and looked at it.

"That hers?" Beau peered at it, and his breath near knocked Mason over. His cousin needed a lot more sobering up before the ceremony.

Mason took a step to the side, not wanting to hurt his cousin's feelings, but hoping to distance himself. "Yep. Got it in Medina. Didn't have a chance to ride to San Antonio or Austin like I wanted. Guess it'll do for a while until she can pick one out." But Mason had it inscribed in case Beth wanted this one.

Mr. Whittaker picked it up and moved it back and forth in an attempt to focus the inscription. "What's it say inside?"

Mason felt his face heat. "Says the date and 'Love Forever' and my initials."

Instead of ribbing him as Mason expected, his father merely nodded. "Nice." Mr. Whittaker slid it back into the box. "She'll like having words inside. Women are crazy for things like that."

"That's the idea." Mason snapped the lid shut.

His father stroked his chin. "Wish I'd thought of that when I married your mama. Reckon I could have something else engraved for her birthday. Maybe a locket."

"Good thought." Mason handed the ring to Beau. "See you remember to bring this to the wedding."

Beau stuffed it into his vest pocket. "I will."

Mason met his father's gaze, and his father winked. "I'll help him remember."

Grandpa cut another slice of ham. Instead of digging into it, he leaned back and rubbed his shoulder. "Gonna rain."

Mason nodded. "I already spread some straw on the chapel grounds. Figure I should have set a washtub of water at the door so folks could clean off the mud."

Grandpa looked up at him. "Not a bad idea. Send one of the hands over there. You got that buggy to pick up and your groom clothes to get into."

Beau didn't move out of his chair, but he stared at the kitchen window. "Looks sunny to me."

Mr. Whittaker walked to peer at the barometer near the back door. "Pressure's falling. Rain's on the way."

Beth cut the thread and admired her work. She had folded the handkerchief into a neat waterfall of lace-edged linen without cutting the fabric. Grandmother Ransom's initials showed at the top of the fold, and Beth thought that worked out as a nice touch. Though the color matched well enough, the difference in the fabrics and style stood out. She sighed. It was the best she could come up with at the last minute without shortening the train.

"It looks odd." Mrs. Pendleton appeared near tears again. "Everyone will know it doesn't belong there."

"I had planned to carry the handkerchief in Grandmother's memory. If anyone comments on it, you can say it was my way of involving my dear departed grandmother in the ceremony."

Mrs. Pendleton sniffed. "What will people think?"

"Perhaps that it's a sweet gesture which leaves my

hands free for a bouquet and Mason's arm." But Beth knew people would speculate, gossip, whisper. She'd heard their vicious comments turn the most innocent of incidents into scandal. What story would they invent for this?

Thunder rumbled in the distance.

"No, that can't be thunder. It can't rain." Beth rushed to the window. Overhead the sun shone, but clouds boiled in the southwest. Dark gray thunderheads. She should have known Mason would foretell the rain or he wouldn't have bothered with the straw. His leg ached worse with a weather change on the way.

Mrs. Pendleton peered out and gasped. "My dress. Rain will ruin my dress. Every drop that hits the silk will leave a horrendous spot." She rushed out, presumably to make arrangements to cover herself from head to toe for this evening's trip to the chapel.

From her second-floor vantage point, Beth watched the progress of a buggy as it raced down the street and turned into the Pendleton's carriage drive. Rachel drove, and from the grim set of her she had bad news. What now?

Six

Mason called after his father's cowpuncher. "It's likely gonna be hot and stuffy inside this evening. You'd best take a big bucket of fresh water and a couple of dippers so folks can at least quench their thirst."

As he and his grandfather had discussed, Mason had delegated one of his father's ranch hands to the chapel to set up a couple of washtubs of clean water by the door. His parents did this for parties in rainy weather so folks who'd traipsed through mud could wash their feet. On those occasions, many guests carried their party shoes and stockings to don after they arrived. In really bad weather, many ladies even changed dresses after they reached the hosts' home, then changed back for the trip home.

Mason had gathered his dress clothes and bundled them into a carpetbag earlier, and now he tied the satchel on the back of a horse in the event he ran late and didn't have a chance to come back by his parents' home.

Mr. Whittaker followed him out of the barn. "What if the rig's not ready? Reckon we should borrow one?"

For a wedding gift, Mason had bought Beth her own buggy and a striking roan mare so she could drive into town whenever she wished. He hoped that wouldn't be too often, but he didn't want her feeling trapped on the ranch. Ransom Crossing didn't have a buggy works, so Mason had ordered the vehicle from Watson's Buggy Works in Medina.

He'd ridden to get the buggy three days ago, only to find the maker had run into difficulty. "Grandpa said I could use his, and he's taking it to the chapel himself as a precaution. But Watson promised to have the new one ready and shined up by noon today."

"Take care, son. We'll see you at the church if you're too late to meet us here."

"Papa, will you see Beau is sober enough to stand up with me? He's broke up 'cause that girl from Bandera took up with someone new. If you don't watch him, he's like as not to drink himself under the table."

Mr. Whittaker stood with his hands in his pockets. He frowned. "I'll try, but I'm not his mama."

Thunderheads gathered and the horizon darkened. Judging the clouds' progress since morning, rain couldn't be more than two hours away. Mason decided he'd best hurry or he'd be caught on the wrong side of the river.

Instead of the road, he followed a shorter trail along the water's edge and made good progress. With only about four miles left, his mount stumbled, walked a bit, and stopped. Mason dismounted and examined the horse. The animal had a stone bruise on the frog of his right front hoof. Mason dug out the stone, but there'd be no riding until the bruise healed.

Loosing a string of curses sure to singe the ears of anyone who heard, Mason set out leading the horse toward town. Like most western men, he hated walking anywhere. His limp slowed him, and a rancher's boots favored stirrups, not the ground. By the time he reached town over an hour later, his uneven gait had jarred him so his hip and back near killed him and his feet begged for mercy.

"Whittaker, you hurt?" Watson polished the tufted leather buggy seat.

"Horse's injured. Had to walk a ways. Soon as I get him to the livery and seen about, I'll be back for my buggy."

Watson took the reins from Mason. "I'll do that for you. Know this is your wedding day." He looked at the clouds headed their way. "You'd better settle up for the buggy and be on your way."

The mare was already hitched and ready to leave. Careful examination of the vehicle met with Mason's approval. "You've done a fine job, Watson. Appreciate it."

Watson pointed out all the special features. "Too bad it don't have side curtains, 'cause you're in for a soaking."

"Reckon you're right. Water's already risen from rain upstream." The buggy required a carriage roadway rather than the narrow trail he'd used getting to Medina, and he'd be longer on the return trip. Mason had stopped at his prospective father-in-law's bank in Ransom Crossing and withdrawn the cash due. He paid Watson, transferred his bag to the buggy, and climbed in.

"Best to you and your bride. She's sure to be proud of your gift." Watson waved as Mason drove away.

The rain started a few minutes later, a drenching downpour so hard Mason could hardly see the road. At the first water crossing, the horse balked. If this were the only place they had to cross a river or creek, Mason would have urged the horse into the water. There were at least four more, and the water in this one had risen almost too high for the buggy to navigate.

Mason turned the horse and headed back to Medina.

"Rachel, only three weeks ago you assured me you could wear the dress or we could have made a new one." Beth looked at the soft pink satin. The rip down the front spanned from neck to the carmago waist, and the fabric on each side frayed.

Rachel sobbed. "I thought I could. I t-t-tried."

"So I see." The jagged tear looked irreparable.

"C-can you fix it? I l-l-love that dress. It's the prettiest one I've ever owned."

Maybe the ruffles could be utilized. Beth turned the dress around. The buttons had popped off—maybe exploded better fit the appearance—and three had left torn fabric. Front and back, the top of the dress was ruined.

Mrs. Pendleton regarded her niece. "How on earth did you get it fastened?"

"It was hard, but I held my breath and Ben did up the buttons. Then, he said something funny, and I tried not to laugh. It-it sort of burst out in a huge cough." Rachel sobbed again. "That's when it happened."

"Maybe you could wear something else. Let's think what other dresses you have?" Beth looked at the green poplin Rachel wore now and remembered a bombazine her cousin saved for Sundays. "What about the lavender moiré you wore last summer?"

"Jamie was sick on it all down the front. I can't get the stains out. I-I loved the dress, but it's ruined."

Beth remembered when Rachel's second oldest had been ill. Rachel had come home from the Pendletons' party to find the little boy burning with fever. She couldn't be blamed for picking up her sick son before changing clothes. His fever had lasted for days, and they'd all feared he'd die. "What else do you have?"

"None except the black Sunday dress. The others are pretty worn and not suitable for a wedding. A married woman on an apple farm needs different clothes than a single woman who lives in town."

Beth sighed. Even in distress, her cousin couldn't resist an opportunity to flaunt her marriage. Beth folded the torn dress. "Let me put this in my room and get my reticule. We'll go to the Mercantile and see if they have anything we can use for repairs."

Mrs. Pendleton sniffed. "Surely you have no intention of wasting time traipsing in public on your wedding day?"

"It won't take long, Mother." She hurried to her room, then back to the drawing room.

Her mother had apparently spent Beth's absence scolding Rachel, who stood in tears with her head hung. Beth's cousin had never been kind to her, but she sympathized with the woman. Mrs. Pendleton's tongue was rapier sharp, and she sliced into people relentlessly.

Beth slid her arm through her cousin's. "Come on, Rachel. We'll find something, don't worry."

The cousins walked the two blocks to the town's

main street. They waved at passersby and spoke to those who called out greetings. On the way, Beth heard Rachel sniff and knew she suffered from Mrs. Pendleton's scolding.

"She's just nervous, you know." Beth patted her cousin's arm.

"Your mother?" Rachel seemed surprised that Mrs. Pendleton might be uneasy about anything.

"Yes. She's afraid Mason will leave me at the altar and she'll be embarrassed again."

Rachel sniffled. "But what about you? She never thinks about your feelings and you'd be hurt."

Beth handed her cousin a handkerchief. "Unfortunately, Mother views all of life as to how it affects her specifically." In an effort to divert Rachel's attention from Mrs. Pendleton's harsh words, Beth asked about the Bigelow children.

For the rest of the walk into town, Rachel related anecdotes about her children. Each pointed out a major flaw in the children's characters or Rachel's parenting, but Rachel saw all the incidents as funny. Beth tried to smile pleasantly and nod as if she, too, thought the Bigelow brats were enchanting.

In the Mercantile, Beth searched the piece goods while Rachel sorted through the ready-made dresses. Beth had bent to sort through the bolts on the bottom shelf when she overheard the loud whispers of two women on the next aisle.

The first gossip spoke loudly. "You know she's jinxed herself this time, don't you?"

Beth froze, and a second voice carried to her. "No, you don't mean this is worse than the man who ran off with another man?"

No matter how she tried to be a good person, rumors like this hurt Beth. How could she fight them? She took food and clothes to the sick, helped the church minister to the poor, attended civic functions, did everything in her power to live a good life serving her community. Nothing stopped the tittle-tattle of malicious people. Absolutely nothing.

Gossip one sounded smug. "Now there's this hurry-up wedding, not even three weeks since they announced the engagement. You know what that means, of course."

The second voice, sounding shocked but amused, replied, "No, you don't mean she's in a family way?"

Beth gasped. Did it never end?

Gossip one said, "What else could it be?"

Rachel stormed over. "It could mean that they suddenly realized they belong together and don't have to prolong their engagement to satisfy a bunch of gossiping old biddies. That's what, so there."

Beth stood, grateful her cousin had stood up for her. She might have known—the two biggest scandalmongers in the state. Beth smiled sweetly. "Good morning, Mrs. Weldon, Mrs. Humphreys." She turned to her cousin. "Did you find a dress you liked?"

Rachel looked at the dress Mrs. Weldon wore. "No, all they had was an awful gray thing with cheap lace." She put her hand on her cheek and pretended surprise. "Oh, I'm sorry, Mrs. Weldon, I didn't realize you'd bought that same dress."

Mrs. Weldon bristled, and her face turned red. "Of all the nerve. Rachel Bigelow, you've lived out on that farm so long you've forgotten your manners."

Rachel shook her head. "No, believe me, Mrs. Weldon, I haven't forgotten a thing."

Beth had moved bolt after bolt of fabric, so she

dusted off her hands. "Excuse us, there don't seem to be any goods here we want."

Rachel and Beth left the Mercantile, and both burst into giggles.

Rachel wiped tears of laughter. "Did you see Mrs. Weldon's eyes bug out? She turned so red I feared she might have a stroke."

Beth looked at her cousin. "Thank you for sticking up for me."

"I hate those two biddies. They have nothing good to say about anyone. What they don't know, they make up and pass along as fact." Apparently Rachel's humor fled and anger replaced it. She almost stomped down the walk.

Beth sighed. "We didn't solve your dress problem."

They crossed the street and turned toward Beth's home.

Beth pointed at the dark clouds almost overhead. "Oh, no. I hope we reach home before the cloudburst."

Both women fell silent and hurried until they reached the Pendletons' massive Greek revival home.

Mrs. Pendleton waited in the drawing room. "Well?"

Rachel shook her head. "Nothing, Aunt Louise."

Mrs. Pendleton tapped her finger against her cheek. "Who do we know who's your size?"

"Widow Braswell, but she only wears black." Rachel shrugged. "The only other person I can think of is that harlot, Sally, at the saloon."

"Hmmm. Perhaps we could send a note to Sally and see if she has anything suitable." Beth didn't realize she'd spoken her thoughts aloud until the other two women displayed open-mouthed stares.

Mrs. Pendleton shuddered. "Bethany, you can't be serious. A harlot's dress in your wedding? What would people say?"

Rachel shook her head. "I couldn't. Ben wouldn't like me dressing in Sally's clothes."

Beth recalled hearing that before Ben courted Rachel, he'd been very well acquainted with Sally. With six kids and an apple farm, Beth doubted he had the time, energy, or inclination to visit Sally now.

Beth grabbed the ruined dress. "Perhaps there's some other way, but we're running out of time. Come up to my room, Rachel. We'll see if there's a dress with fabric we might use to redo the bodice."

In one of the armoires in her bedroom, Beth pulled out a dark pink China crepe. When it was made, she had loved the dress, but hadn't worn it since the ball at which her brief engagement to Fred Mahoney was dissolved by the arrival of the U.S. Marshal. She held the ruined dress next to the China crepe. The combination might not be ideal, but it beat green poplin, stained moiré, black bombazine— or anything Sally might offer.

Beth tossed both dresses across her bed. "Can you stay and help me?"

Rachel nodded. "I told Ben I'd meet him at the chapel. His mother will see the kids are clean and decent."

Beth turned to Rachel. "We'll have to hurry." She reached under her night table and retrieved a stack of *Harper's Bazaar* magazines. "Let's look through these. I think I saw a style we can use."

"You've been sewing—I see your things are out."

Beth sighed and told Rachel about her wedding

dress and the hasty repairs while each leafed through
one of the magazines.

"A mouse in your home? I wouldn't think Aunt
Louise would allow it."

Beth smiled. "Likely she'll be making war on the rodent world. Now that I know it's repaired, it seems
humorous. It'll be something to tell my children and
grandchildren, won't it?"

"You've always been a wonderful seamstress. My
stitches are never neat." Rachel turned a page.

"Oh, see this one?" Beth pointed to an illustration
of a riding habit. "It says it's made in red habit cloth,
so that's what I used in the one I made for the ranch.
Mason's teaching me to ride."

"I can't picture you on a ranch. Are you sure you
can adjust?"

Beth nodded at the trunks. "Oh, yes. I'm looking
forward to it. I have lots of linens for the house, of
course, as well as pictures and prints and things I've
collected all these years. Mason's hired Delia Boone
to help me with the house, but I wouldn't mind doing
everything myself."

Rachel gave Beth a measuring look. "You'll need
different clothes for the ranch."

"Yes, and I've made several dresses the past three
weeks." She hurried to a trunk and pulled out a modest dress of blue calico. "This one is the latest. I think
it will be cool for the summer."

Rachel put down her magazine. "What else?"

Beth laid the blue gown on the open lid and held
up several others for Rachel's inspection. "I don't
have a lot, but I'll need several changes plus plain petticoats and bloomers. See this, it's modeled after one

that I saw in *Harper's* from Princess Beatrice's trousseau."

She laid them back in the trunk and closed the lid. "We'd better get busy on your dress. I think I remember where I saw that drawing." Beth hurried to the bed and picked up a magazine. "See, this one would work."

Rachel clapped her hands. "Oh, it's wonderful. Can you really do that in so little time?"

"I hope so, but I'll need your help with this bottom ruffle."

Thunder rattled the windows, and the first raindrops fell. Surely nothing else would go wrong with this wedding day. Beth wondered if the rumors were true. Was she jinxed?

Seven

Mason fought his way through the storm. Back in Medina, he stopped at the livery for his saddle and checked on his father's horse he'd brought into town earlier. True to his word, Watson had given instructions for the horse's care. Mason threw the saddle into the buggy and headed for the Buggy Works.

He got under cover of the buggy works' wide portico. "I'll send someone for this rig after the water goes down."

Watson appeared with a large chamois. "I'll dry it down for you."

Mason unhitched the mare and threw his saddle and bridle on her. When he'd cinched her down tight, he tied his satchel on and mounted. He'd wasted precious time walking the injured horse into town earlier and on the aborted buggy trip. From having plenty of leeway, he'd wound up not being sure he could make it on time for the wedding.

Damned if he'd leave Beth standing alone at the altar. He took off through the downpour at a gallop.

* * *

Beth's fingers were sore from hasty stitches. She'd cut a new bodice from the China crepe and left the satin sleeves. "How are you doing with the ruffles?"

Rachel sat in a chair by the window and sniffled. "I can't get it right. You've ruined your dress for nothing."

"Keep trying. The bodice is almost finished." Beth fashioned a rose from the ruined fabric and tacked it to the vee of the new neckline. She hoped Rachel avoided coughing or laughing in this dress until after the wedding. Just in case, she'd left plenty of room. Rachel could probably wear it without a corset if she chose.

"Here's the ruffle." Rachel handed over a long piece of gathered China crepe.

Beth didn't say it looked as if it had been fashioned by a drunk or a child. Instead, she took it and sewed it in place of the satin one she'd removed. "Make a couple of crepe bows to go at each side of the panier puffs. Then I think you can try it on, and we'll see if it's going to look all right."

Rachel fashioned the bows while Beth sewed on the ruffle. When the dress was ready for Rachel to wear, Beth helped her into the modified creation. Rachel stood in front of the cheval glass and preened.

Beth cocked her head and walked on each side of her cousin. "It doesn't look bad. No one will know that's not how it was originally."

"It's even prettier than the first one." Rachel held out her skirt and twirled back and forth before the mirror. "Wait until Ben sees me in this."

Rachel's face turned serious, and she bit her lip. "I'm sorry you had to ruin your dress. I remember when you wore it at your parents' party last year. I thought it was the prettiest dress I'd ever seen."

Beth remembered. "But that party's not a pleasant memory, so it's just as well we were able to make use of the crepe. I don't think I'd have been able to force myself to wear it again."

Rachel took a deep breath and gulped. "I-I've said mean things to you. I want to apologize."

Beth couldn't have been more surprised if Rachel had declared she intended to run off to join the circus. She waved a hand in dismissal. "It's not necessary."

Rachel met her gaze in the mirror. "Yes, it is. I've been jealous of you as long as I can remember because your folks had more money than mine. Then both my folks and my brother died, and both your folks were alive and healthy. I guess I had to remind myself I had things you didn't to make up for the things I didn't have. Now that you're really getting married, you're not even spiteful back."

Beth had no idea what to say to her cousin's revelation. She decided honesty always worked best. "Sometimes when people say mean things to me, or about me, I want to lash out, but I can't let myself. It—it isn't something I ever learned. Hours later I think of the perfect thing I might have said, but then it's too late." Beth sighed. "Besides, you're my cousin, and I guess you're as close to a sister as I'll ever have."

Rachel turned, and tears ran down her face. "You're a better person than me, and I guess that's made me resent you even more. I'm truly sorry, Beth. I'll be a better cousin in the future."

"Rachel Bigelow, don't you dare drip tears on that fabric." Beth rushed to a drawer and pulled out a handkerchief. "Let's get you changed and eat some lunch. You can help with the rest of the preparations. I've yet to make the bouquets. The flowers are cut and waiting in the kitchen."

The two cousins went downstairs. The rain battered against the house relentlessly. They each took a seat at the kitchen table while Beulah and Emma worked and Mrs. Pendleton picked at her plate.

Beth thought of Mason, who usually worked out-of-doors. "I'm glad Mason planned to go to his folks so he won't be out in this weather."

"Mason? You might have a thought to me." Mrs. Pendleton glared at Beth. "All this rain will make the river and creeks too high to cross. Some guests won't be able to get to the chapel in spite of all my planning. There'll be only a handful at the reception."

"It's hardly my fault, Mother." Beth took a helping of the potato salad and ham Beulah had set out.

"Don't either of you eat a lot or your dresses won't fit. A corset can only do so much, as Rachel found out."

Rachel took a healthy helping of potato salad. "Don't worry, Aunt Louise. Beth left plenty of room in the new bodice."

Lightning flashed and thunder shook the windows. Beth and Rachel arranged containers of flowers throughout the downstairs, then came back to the kitchen to make their bouquets.

Beth tied her bouquet with a blue ribbon. "Lucky we didn't have this weather yesterday or the flowers would have been too beaten to use."

Finally, it was time to dress for the wedding. Beulah did Beth's hair; then Beth arranged Rachel's while Beulah helped Mrs. Pendleton.

Rachel admired her coiffure in the hand mirror. "I

wish there was a room at the chapel where we could dress. It'll be hard to keep dry in this weather."

"Daddy will let us use the closed carriage, but it'll be a tight squeeze for all five of us." Beth laid out her undergarments.

"Five?" Rachel counted on her fingers. "You, me, your parents. That's four."

"And Beulah. She has a new dress."

"You're having your maid at the ceremony?"

"She's not a maid; she's our housekeeper. Has been as long as I can remember, and she's a part of my family."

Usually Beth conformed to society's stilted rules, but on this one thing she didn't care what folks thought. Beulah had been more a parent than either of her real parents. Beth wanted Beulah in the chapel to see the vows.

"It's your wedding. I guess you can do whatever you wish." Rachel slipped out of her dress and prepared to don her remodeled attendant's dress. "Have you packed the things you're moving to Mason's?"

"Yes, I finished the trunks this morning, and Daddy will send them to Mason's ranch tomorrow. All I need is the carpetbag there in the corner with tonight's things and a dress for in the morning."

"Do you have a fancy nightdress?" Rachel's brown eyes sparkled.

Beth didn't want to display it, but she nodded. Rachel rushed to open the satchel. The lace and batiste nightgown lay on top.

Rachel held it up. "Ooooh, Mason will love this. You can see right through it."

Beth blushed. Valenciennes lace trimmed the neck with narrower lace at the armholes. A ruffle trimmed in the wide lace circled the hem. "It's scandalous, nothing more than a long chemise. Mr. Henrí assured me it was proper for a bride, but I included a modest gown in case I lose my nerve and can't wear the, the thin one."

Rachel dug into the bag and tossed the long-sleeved gown with a high neck onto a chair. "You won't need that. This is the one that will please your husband." Rachel cocked her head. "Has he kissed you?"

Beth nodded.

"Did you like it?"

Heat suffused Beth's face, but she smiled. "Yes, I liked it a lot."

"That's a good sign. And what else did he do?" Rachel rose from her perch on the floor and came closer.

Beth wondered if she should admit it. She took a deep breath. "He, um, he put his hand on my breast. And he pulled me close by wrapping his palm against my, um, my bottom."

Rachel smiled. "How did that make you feel?"

"I tingled all over, and had the most scandalous thoughts. I had the feeling he shared those ideas."

"Oh, of course he did. Men are randy as goats most of the time. I expect Mason can hardly wait until tonight."

Dare she ask? Beth took a deep breath. "Do, um, is there anything you can tell me about your wedding night? I mean, all Mother says is that it's something a woman has to suffer through and for me to endure it as best I can." Beth took another deep breath. "Th-that doesn't sound at all encouraging."

Eight

Rachel looked surprised. "Do you think I'd have six children in eight years if it was that unpleasant? If Mason's as caring as Ben, you'll be in heaven before morning."

Beth hadn't realized she'd held her breath, but now she released it with relief. "He's a caring man. He said today that he's always loved me but didn't feel worthy of me. Can you imagine?"

Rachel stepped into her dress and turned for Beth to do up the buttons. "I'm not surprised, but knowing how Uncle Howard and Aunt Louise hate his folks, I couldn't believe it when they agreed you could marry Mason."

"They wouldn't have years ago, but with all the gossip about me being jinxed and three cancelled weddings, they're desperate. I think they'd given up on ever marrying." Beth turned and held on to the bedpost so Rachel could tighten her corset. Ordinarily she didn't wear a corset, at least she hadn't for the past few years. Her mother insisted she wear one with this dress. "I just hope he never learns about our bet. He'd be hurt and angry."

"He won't hear it from me or Ben." Rachel pulled hard on the strings until Beth could hardly breathe.

She gasped. "You mean Ben knows?"

"Well, of course. When you love a man you tell him everything. But he won't tell anyone because I asked him not to." Rachel had cinched the corset and tied it.

Beth stepped into the mended wedding gown. "Rachel, what do you suppose Sally does to please men?"

"Well, Ben told me she does lots of things, some of which I'd guessed. Some surprised me. One is, she sometimes puts their, um, you know, right into her mouth and sucks on it." Rachel started fastening the thirty buttons down the back of Beth's dress.

Beth almost stumbled. "You can't mean it? Men pay her to do that? Why, I wonder?"

"I couldn't believe it myself." Rachel looked smug. "At least not at first. Ben told me lots more she does— and showed me. I was mad at first that he'd ever visited Sally, but maybe it's good because he learned things I like."

"Do you suppose she enjoys the way she earns her living?"

"Maybe some of the time, if the man is nice and clean and handsome. But can you imagine being with Old Mr. Handley?" Rachel finished the last button and stepped away.

Beth made a face. "Eeuww, no."

The two stood side by side and stared at their reflections in the cheval glass.

Rachel turned sideways. "Don't we look wonderful? I can hardly wait for Ben and the kids to see me. And won't his mother be stuck for something to criticize this time?"

"You look lovely, Rachel. I think you're right, we do

look wonderful. I hope we can stay dry until we get inside. Any guests who make it through the storm to the chapel will be waiting for something bad to happen, and I mean to disappoint them."

"You can count on Mason. He'll be there."

"Yes, I can. Today and always." Beth took one last look around the room. The package near an armoire caught her attention. "Rachel?"

"Yes?" Rachel looked at her.

She nodded at the bundle. "The bolt of silk is tied with brown paper ready for you to take home. I want you to have it."

"You can't mean it." Rachel's hand went to her throat, and she beamed.

"Yes, I do. I could never enjoy it. Every time I saw it I'd think of that silly bet."

Rachel frowned. "But you'll see me in it."

"It's not the same. I want you to have it. There's some brown foulard and trims to go with it as well. If you want me to, I'll help you make it up."

"After all the things I've said to you these past few years? I don't know how to thank you."

"No thanks are necessary. It'll look nice with your coloring." Beth took another look around the bedroom.

Rachel followed Beth's gaze. "Will you miss this house? It's such a beautiful place."

"Maybe a little. I look forward to being with Mason on the ranch, but I've lived here since I was eight." She ran her hand along the side of the dark cherry highboy.

Rachel met her gaze. "Yes, that's when we moved into your old house."

Beth gasped. "I-I never realized you minded,

Rachel. Mother and Daddy wanted your parents to have it, much better to have family instead of strangers living there, but we never meant you to feel bad."

"I know, and we were glad to move into it. I loved the nice yard and having my own big room." She looked at the floor. "I guess it was just me. I felt I lived in your shadow."

Rachel raised her face. "People have always talked about how pretty you are, how smart, and you had this wonderful house. You went away to school and came back looking like a princess. I felt dowdy and plain by comparison."

Beth hugged her. "Oh, Rachel. I never knew that. How terrible that I wanted to stay home but went away to school while you wanted to go away but stayed here."

"But if I'd gone, I might not have married Ben, and that would be bad because I do love him. Guess I was needlessly jealous of you all these years." Rachel pointed to the trunks. "Soon you'll be unpacking those at your new home. You'll be a married woman."

Beth smiled. "When I come up here to change during the reception, I'll be Mrs. Mason Whittaker."

"It won't be long now." Rachel folded her day dress and picked up her shoes. "Do you have a long wrap I can use?"

The two went downstairs where Mr. Pendleton and Beulah waited. Beth's father looked impressive in his dress clothes. Beulah wore pale green cotton sateen trimmed with Irish point embroidered lace.

Beulah clasped her hands to her chest. "Don't you look good enough to eat? I knew you'd be the prettiest bride I ever did see." She gasped. "Begging your pardon, Miss Rachel, but you know I'm as partial to Miss Beth as if she was my own."

Mr. Pendleton kissed Beth on the cheek. "Lovely. Bethany, that boy doesn't deserve you."

That was the closest her father had ever come to a compliment. "Daddy, you'd best change your mind about Mason. He's here to stay, and he'll be the father of your grandchildren."

"Hmph." Mr. Pendleton stuck out his lower lip. Beth couldn't say whether his displeasure stemmed from knowing Mason would father his grandchildren or from the fact that her father suddenly realized he might soon be a grandfather.

Emboldened by her near wedding, Beth faced her father and asked something that had bothered her for years. "Why don't you like the Whittakers? They're nice people and have always acted friendly toward you and Mother."

"With all their money, you'd think they'd fix up their home and set an example for others. Instead they live out there in that house that's grown all higgledy-piggledy, and they dress like ranch hands. Socialize with them, too. Not at all the proper way for people of substance to act."

Beth stared at her father. "You mean Mason's parents have as much money as you do?"

"Hmph. Reckon they don't know the responsibility wealth carries. Have to set an example."

"Daddy, I expect they believe they are setting an example. They treat everyone the same and make everyone welcome."

Mr. Pendleton shook his head. "Not the proper thing, not at all. Have to observe the rules, social order. It's how the country is organized."

From the top landing, Mrs. Pendleton cleared her throat and started her descent. When Beth turned, she caught her breath. Her mother wore possibly the ugliest dress in all creation. The dark yellow dress of silk brocade turned her mother's beautiful skin a shade resembling someone with severe jaundice.

The dress hugged her mother's small waist, but her mother swam in yards of Chantilly lace in the same sickening color. Lace epaulets graced the shoulders, and a matching ruffle fell at the end of the long sleeves. Several strands of beaded ribbon hung from the epaulets, and the same beads decorated the front of the brocade vest.

The expensive lace formed ruffles at her hips and down the front of the dress, and around the base of the skirt. Silk bows decorated the ruffles. The effect was of gaudy and ostentatious excess. Beth's mother looked like a joke, a caricature of bad taste.

"Mother, that's not the dress that Mr. Henrí made for the wedding."

"I wired Mr. Henrí the day you told us of your engagement to Mason. This arrived by courier only yesterday. It's the very latest thing from Paris." At the bottom of the stairs she held the skirt out. "Mr. Henrí insists this color is the rage in Paris and New York. I'll be the only one in Ransom Crossing to have it."

Everyone in the room stared at Mrs. Pendleton, apparently each of them rendered speechless by the horrible dress.

Beth thought Mr. Henrí had a lot to answer for and suspected he'd simply found a way to rid himself of unwanted piece goods, probably at an outrageous price. "But, but it's, um, sort of a dried-out mustard."

"Bethany, what nonsense. Show some breeding

even if you are about to become a provincial ranch wife. This color is Imperial Chrysanthemum." Mrs. Pendleton checked her elaborate hairdo in the mirror over a wall table. She turned this way and that admiring herself. "It's new this season, so it's not a color you've seen me wear."

And thank heavens for that. Beth remembered the tasteful dress she'd chosen to be made for her mother. The color had complemented her mother's hair and set her complexion to glowing. "What about the lovely gray silk with the imported lace trim?"

Her mother pushed a curl into place. "That? Well, I'll wear it some other time. There'll be plenty of occasions. Your father and I plan a trip to Europe now that you're to be wed and not in need of us as chaperones." Then she spotted Rachel and narrowed her eyes. She marched over and examined Rachel's dress. "Bethany, surely that's not fabric from your China crepe gown?"

"Yes, and I think it turned out rather well, don't you? I like it even better than the original."

Over the yellow cast of her skin, Beth's mother reddened with anger. "Do you realize how much that cost? You've ruined a Paris gown to repair one that will never leave the county."

Tears welled in Rachel's eyes. Beth put her arm around her cousin. "But Rachel looks lovely enough to grace any Paris ballroom, doesn't she?"

"Hmph, yes, yes." Mr. Pendleton rubbed his hands together. "Well, then, let's get on our way. The carriage is waiting under the portico."

The women swathed themselves in long cloaks and held their skirts up. With the strong wind blowing outside, Beth bundled her veil under her wrap. Once she was safely inside the chapel, she'd have someone help her set the silk orange blossom crown on her head. Though the portico was covered, Mr. Pendleton carried umbrellas for their use at the chapel.

The closed coach set off with all five of them crowded inside. Beulah and Mr. Pendleton sat facing the other three.

Beulah shook her head. "This rain done ruined my frosting. Turned the sugar all grainy. I told Emma to watch it. Like as not it's gonna run right off them cakes."

"It'll be fine, Beulah, and your cakes always taste wonderful." Frosting was the last thing Beth cared about right now. "With this kind of weather, probably not many people will show up anyway."

Rain lashed against the sides and trickled in at the windows. Beth pitied the poor driver—as well as any guests traveling in open vehicles.

Mrs. Pendleton adjusted her cloak to ward off the window's leak. "We should have put up a screen at the back of the chapel so people could change there."

Mr. Pendleton stared at the window. "Too late now, Louise. I'm sure people will make provisions."

After a short but rough ride, they reached the chapel. Dozens of wagons and buggies ringed the churchyard. Much of the straw Mason and Rowdy had spread floated on puddles or ran on the rivulets down the slope.

Mr. Pendleton opened the door and stepped out. "Bethany, you wait here until time for the ceremony. I'll come back to get you and Rachel."

Beth leaned forward. "This coach is stifling with the windows up. Hurry, or we'll boil."

Mrs. Pendleton pulled the hood of her cloak up

and gathered her bunched skirt up under her cloak. Mr. Pendleton held the umbrella and offered his arm. Beulah carried her own umbrella and made a dash for the door. Halfway up the steps, the wind caught the Pendletons' umbrella and turned it inside out. Mrs. Pendleton screamed and rushed into the sanctuary behind Beulah.

The driver moved a few feet away so the steps were clear for other arrivals. Soon Mr. Pendleton appeared carrying what must be Beulah's umbrella over two dippers of water. "Here, this will cool you a bit."

Beth laid her bouquet on the seat beside her. "Thanks, Daddy." She took a long drink, then sipped the remainder before she handed the empty dipper back to her father.

"Neither your groom nor his parents are here yet, but old man Whittaker is sitting right up front."

Beth fought the panic his words created. "Likely the storm slowed the others."

Mason won't let me down. Mason won't let me down. She repeated the litany in her mind to still the butterflies in her stomach.

Rachel drained her dipper and handed it back to Mr. Pendleton. "Thank you, Uncle Howard." She licked her lips and appeared puzzled. "Tasted odd, didn't it?"

He closed the door and went into the chapel. Beth leaned back and closed her eyes. "Yes, it did."

"Suppose someone spiked it?" Rachel licked her lips.

"I—I don't know. How could we tell?"

Rachel shrugged. "Don't know. Probably doesn't matter. No more than we had, it won't make us tipsy."

Time dragged while they waited in the sultry coach.

Beth scratched at her neck. It itched. Then the itching spread.

She looked down at the bare skin above her low neckline. Red welts had sprung up. On the bare part of her arms above her long gloves, more angry hives showed.

"No, this can't happen."

Rachel's eyes widened. "My stars. Beth, you're breaking out in hives. Maybe it's nerves because of the wedding, or the heat. Should I open the door?"

"No. The odd-tasting water." Beth panicked. "Gin makes me break out like this." She pointed her gloved hand at her chest. "If someone poured gin in the water and I drank it, this would happen."

Rachel's eyes widened. "How can you be allergic to gin?"

"Juniper berries. Gin's made from them." Beth thought she might cry. Her dress, Rachel's dress, Mason falling, the rain, the cake frosting—the day's events wore on her, and she wanted to curl into a ball and cry. How could so many things go wrong with one ceremony?

"Oh, my gosh. I remember when we were kids and picked all those juniper berries at Grandma's so we could string them for our make-believe Christmas tree. And your eyes swelled and your nose ran and you broke out in—"

"Hives." Beth pointed to herself again. "Just like these."

"What will we do? I keep soothing lotion at home, but no one will have anything here."

Beth closed her eyes and fought against tears—or a scream. "I'll pretend it isn't there. If I ignore the welts, maybe they'll fade." But already she itched on every part of her body. "Are they on my face, too?"

Rachel bit her lip and nodded. "Sorry, Beth."

"Why do all these terrible things have to happen whenever I plan a wedding?" Beth wriggled in her seat. She itched everywhere, even her bottom.

Rachel shook her head.

At that moment, another carriage drew up. Rachel polished the steam off the glass and peered out. "It's Mason's parents, but he's not with them."

"Thank goodness they're here. At least that should cut short some of the speculation that's bound to be going on in there."

Rachel leaned back. "Yes, I'd guess the bets were increasing."

"Bets? You said you kept our bet a secret and only told Ben."

Nine

Rachel nodded to Beth's question. "Oh, I only told Ben. Well, maybe the kids heard, but they never pay any attention."

Beth wanted to scream, but she took a deep breath. "Then what bets?"

"Everyone in town's betting whether or not Mason will show up and, if he shows, whether or not he'll go through with the wedding. I figured you knew."

"Well, that takes the cake." Beth crossed her arms. "I hope they all bet that he wouldn't show so they'll all lose their money."

"So do I. Ben's holding most of the cash."

"Rachel! You can't mean my own cousin's husband has encouraged bets against me?"

"Don't get mad at us. We figured Mason's a sure thing, and some bet a considerable amount. You know how gossipy folks are, and we thought it would serve them right to lose."

"And so it will. I hope all the talk about me being a jinx will die off now." She fisted her hands. "I can't tell you how sick of it I am."

"You never let on it bothered you."

"Of course it bothers me! How would you feel if

half the county talked about you? If they gossiped night and day about silly things?"

"I reckon they have." Rachel laughed. "You remember our oldest was born, um, a few months early."

"Oh, that." Beth clasped her hands to keep from scratching. "Let me guess. Mrs. Weldon and Mrs. Humphreys spread that tale."

Rachel giggled, as if remembering the incident in town today. "Right you are, the sour-faced old biddies."

"As if yours were the first eight-pound premature baby born in this town or any other. For heaven's sake, it's not as if you were running around with half the men in town. Everyone knows you and Ben loved each other and had planned to marry anyway."

"Why, thank you, Beth. No one ever defended me before. Ben's mother acts as if I have horns and a forked tail because I trapped her precious boy."

Though she'd never said so to anyone, Beth disliked Rachel's mother-in-law. "The old cat. Has it ever occurred to her that maybe her dear son trapped you?"

Rachel laughed. "No, her adorable, perfect boy can do no wrong. Didn't you know? I hope Mrs. Whittaker isn't like that."

"Me, too, but I don't think she is. She's always been very nice to me and seems pleased Mason and I are getting married."

Rachel chewed her lip and hesitated. "Um, Beth? You heard Mrs. Weldon, so you know the latest gossip?"

"Latest? You mean her remark that I must be in the family way. You mean that wasn't the first time that had been discussed? Oh, forever more! I am so sick of people gossiping. You'd think they could find something better to do with their time than make up stupid rumors about me."

"I wanted to be sure you understood, so you'd be prepared in case she says something to you at the reception."

Those women and others like them made Beth angry. She tried to take a deep breath to calm herself, but her darned corset wouldn't let her. "Does no one read the newspaper? Can't they discuss the weather, what about Governor Ireland's or President Cleveland's policies or other current events, anything besides me?"

Mr. Pendleton chose that moment to open the door and climb in. Beth had never seen him in such disarray. In spite of his oiled coat, his jacket appeared soaked and his hair plastered to him. Mud and straw coated his shoes.

"Driver's pulling the coach back to the steps so we can get you and Rachel inside. Everyone's here but the groom. His parents said he's picked up a horse and buggy in Medina to give you for a wedding gift and is on his way. He'd damned well better show."

Pleasure shot through Beth, and she clasped her gloved hands. "He ordered me a buggy? Isn't that sweet of him?"

Her father glared. "Not unless he shows up."

Beth smiled, considering her groom's kind nature. "He'll be here, Daddy, you can count on it. Mason won't let me down."

The carriage stopped, and her father climbed down. The rain had slowed, but he opened another umbrella. "Rachel first. Steps are slippery so let me help you. Bethany, you wait here and I'll be back for you."

He closed the door, and Beth waited, willing herself not to scratch. She looked down at her chest, but the welts looked even worse since a few more had popped out. The stifling heat took her breath away, and she feared she'd pass out. Some bride she made, but she pulled her duster around her and prepared for her dash to the chapel.

Her father opened the door and held the umbrella for her. "Lucky for us Whittaker put down the straw. Otherwise the buggies would have stuck."

"He's very thoughtful. Daddy, he really is a wonderful man. I hope you'll realize that soon." Beth rolled her train up until she had it and her veil covered by her wrap and held her skirt up so far her ankles showed. She hoped she didn't drop her bouquet. Her father gripped her arm and guided her up the steps and into the back of the church.

Her mother waited there with Beulah, Rachel, and Rachel's husband and oldest son. Rain and wind had ruined Mrs. Pendleton's elaborate coiffure, and Beulah repeatedly tucked Mrs. Pendleton's curls back into place. Ben wore his best black trousers and a coat that almost matched. Ben, Jr., wore his usual church clothes of shirt and dark britches.

Mr. and Mrs. Whittaker and Mason's cousin, Beau, stood nearby. Mrs. Whittaker wore a dress of turquoise blue lampas trimmed with turquoise satin and pale straw-colored surah. The color deepened the shade of her eyes and contrasted with her sun-kissed skin and dark hair in an attractive way. Mr. Whittaker and Beau wore dark suits, but not a tuxedo like Mr. Pendleton.

From the front of the chapel, Rachel's next oldest, Jamie, yelled. "Hey, there's Cousin Beth. Reckon her man's gonna show up this time?"

Beth wanted to melt into the floor when chuckles rippled across the chapel. Instead, she held her head high.

Rachel marched forward and pinched her son's arm.

"Ow-w-w-w, Mama. I didn't do nothin'." He held his arm as if it were broken.

"You be quiet, Jamie Bigelow, or I'll tan your hide when we get home." Rachel whirled around and walked to the back where her husband waited.

Mrs. Weldon and Mrs. Humphreys pivoted in their seats to smirk at her. Mrs. Weldon had wet leaves stuck to her bonnet. Mrs. Humphreys' hair straggled in limp, soggy curls beneath her hat. Beth looked through them with her coldest glare. Both women quickly faced the front of the chapel.

Beth unfolded her veil and plumped the circle of silk orange blossoms to which the veil attached and set it firmly onto her head. Beulah came forward and adjusted the tulle so that it flowed gracefully down from the crown.

Mrs. Pendleton's eyes widened in alarm. "Bethany, what on earth is wrong with your skin? You look awful. For goodness sakes, do something to repair yourself."

"What can I do, Mother? I have hives. Rachel and I think the water is spiked with gin. You know how allergic I am to it."

Mrs. Whittaker glared at Beau. "You didn't?"

Beau blushed and stepped back. "Thought it might relax folks. Didn't know Beth would break out in red dots."

She leaned close to his ear and hissed so loud Beth heard. Probably everyone in church heard. "I'll show you relaxed when we get home, young man. You're lucky I didn't find out about this earlier or I'd of poleaxed you myself."

He looked down at the floor. "Sorry, Aunt Millie. Beth, I 'pologize. My thinkin's all messed up 'cause everything about this wedding reminds me Amy doesn't love me. Thought we'd be gettin' hitched, but she's marrying a fellow she met at her aunt's. Tears my heart to pieces."

He looked so forlorn that Beth had to say something nice, even though she'd like to bang his head against the wall.

"It can't be helped now, Beau. I'll be fine in a day or two." She glanced at the delicate watch pinned to her mother's ugly dress. Straight up seven. Beth looked at Mrs. Whittaker. "Mason's late and that's not like him. It's a bad storm. What if something bad has happened to him?"

Mr. Pendleton sniffed. "Boy doesn't deserve Bethany anyway, but he'd better show up."

Ignoring him, Mrs. Whittaker patted Beth's hand. "Now, dear, don't worry. Mason is crazy about you, and he's resourceful. He's sure to be here as fast as he can." She fished in her bag and brought out a jar. "I brought this in case he needs more for that bump on his head. Let's put some on those hives. It smells awful, but it works."

Mrs. Pendleton wrinkled her nose in disgust. "Eeu-uwww. Millicent, you cannot put that awful stuff on my daughter. It would ruin her gown, and it smells to high heaven."

Mrs. Whittaker unscrewed the lid. "Nonsense,

Louise. Beth's uncomfortable, and this will ease her itching."

Beth held still while Mrs. Whittaker rubbed her exposed skin with a concoction whose fumes brought tears to her eyes. But the smelly goo cooled the burning and itching wherever it touched. "Thank you. It does feel better. I wish it were everywhere."

Mrs. Whittaker slipped the jar back into her bag. "I'll send it with you after the reception. What you need is a nice warm bath, and then Mason can rub this on you." She nudged Beth and leaned near, her eyes twinkling. "Doesn't that sound interesting?"

Sure her face turned bright red, Beth barely nodded.

Mrs. Pendleton gasped and bristled. "The nerve. She will do no such thing. My daughter is a lady, and no man, not even her husband, will ever see her in her bath or put his hands all over her."

Beth weighed her mother's words against Mrs. Whittaker's. Her mother cared only what people thought. Mrs. Whittaker actually cared for Beth's comfort and welfare. Her mother thought relations between a man and woman something to suffer through. Mrs. Whittaker thought they were interesting.

Beth faced her mother. "You care more about what folks think than how I feel. You always have, Mother. It's time you learned that the way you treat people is more important than your social status."

Her mother clutched at her heart. "Bethany! What's come over you?"

"Nothing. I've set my priorities, and being a good wife to Mason is first. If you want to see me in the future, you and Daddy had better be nice to Mason and his family. He's a fine man, the best I've ever known, and he deserves your respect." She turned and smiled at her future mother-in-law. "Thank you for the ointment, Mrs. Whittaker. I appreciate your thoughtfulness."

Mrs. Whittaker patted her hand. "Now, dear, you call me Mama, just like Mason does. Can't tell you how I've looked forward to having a daughter."

Beth sighed. "Thank you, um, Mama. That's very kind of you." She hoped her parents would come around. Maybe when they returned from their trip they'd see how happy she and Mason were and be glad for her. Whether they did or not, she was fortunate to become a part of the Whittaker family.

Beside her, Beth's father snorted. "Hmph, no point in calling her Mama if that boy doesn't show up—not that he deserves you, Bethany."

Mr. Whittaker stood with hands in his pockets and a shoulder braced against the back wall of the chapel. "He'll be here. Unless some jinx has kept him from it."

Mr. Pendleton stepped forward, but Mrs. Whittaker reached her husband first. She hit him hard on the arm.

"You stop that talk right now, Glenn Whittaker, or you'll be sleeping in the barn with the other jack-asses."

Mr. Whittaker rubbed his arm and looked at the floor. "Beg your pardon, Beth."

Rachel removed her cloak, and Ben stared.

"You look awful pretty, hon. I reckon that's even prettier than the other dress."

"Yeah, Mama, you look nice as candy." Ben, Jr., was

of an age where he compared everything to horses, dogs, or candy.

"This *is* the first dress." Rachel looked at Beth, and a look of understanding passed between them. "Beth fixed it with one of hers."

Mrs. Pendleton harumphed. "Wasted a perfectly good Paris gown."

"No, Mother, we made good use of it." Beth smiled at Rachel.

"Your dress is beautiful, Beth." Mrs. Whittaker touched the skirt's beadwork. "Such an unusual and clever design. And the little lace at the bottom is so interesting."

Beth's mother moaned.

Beth announced loud enough that Mrs. Weldon and Mrs. Humphreys would be certain to hear, "That's my late Grandmother Ransom's handkerchief. I'd planned to carry it in her memory, but this keeps my hands free for my bouquet and Mason's arm." She leaned near Mrs. Whittaker's ear and whispered, "I'll tell you the rest about it later."

An elderly woman two rows up turned around and struggled to stand. "May I see, dear. Your grandmother was one of my closest friends."

"Oh, Mrs. Vanderpool. How nice you could come, even with all the rain." Beth moved a few steps up the aisle to greet the woman.

"I wouldn't miss it for the world." Mrs. Vanderpool adjusted her spectacles. "Oh, Beth, you're as lovely a bride as I thought you'd be. You look exactly like your grandmother at your age. What a beauty she was."

"Thank you so much. That means the world to me." Beth thought she might cry.

The elderly woman looked at Beth's dress. "Oh, I

see the handkerchief with her initials showing. What a nice touch, my dear. She would be so proud of you."

"I hope so. She was a wonderful person."

"Yes, she was so kind and compassionate and did many good works about town—without her husband's knowledge, of course. I've heard you carry on that tradition, dear, and help many of the unfortunate in our community. Bless you." Mrs. Vanderpool smiled. "Don't worry, that boy will be here. He's a smart young man, and no man in his right mind could resist you, my dear." She sank back onto the pew.

Beth thanked her again and moved to the back of the church holding back tears of happiness and sorrow. Sorrow her beloved grandmother had passed on but happy that finally, someone besides Mason had something good to say about her.

Mason was never late for anything, and Beth feared he might have been injured in the storm. She pictured all sorts of disasters—he could have been struck by lightning, a tree branch could have fallen on him, the lump on his head from this morning could have made him ill.

Still near tears, she asked his parents, "When did Mason leave?"

Mr. Whittaker met her gaze. "He left at noon. Took my horse to Medina. Watson's Buggy Works didn't have the buggy ready when he went three days ago, but Watson promised to have it ready and waiting today. Reckon this storm's slowed him."

Beau wove to look out the window. "River's too high to cross." He took a flask from his pocket and took a swig. "Might have had to turn back and leave the buggy, then ride here."

Beth hugged her arms. Had she turned into a jinx

after all? She counted the travel time on horseback to Medina, then added the time back by buggy, and threw in an extra hour for the storm. Mason should have arrived by now. What if he'd fallen into the river, or the axle had broken? She took a deep breath and battled light-headedness.

"Now, dear, don't fret." Mrs. Whittaker patted her arm again. "Nothing could keep Mason from showing up here and marrying you."

Mr. Pendleton crossed his arms. "Boy doesn't deserve her, but he'd damned well better show up, and fast."

Beau took another swig from his flask, and Mr. Whittaker scowled at Mr. Pendleton.

Beth felt trapped in a nightmare. What if Mason didn't come? Beth fought for air and saw white circles swirling in front of her. Maybe her corset was too tight. "I think I'd better sit down."

People on the back pew scooted together and made a place at the end, and she sat on the hard bench. Someone produced smelling salts, and the acrid scent combined with the awful odor of the ointment. Her nostrils stung and her eyes watered, but the dizziness decreased. If only Mason were here, she'd be fine.

Beth heard the murmurs through the small sanctuary. Though she couldn't understand much, she picked out the words "bet," "jinx," "again," and "family way." Everyone thought Mason had decided to run out on her, leaving her with a baby on the way. If he didn't show, it would be because he'd been injured—but wouldn't that prove she was a true jinx?

Ten

The door burst open, and Mason limped in—
maybe fell in was more accurate. Everyone in the
sanctuary turned around, and a murmur rose in
waves across the chapel. Beth sighed with relief and
stood to greet him. She wanted to rush into his arms,
but there were too many people between them. She
pushed her way through.

"Mason, you poor dear, you're soaked." He wore
what looked like the same work clothes he'd worn this
morning, but she didn't care.

He stood in front of her, water from his hair running into his eyes and every part of him dripping onto
the floor in a growing puddle. Grabbing her hand like
a lifeline, he looked at her. "Aw, Beth, honey, what
happened to you? I'll bet you're miserable." He
leaned forward. "Smells like Mama's goo."

"I broke out in hives. Your mother put the ointment on the skin that's not covered by dress and
gloves. It eased the itching." She wanted to add the
part about him rubbing it all over her later, but
couldn't with all the people around them.

Beau looked at the floor. "Soory, cuz. I mean, sorry.
Poured gin in the water bucket. Thought it'd relax
folks. Didn't know Beth couldn't take gin."

"Beau, have you lost your brain? I take back what I said. I'm not one bit sorry I hit you this morning."

Beau hung his head. "Know I'm acting crazy, but can't think straight. Glad you're marrying Beth after wanting her all these years, but I can't think about anything but Amy leaving me."

"I know, Beau." Mason exhaled and smiled at Beth. Love shone from his eyes. "Don't worry, Beth. You look pretty as a picture."

Beth looked down at the angry welts across her skin and knew she looked a fright. "You always say nice things to me. Thank you."

"Papa, your horse is at the Medina livery with a stone bruise on the frog of his right front hoof." Mason looked at Beth while he spoke, and clasped her hands in his. "Beth, for your wedding present I bought you a pretty new buggy and a roan mare to pull it."

Another murmur rippled across the room.

Beth smiled up at him. "Your folks told me. It was awful sweet of you, but you've always been thoughtful."

"Couldn't get the rig across the creeks. Had to turn around and take it back to Medina. We'll send for it when the water goes down."

"Thank you for thinking of it, Mason. But, if your father's horse is at the livery, how'd you get here?"

"Had to ride the new roan I bought you. She's buggy trained but not saddle broke, and she fought me." He looked down at his clothes. "Somewhere along the way I lost my hat. My satchel came loose and fell off the back of the horse. Lost my good suit, boots, and best shirt, but didn't have time to go back."

Mr. Whittaker took off his own jacket. "Here, son, wear this. Beau, give Mason a drink from that flask."

Mason accepted a nip from the flask. Taking the coat his father offered, Mason pulled it on over his wet shirt.

Reverend Moseley cleared his throat. "Shall we get on with the ceremony? Mason, would you and the best man take your places at the front?"

Mason's boots squished when he walked. When he and Beau were at the front, Rachel's husband acted as usher and seated the Whittakers on the front pew next to Mason's grandfather, who slumped as if he'd dozed off. When the Whittakers sat beside him, Mr. Whittaker nudged him.

The elderly man started awake. "What happened? Oh, I see Mason finally made it." He pulled out his pocket watch and peered at it. "Damned well time he showed up."

Ben returned and guided Mrs. Pendleton to the front pew across the aisle from the Whittakers and down a space to leave room for Mr. Pendleton.

The accompanist played the little pianoforte that Mr. Pendleton and two other men had hauled to the chapel. Beside the pianist, Mozelle Darby straightened her shoulders, thrust out her bosom, and broke into song. Off key. Apparently the screech startled the accompanist, and she missed notes of her own.

Beth gritted her teeth against Mrs. Darby's shrill voice and ignored the titters that rippled across the guests. Mrs. Pendleton had insisted they use Mrs. Darby because the woman had once sung solos at a large church in Austin. It must have been years ago, for what little voice the woman may have once possessed had long since departed. Mrs. Darby finished the first selection and broke into a second. The accompanist raced to keep up. Thunder rumbled outside and appeared to punctuate the soloist's vocalizing.

Rachel, standing in front of Beth, turned around and rolled her eyes. Some people laughed openly at Mrs. Darby's attempts at vocalization. A couple of children covered their ears. Beth would have liked to, but she stood rigid beside her father. Finally, Mrs. Darby took her seat. The accompanist played alone.

Ben took out a match safe and lit a long taper he handed to Ben, Jr., who carried the lighted candle and used it to start those at the front of the chapel.

Halfway through, he yelped, "Hot damn," and dropped the lighted candle. The boy danced first on one foot and then the other while shaking his hand. Ben rushed toward his son. Mason scooped up the candle and stomped out the burning floor. Smoke rose, and Beth smelled the scorched wood.

Mason struck a match and lit the candle again. Ben held his son so he could reach the remaining candles without hot wax dripping on his hand. They blew out the candle they'd used to light the others and placed it on the floor. Then he and Ben, Jr., took their places on the second pew beside Ben's mother and father and Rachel's other five children—Jamie, Angus, Bart, Liza, and baby Becca.

Rachel glanced over her shoulder, and Beth nodded to signal she was ready. Rachel walked slowly toward the front.

"That boy doesn't deserve you." Mr. Pendleton's stage whisper carried through the chapel.

Mason's gaze met Beth's, and he smiled.

"No, Daddy, it's I who don't deserve him." She

placed her hand on her father's arm and began the walk down the aisle.

Mason heard the murmurs. Bets. Jinxed. All sorts of vicious gossip floated toward him. At this point he didn't care. The day he thought would never come, the day he thought barred to him, the day he would wed Beth had finally arrived. In a few minutes she'd be his wife.

He watched her walk toward him and beamed at her. No woman on earth had ever looked so lovely. The dress hugged her figure the way he intended to in a few hours. The long train probably picked up plenty of mud and water as she came toward him in spite of the washtubs at the door, but Beth had never looked lovelier. Even Rachel, walking a few steps in front of Beth, looked pretty in her pink dress.

Beside him Beau seemed to weave, but Mason ignored his cousin and kept his eyes focused on his bride. Rachel, Mr. Pendleton, and Beth came forward. Halfway in their walk down the aisle, Beau keeled over and took out both of the large flower urns as he fell flat on his face. The accompanist crashed her fingers against the keys and stopped playing.

The first urn's contents spilled across Mason's already soaked britches and boots and splashed onto Reverend Moseley and the lectern. The minister stepped back; his eyes widened in horror as he watched the second container reach its destination.

Mrs. Pendleton shrieked as water and flowers showered her. "My dress! My gorgeous Imperial Chrysanthemum silk brocade is ruined. Ruined." She held out her skirts and shook them as she sobbed. Flowers flew off the skirt or tangled in the lace. Water soaked the front of her dress.

Mr. Pendleton deserted Beth halfway up the aisle and pushed by Rachel to rush toward his wife. "Louise, are you all right?"

Mrs. Pendleton sobbed. "First my own daughter turns against me, and now my special new dress is ru-uuuuined." She accepted the handkerchief her husband offered. "This is the worst day of my life. This is the worst wedding in history."

Mr. Pendleton glared at Mason, who ignored him and bent to retrieve one of the urns. He dumped what remained of the water onto his cousin's head. Beau didn't move. Mason placed the empty urn back where it had set earlier.

When Mason saw Beth shaking with her hand over her mouth, at first he thought she was crying, and he started to go to her. Rachel, who had missed the water by only a few steps, hid behind her hand as well. Then he realized that Beth's anxiety had apparently shattered her demeanor, and she pressed her hand to her mouth in what looked like an attempt to stifle laughter. Both women shook with suppressed mirth. He had to admit it was pretty funny that Mrs. Pendleton had received her comeuppance, but he kept a straight face.

Rowdy appeared and took Beau's feet while Mason grabbed his cousin under the arms. They dragged him to the side. Apparently out cold, Beau never so much as moaned.

Rowdy grinned as if he'd heard a funny joke and wanted to bust out laughing. "Reckon the jinx is on your cousin."

Mason agreed and smiled. "Thanks for your help."

Rowdy went back to his seat. Mason felt in Beau's pocket for the ring and nodded to his father.

"Papa, I think you'll have to fill in for Beau. He's out for a while."

Mr. Whittaker came forward and took the ring. Mr. Pendleton seemed to suddenly remember he'd left his daughter midway up the aisle and went back for her. The accompanist resumed playing, and Beth and her father stopped in front of the minister.

"We are gathered here today to . . ."

Beth tried to follow his words, but too much had happened. The red spots on her itched, and those white spots danced in front of her eyes again.

"Who gives this woman?"

Mr. Pendleton glared at Mason. "Her mother and I do." He handed her to Mason and stepped back.

Beth felt the train tear when she turned toward Mason. She looked back, and her father's large, muddy footprint was smack in the middle of her train. She felt a draft at the waist where the train had come loose. Beth handed her bouquet to Mason and reached behind her to poke at the seams.

Rachel peered around to look at the train. "It's torn, but nothing shows through."

Her mother broke into wails. "Mr. Henrí's beautiful dress. I hate this wedding!"

Beth heard her mother's sobs, but she didn't care about anything but marrying Mason—and maybe getting into that warm bath Mrs. Whittaker mentioned. She took back her bouquet and nodded at the minister. Reverend Moseley launched into the rest of the ceremony.

Once again Beth tried to pay attention, but she thought she might pass out. The heat from the candles seared her. The corset stays cut off her air in the sultry humidity. Her hives itched fiercely, and her shattered nerves threatened to overwhelm her. She clung to Mason's arm. He put his hand over hers and gave her hand a gentle squeeze. Amazing how he reassured her, how his touch calmed her.

"Do you, Mason Glenn Whittaker, take this woman to be your lawfully wedded wife, in sickness and in health, for richer or poorer, until death do you part?"

Mason smiled down at her. "I do."

Behind them, Ben, Jr.'s, crystal clear voice sounded. "Mama, you done lost the bet with Cousin Beth and now you got to give her that new quilt."

Eleven

Beth almost died right there. She wanted to sink into the floor, right after she smothered Ben, Jr., to death.

"Bet?" Mason looked at Beth and frowned. "What bet?"

A fountain of unwanted information, Ben, Jr., stood. "The one where Mama has to give Cousin Beth her new quilt if Cousin Beth gets married before the end of June, and if Cousin Beth don't, then she has to give Mama some new silk from New York."

Rachel stomped over to her son. "Sit down and shut your mouth, young man."

But the damage was done. Beth saw the hurt and anger flash in Mason's eyes.

"You asked me to marry you so you could win a quilt?"

Beth knew he'd never listen. Not now. "It wasn't like that. Honest, Mason. Rachel and I did make a bet, but who else would I want to marry? You're the one I always turned to, the one who understood me all these years."

He stepped back from her. "I thought you'd finally realized you love me. What a laugh." He shook his head. "You asked me to marry you because of a bet with your cousin Rachel?"

Beth stepped toward him, her hand still on his arm. "Mason, you have to understand. I didn't know how much I loved you before. I was so tired of everyone making a joke about me. I thought if we married, the talk would die down."

"As if that's any better? You proposed just so the gossip would die down? What a fool you played me for." He removed her hand from his arm and stepped back.

"No, Mason. Listen to me. No matter how it started, you're the one I love and want to marry."

Mason shook his head again. "No, that's it. I thought that after all these years you'd finally decided to make your own choices instead of letting your parents decide everything for you. Now your cousin is making decisions for you. The gossips in town make decisions for you. What next? No more, Beth. I won't play second fiddle any longer. This wedding is off." He turned and walked toward the back of the church.

Mr. Pendleton rose. "Now see here. You can't leave my girl like this."

Mason called over his shoulder. "Just watch me. A marriage can't stand on a foundation of bets and lies—or with a woman who doesn't know what she wants."

Beth picked up her skirts and ran down the aisle.

Her mother called, "Bethany, what are you doing? You cannot chase after that man. I forbid it."

She ignored her mother and reached Mason as he put a hand on the knob. She threw herself to knock his hand from the door and bar him from opening it.

"Mason, I love you, and I know exactly what I want.

I didn't know how much until after I'd proposed, but I've loved you all these years and want to spend the rest of my life with you."

"Of all the nerve." Mrs. Pendleton stood. "Bethany Pendleton, do not debase yourself begging that man to marry you. Get right back here with your father and me."

"Mother, stay out of this. This is between me and the man I love."

Mason watched Beth with his jaw set. Anger and pain showed in his eyes.

Beth never even glanced at her mother, but kept her gaze on Mason. "I never meant you to know about the bet. I should have told you. I started to a dozen times, but I was ashamed."

She put her hands on his arms. "All those other times, I felt like a woman in jail about to be hanged. I was relieved when the other engagements were cancelled. But, Mason, after you agreed to marry me, I was so happy. Happier than I've ever been in my life."

She looked around Mason at those gathered in the sanctuary. "And all of you who gossiped about me behind my back"—she looked directly at Mrs. Weldon and Mrs. Humphreys—"do you think I didn't know or that it didn't hurt my feelings? Well, I knew, and it hurt a lot. When I tried to hide the pain, you added the label of Ice Queen. How can you people sleep at night knowing the harm you've caused me and others?

"I know you'll all be gossiping about this wedding, talking about what a disaster it's been. Well, I don't care. This time I really don't. All that matters is that Mason loves me and that we're married."

She stepped forward and rested her hands on his

chest. "This wedding isn't about bets any more than it's about Paris fashions. This is about you and me and our future together. It doesn't matter what anyone else thinks. They can talk all they want, but it won't alter the fact that our marriage and us being together is the right thing."

He removed her hands and crossed his arms, but at least he was listening.

"You know how I always came to you when I was upset or happy? Why do you think that was?"

"Ha. You said I was your best friend, like a brother." He spat the words like a curse.

"But now I realize it's because I've loved you all this time. Not like a brother, but like a woman loves the only man for her—the other half of her soul." She wiped at the tears streaming down her face, and goo smeared her gloves. She hoped she had the right words to convince him. Nothing had ever been so important in her life.

"Mason, you said I could count on you. Please mean it. You've always been honest with me, a solid rock I can depend on."

She saw the emotions warring in him and pressed her case. She stepped toward him and put her hands on his. "Please, Mason, you're too fine to pretend you don't love me. I love you as much. We belong together. Please marry me."

He exhaled. "I'd planned to ask you when the house was finished and furnished inside. Why else do you think I built it and painted it your favorite color? So, reckon I'll do the asking now. Beth, will you marry me?"

Tears streamed down her face, but now they were

tears of joy. "Oh, Mason, I would be honored to marry you."

He pulled her into his arms. She'd never been so happy or so relieved.

The guests cheered.

From the front of the chapel, Reverend Moseley called. "Do you, Bethany Louise Pendleton, take this man to be your lawfully wedded husband?"

Mason looked into her eyes. "You bet she does."

The minister snapped his book closed. "I now pronounce you man and wife. You may kiss the bride."

And Mason did, a long, sweet kiss that curled her toes.

Those attending sent up another round of cheers accompanied by whistles and applause.

Mason and Beth rushed out the door. The rain had stopped, but the churchyard was a sea of mud and puddles.

Mason set her on the porch. "Grandpa's buggy is right over there. Wait here while I fetch it."

Beth shook her head and hiked up her train and skirts. "Oh, no, you're not leaving me, Mason Whittaker, not ever."

He took her arm. "Then hold on to my arm. The steps are slippery."

Folks leaving the chapel poured out. Ben, Jr., and Jamie Bigelow raced into Mason, hit him in the back of his legs, and his knees buckled. He went skidding down the steps to land in a mud puddle with a splash.

Beth tumbled after him and landed in his lap. Her crown of orange blossoms skewed like a crooked halo, and the pristine tulle floated with stems of straw on the murky water puddle. Mud splatters covered them both. They looked at each other and burst out laughing.

Mason kissed her gently. "Reckon this is the end of the jinx?"

The clouds parted, and rays from the setting sun spotlighted them.

She smiled at her husband. "Certainly. Remember? Happy is the bride the sun shines on."

Epilogue

June, 1890

Beth wakened to sunshine pouring in the window. Oh, no, she'd overslept again. This pregnancy drained her energy more than the others had, and she needed extra sleep. Thankfully, once her term ended the other babies had popped out as if she was created for childbearing.

Beside her, Mason pressed his lips to her shoulder as he splayed his fingers against her rounded stomach. The babe inside her kicked.

"Baby's running races this fine Saturday morning."

"I hope this one's a girl so Millie won't be the only one." Beth's husband didn't seem to mind that she'd overslept. She turned to face him. "You're dressed. What time is it?"

"After seven. The right time, Beth." He stood and unbuttoned his shirt and tossed it onto the floor. His denim pants and drawers followed, and he slid between the sheets beside her.

She looked at the door. "Um, the door. Where are—"

"I locked the door." He feathered kisses across her face and nipped at her lips. "Rowdy's gone to town for supplies and to spend part of his paycheck. Probably come back broke, drunk, and satisfied. Wish he'd find a good woman and stay home like his boss."

The only thing better than going to sleep with Mason beside her was waking with him. "The children need their breakfast—"

"Beulah's fed them and said she'd look after them for an hour or two before she starts baking."

Beth smiled and arched a brow. "An hour or two? My, my, am I married to Samson?" They'd made such sweet love last night. No wonder she'd slept late this morning.

"May take longer." He grinned. "If I have to suffer, I'm willing."

He pushed her nightgown up until he worked it over her head and tossed it aside. "Mmm, I love your body. Never tire of looking at you." Leaning on his elbow, he trailed his finger between her breasts and down to circle her bulging belly button.

She met his gaze. "Mason, I'm over six months pregnant. I know I'm fat and ugly."

"Uh-uh. You're beautiful. Always have been, but you get this extra glow when you're expecting a babe."

She gave thanks every day for this man. "What I get is fat and sluggish. You only think I'm beautiful, dear, because you love me."

"I do love you, and that's a fact known far and wide." He rained kisses across her shoulders, down her breasts, and across her stomach. "Let me show you how much."

He laved her nipple with his tongue while he moved his fingers to tease her other breast.

She pressed him to her. "I love when you do that."

Around her nipple, he laughed. "That's the idea." His hand slid to the mound at the apex of her thighs. His finger worked magic there, delving in and out in cadence with the strokes of his tongue.

Her breath increased to pants, and she delighted in the effect of his lovemaking. His caresses sent her into throes of ecstasy. The sensations built until she exploded in a burst of golden pleasure.

He stretched out beside her and caressed her breasts. "I love you more each day."

"As much as I love you." She pulled his arm across her. "Come here and make love with me."

"I can do that, ma'am, if you insist." He moved on top of her, careful not to press hard on her bulging stomach.

She opened to him and he filled her. She raised her hips to meet his thrusts. They matched their bodies, by now finely tuned to each other's needs. Higher and higher she flew, soaring toward heaven. Stars exploded around her, and she floated back to earth. The warm flow of his seed signaled his completion. He exhaled and lay beside her, cuddling her close.

Nuzzling her neck, he kissed her where her shoulder began. "I'm the luckiest man alive."

She turned and looked at him. "We've done well so far, haven't we, in spite of the jinx?"

He chuckled. "No jinx. An enchantment is more apt."

Later, they heard giggles outside their room. Mason rose and dressed and tossed Beth her gown. When they were both presentable, he unlocked the door.

Three-year-old Howie and four-year-old Glennie ran in.

Glennie rushed to the bed. "Mama, Papa, Millie's trying to walk."

Mason handed Beth her wrapper and slippers. "Let's go see, shall we?"

They moved to the kitchen and watched their daughter take her first steps. When she fell on her bottom, she let out a wail. Millicent Louise had her mother's gold hair and blue eyes, but her father's temper. He'd conquered his quick anger, but his little girl had not.

Mason scooped up his daughter, and Millie stopped crying to flash him a coquettish grin.

He laughed at her antics. "Good thing her brothers are more easygoing like their mother. I think this one's going to be a handful."

"I repeat, let's hope the next one's a girl. Otherwise, with no competition Millie will twist all you men around her little finger."

Mason had finished the addition to their house, and it now contained enough bedrooms for all the children, plus two extras and a small suite for Beulah, their housekeeper.

Beulah handed Beth a glass of milk. "You got to drink plenty of this stuff so our baby grows right. But take it outta the kitchen." She made shooing gestures with her hands. "I'll bring you breakfast somewheres else. I gots to get tomorrow's baking done in here, and I can't with all you folks flitting around in my way."

Mason carried Millie while the boys walked on each side of him into the main parlor. Beth took a seat on the sofa. She loved this room.

The fireplace kept them warm in winter, and the large windows cooled the room in summer. A large rug covered the plank floor, and ivory lace curtains hung at the windows inside open heavy jacquard drapes. This morning the lace fluttered in the breeze.

Four-year-old Glennie curled up beside Beth. "Tell us the story again, about you and Papa."

Beth followed his gaze to the quilt hanging on the wall.

Three-year-old Howie plopped at her feet. "Yeth, Mama. Tell uth how you got our Papa for a bolt of thilk."

Beth met Mason's gaze and reveled in the love that shone there. She might have experienced misfortune in her life, but for the past five years she'd been the luckiest woman on earth.

She smiled at her husband, then began the story her boys loved. "Once upon a time, there was an unlucky woman whom no one wanted to marry . . ."

Promise Me

Yvonne Jocks

In memory of John Bruce Jocks
1923–2004.
Love never dies.

One

The Promise House, brick fronted and three stories tall, could have been another Market Street parlor house but for one significant difference: the sign on the front door read, *No Men Allowed*.

Dr. Joe Erikson rapped sharply beside the sign and waited. He fisted the gloved hand not holding his bag and tucked his chin against the spring chill. For visits like this he wore plain, mail-order clothes, both for politeness and—according to his grandparents—a certain amount of safety. Nobody at the Promise House for Reformed Women or any of the other poor homes he visited knew him as anything but a young doctor doing charity work. He liked it that way.

But over the last few months, he'd begun to enjoy this particular house for even more reason than that.

Then the redheaded girl who called herself Dixie opened the door and announced, "Miz Prescott up and eloped, Doctor!" And Joe's good mood died on the table.

But she was already married . . . wasn't she?

He felt his mouth forming Mrs. Prescott's Christian name—*Alice*—even as his head reminded him that he had no right to use it. His head, however, was fighting a losing battle if she had in fact gone. Luckily, his voice had deserted him, too.

"We all figured she musta had herself some big society wedding," continued Dixie, backing into the plain foyer so that Joe could enter. "But when Rose asked her about it, Miz Prescott said she and that lousy husband of hers eloped! She said that was proof he was no good, that even *us* kind of girls should always demand a proper wedding."

Oh. Dixie meant the bastard who had deserted Alice over a year before. Joe's racing heart eased into mild confusion as he came in from the cold, removing his snowy hat. Why should he care so intensely whom Mrs. Prescott married?

It wasn't as if he had any real claim to worry about what Alice Prescott did. Even if spending time here had become the high point of his every week. Even if she was the embodiment of everything Joe ever imagined in a perfect woman. Gracious. Charitable. Beautiful inside and out.

Married, he reminded himself with a private grimace. She was also legally married, no matter to whom.

But despite his philanthropic ways, Joe had more than enough devil in him to add, *abandoned.*

"It just goes to show," continued Dixie, leading the way toward the kitchen's warmth where Joe would conduct his examinations. "Folks can surprise you. Us girls would've bet gold money that Miz Prescott had herself some high-falutin' society wedding."

"Except," came a gentle voice from near the stove, "that gambling isn't allowed at Promise House. You haven't forgotten the rules, have you, Dixie?"

The redhead laughed, a brazen sound better suited

to her former occupation than her current attempt at redemption. "No ma'am, Miz Prescott. No men, no boozing, no medicine but what the doc here gives us, and no gambling. But I didn't reckon that last one applied to sure things. That just don't seem right, ma'am."

Joe just swallowed, hard, at his first sight in a week of the perfect woman . . . or as close as anyone could get.

What he most admired about Alice Prescott was not, in fact, her beauty. She wore her golden hair tied back like a spinster's and hid her voluptuous young curves beneath plain and inexpensive frocks, though she couldn't hide her wide blue eyes or thick lashes or full lips . . . or the blush that tinged her cheeks when their gazes touched. He admired the good she did for the needy women of Denver's red-light district, single-handedly running the Promise House on donations and willpower. Compared to Alice's sacrifices, his own donation of time and skill felt paltry. But even that was not what most drew him.

No, what made Joe feel so differently about her more than any other woman was an odd sense of con-nection. He couldn't explain it, but for months now, neither could he ignore it.

Joe wasn't a man who wasted time second-guessing himself.

"Good afternoon, Mrs. Prescott," he said. It came out appropriately formal, even if his heartbeat was speeding far more enjoyably than it had on the stoop.

He was pleased she hadn't eloped *recently*, anyway.

"Dr. Erikson," said Alice, ignoring the ladle in her hand. She wore an apron over her plain dress, and steam from the cookstove curled at tendrils of her golden hair, flushed her face. "Thank you for coming in this weather."

March, in Denver, could be as harsh a month as January. Perhaps worse, because of how desperate everyone became for a breath of springtime.

"It would take worse weather than a little snow to keep me away, Mrs. Prescott," Joe assured her, holding her gaze. Then, before he did anything scandalous in front of Dixie, he shrugged out of his overcoat, put his black bag on the freshly scrubbed table and added, "Especially with Rose so close to her time."

Alice nodded and glanced toward Dixie. "Would you please fetch Rose? Be sure to help her on the stairs."

"Only if Dr. Erikson promises to give me a look-see later," said Dixie. "I ain't so sure we cleared up that problem I come in with."

Joe reined back a laugh. Unless the girl had snuck back into the trade, which would get her expelled from the Promise House, Dixie was disease free. But by the time she'd healed from the broken bones that had brought her here, compliments of a jealous customer, the reformed Cyprian had taken to inventing any excuse she could to spend time with her physician.

"With the proper chaperone," he agreed with an amiable smile.

"Why, Doctor, shame on you. I am a changed woman!" But again, Dixie used a throaty voice more fitting to her former boardinghouse career.

"I'll start believing that when you tell us your real name," warned Joe, as she left to fetch her pregnant friend.

Then it was just he and Alice, alone—for a moment at least—in the home's warm, cinnamon-scented kitchen.

So he kissed her.

Just like that, Joe scooped her into his arms and ducked his face to hers, captured her mouth, and kissed those full lips as he'd longed to for a week.

It wasn't like they had a lot of time.

With a mew of assent, Alice opened her mouth to his. At moments like this, Joe couldn't even hear the voice in his head warning him that she was married—if abandoned.

Warning him that he knew almost nothing about her past, or the reasons for her concern about fallen women.

Warning him that worse, she knew almost nothing about his . . . such as the fact that he was one of the richest young men in the country. If he told her that, she might stop kissing him. Or worse yet, she might kiss him for the wrong reason.

And that, Joe couldn't quite risk.

All morning Alice had told herself—quite firmly—that this time, she would not succumb to the handsome doctor's dark charms. Not like that first stolen kiss, three weeks ago . . . one that had happened so quietly, so inevitably, that she still wasn't sure who had stolen it. Not like the half-given kiss a week after that. Certainly not like one week past, when she'd not protested the tiniest bit. . . .

This time, she succumbed in a wholly different manner. This time, as Joe surged forward, Alice met him halfway, as brazen as any of the girls she tried to help. In a moment he was holding her in his hard, winter-cool arms; kissing her with his clever, sensuous mouth; sending sensations thrilling through her that she'd never even imagined could exist, much less could set her to shivering this close to the hot iron cookstove.

Unguarded, her mind raced. Gilbert Prescott, her erstwhile husband, had never made her feel this way. Nor had her first fiancé, the man who'd promised and then stolen her one chance at a perfect wedding. Once her family lost their fortunes in poor business deals, he'd wanted nothing of them or her.

But even he had merely stolen her wedding; he hadn't broken her heart. She'd been something of a cold fish back then. Until these kisses with Joe Erikson began, she'd believed herself fully frozen.

She was hardly frozen now. Now she was thirsty. For him. Her lips parted to drink him in. His breath seared her cheek, and his embrace tightened. Yes. . . .

Oh, her mother would never have approved.

Had it simply been her upper-class surroundings, her upper-class beaus that had kept her cool? Had part of her simply been waiting for a man of humble immigrant birth to wake her to such earthly pleasures?

Dr. Joe's hair, raven black and curling softly between her greedy fingers, was as lower-class as his swarthy olive skin. Neither his flashing Italian eyes nor his strangely Norwegian name spoke of any advantages except quick intelligence and good character. Those, she felt sure, deserved credit for his rise from clearly modest origins into a respectable profession. She admired him for that.

His tongue touched hers, startling her, searing her. Oh, yes, she admired him for many things. But. . . .

Surely there were more appropriate ways to show

her admiration! This was exactly the kind of behavior that Alice was asking the Promise House residents to reject!

Somehow, she managed to turn her head so that Joe's kisses fell not on her open mouth but her ear . . . then her neck . . . then her shoulder. . . .

Oh, my. Yes. Rather, *no.*

"No," she gasped—and blessedly, horribly, that was all it took. Joe—Dr. Erikson—drew a deep, tickling breath from near the collar of her gown, then graciously stepped back.

"My apologies," he said, so formally she almost felt certain of the world around her again. Almost. Then he had to flash those white teeth and black gypsy eyes at her and add, "I know I said that last time, too. And before that . . ."

"And before that as well." She cleared her throat, smoothed her skirts, and hoped her blush wasn't as bright as it was warm. Her tingling lips felt lonely. "Yes, I remember."

"So I could understand you not fully believing in my repentance," continued Joe, his hands flaring and then fisting, moving with his words. "But I *am* sorry, Mrs. Prescott. If not for kissing you, then I'm sorry for any insult or discomfort I might have caused you. Truly."

Did the sense of loss that tingled through her count as discomfort? "As am I," she managed, clinging to vague memories of her proper upbringing, of her advice about trusting men. "Regretful of any discomfort . . ."

Oh, dear, that didn't sound appropriate at all!

Joe said, "Alice . . ."

At her given name, she looked up sharply. She

liked how it sounded from him, yet it was so terribly improper. . . .

Some people thought propriety ought not matter in a house this poor, surrounded by women who'd tasted such extremes of indecency.

Alice usually argued it mattered all the more, here.

"Let me call on you," pleaded Joe, his eyes liquid in their entreaty. "You deserve better than stolen kisses and . . . and elopements."

She hated that Dixie had told him of her elopement. It was the talk of the house, ever since Alice had confessed to it in an attempt to convince several residents to hold themselves more dearly than they had in the past. She hadn't realized—

If she'd imagined that Dr. Joe would find out, she might not have been so forthcoming. That elopement was the single worst mistake of Alice's life, a childish protest against losing the life and the society wedding she'd always dreamed of. She'd paid for it dearly, deflowered and deserted and too ashamed to contact a family unlikely to help her anyway.

But for the grace of God, and the assistance of a Kansas City house very much like the one she now ran, Alice could easily have fallen as low as these women she now tried to help. She hated the foolish, selfish girl she'd been.

Worse, she hated that some part of her still dreamed those dreams. Some haughty part of her that she'd not exorcised, no matter how hard she worked, still listened to what her mother would have said—and her mother would have surely rejected being courted by an immigrant doctor in mail-order clothes who, with all this charity work, likely couldn't afford his own room in a boardinghouse, much less a wife.

As if Alice were any great catch, or had ever been.

For the first time since that awful elopement with Gilbert Prescott, Alice owed something to her husband. Gil gave her the excuse to simply say, "I am a married woman, Doctor."

Joe held her gaze a searching moment longer, his disappointment palpable. Then he nodded, and turned away, and began to arrange his instruments on the clean table.

Thanks to Gil, she did not need to know whether her fear of saying yes was due to hard-earned pragmatism . . .

Or that old snobbery that she still feared she might never escape.

Then Dixie arrived with the very pregnant Rose, and Alice did not have to worry the matter any further. For now.

But she knew from over a month's experience that she would be cold and lonely in her bed tonight, wondering what she was missing.

Two

Joe used the servants' entrance to his aunt and uncle's Denver residence, winked at the cook, and took the back stairway to the room they kept for him. He wanted to clean up and dress more appropriately before presenting himself in the parlor.

This was the Capitol Hill neighborhood, after all. One never knew what important personage might be calling on Senator Barclay or his wife.

To Joe's relief, nobody was in the parlor but his Aunt Charisma. Just who he wanted to see.

Once upon a time, Joe had been a lost Italian orphan named Gio. Then the gods had smiled upon him, granting him a new family. That Jon Erikson, a Norwegian miner, would settle down to raise a foundling like him had been blessing enough. But when the man married Grace Sullivan, "Gio" found himself not only with perfect parents, but affectionate Irish grandparents and two sets of loving aunts—Grace's sisters—and uncles. The wealth of his adoptive mother's family, the Sullivans of Colorado Springs, quickly came to mean far less to the orphan boy than the fact that they accepted him with open arms.

Even before Jon Erikson's own gold strike, in Cripple Creek, made them rich ten times over.

Now, as the handsome Charisma Barclay looked up from her writing desk with a welcoming smile, Joe thanked his lucky stars yet again.

"Good afternoon, Aunt Charisma," he said, kissing her offered cheek. "Are the children still in school?"

"Mmhm." The strawberry-haired Charisma hardly looked old enough to be the mother of two girls and two boys, especially when she teased, "You're home early. Didn't you want to linger down Market Street?"

Joe groaned at her mention of Denver's most notorious thoroughfare, even if she didn't realize he *would* like to linger. Or why.

He sank onto a velvet-upholstered chair near hers. "You haven't told Nanna where I'm working, have you?"

"We have a deal, Joe. I don't tell my parents just how far down Market Street you make calls, and you don't tell them that I'm spending some of the Sullivan Foundation money on family limitation."

For as long as Joe could remember, Charisma had supported causes like a woman's right to vote, to work—and to have access to birth control. As a physician, Joe wholly agreed with her. That was why he shamelessly broke the Comstock Law every time he gave contraceptives to poor, desperate mothers and even hardened prostitutes. In theory, he supported the popular Purity Movement as much as the next fellow. But in practice . . .

In practice, he'd already seen too many dead babies.

"Just checking," said Joe, shrugging off his unusual paranoia. "Everything went fine today. But I was curious . . . you led the committee that approved funding for the Promise House, right?"

"Gladly so. Is there a problem there?"

"No! I just—" Oh, hell. He'd never been a coward before; why start now? "What can you tell me about Mrs. Prescott?"

"Hmm." Charisma put down her pen to give Joe's question full consideration. "Alice Prescott is a surprisingly strong woman, considering her youth. Her residents like and respect her. She seems honest—"

"But where's she from? What kind of man was her husband?"

Charisma blinked at Joe, then gentled her voice with understanding. "You mean, what kind of man *is* her husband."

Joe didn't bother to look away. "There has to be some kind of legal option for a woman who's been abandoned."

"There is. I'm afraid it's called a divorce."

Joe had to admire his aunt's frankness, even as he rejected her answer. "I doubt a lady like Mrs. Prescott would ever file for divorce."

Though more common in the West than back East, divorce still left a woman with a reputation barely better than that of the fallen frails that Alice helped.

"There are other kinds of scandals, Joe. Perhaps you should consider giving Mrs. Prescott no more than your professional attentions."

"Please?" said Joe.

Charisma bit her lip, wavering.

He ducked his head, widened his eyes. "*Please,* Aunt Charisma. Is there nothing else you can tell me about her?"

His aunt sighed. "Mrs. Prescott was quite forthright

in her interview. She comes from a good family in Wyoming, but was sent to live with an aunt in St. Louis after her father lost their fortune to legal problems. His ruin made her vulnerable to Gilbert Prescott's promises of reviving her place in society. She didn't realize the only thing respectable about him was his family name until after she'd married him."

Eloped with him, thought Joe angrily. The bastard had seduced her away from everyone she knew.

"When he realized she had no money either, he left her in Kansas City, penniless and alone. She was too ashamed to go back to her family, and in any case she doubted they would accept her back after she'd behaved so rashly."

Oh, God. He'd heard too many similar stories from the working women of Market Street. "She didn't . . ."

"Why do you ask? Would you think differently of her for staying alive however she could?"

Joe swallowed uncomfortably. "I hope not."

His aunt took pity on him. "Well, she didn't. But she was near starving when a woman of the streets helped her to a reform home similar to the Promise House. Soon Alice was learning to run the place and looking for a city that didn't have one. That's when she came to Denver."

"She's incredible, isn't she?"

Charisma leaned forward to catch his hand in hers. "And she is married. And since you needed to find out all this from me, instead of her, I assume that she may be less willing to overlook that fact than you seem to be."

"But—"

"Anything else you want to know, you really should ask her."

And when his aunt set her back like that, no matter how nicely, Joe knew that even big eyes and a *please* wouldn't avail him further.

Normally, considering the kind of residents her home brought in, trouble came to the Promise House at night.

This time, it surprised Alice in the middle of the day. She was in her own room, what had once been a tiny maid's room, with her old leather chest open, looking at the memory book she and her mother had created for her wedding.

The first wedding. The one that had never happened.

She'd dreamed of it all her life and had held it in her grasp when, after a tour of Europe, she'd become engaged to a New York society banker.

A banker who'd left her after her father's ruin.

Alice still had a copy of the gilt-lettered invitation. She'd kept swatches of material—silks and satins and organdies—and pressed flowers from the samples of what she'd meant to use in decorations. She had lists of music the orchestra would have played, and the planned dinner menu, and all the places she and her husband would have gone on their six-month honeymoon.

Foolish to keep such souvenirs for an event that never in fact took place. But every once in a while, she liked to turn through the fat pages of the memory book and remember those few, brief times her mother had seemed happy with her, or to imagine what her life could have been like. Some of it she'd already known—balls, beautiful clothes, delicious and plentiful food. Some of it, she'd only dreamed of—running her own extensive household, planning society galas, having her own children. Little babies of her own, to hold and dress . . .

And pass off to nannies.

Alice hated that the memories and lost dreams could still hurt so poignantly. It wasn't as though the spoiled girl she'd been had done anything to deserve dreams-come-true. In fact, she'd deserved them less than many of the women now in her care, women who'd seen their lives brought far lower than Alice's. She'd just assumed it was her right.

Money, she'd since decided, could be as corruptive as poverty. Wealth made a person lazy, selfish, and small-minded. She was well rid of it!

So why did a swatch of beautifully patterned silver brocade in her memory book still bring tears to her eyes? Her mother would hardly write to her, after Alice's elopement and desertion, she'd been so disappointed.

As she knelt beside her bed, running her work-roughened fingertips across the gleaming material and remembering happier times, Alice almost resented the intrusion of a door slamming.

Then Dixie, downstairs, yelled, "Lock the doors!"

Alice forced herself out of the beautiful and painful memories and back into this harsher but more important life.

She wished she did not occasionally resent it so.

As she ran down the stairs, she called, "*Why* must we lock the doors, Dixie?"

But that was when the pounding began.

"You're mine, damn it!" screamed a man from the street. "Come out of there. You're mine!"

Dixie, one of three women with their backs pressed against the bolted door as if to give it extra support, lifted guilty, unhappy eyes to Alice. "It's Quentin Moore. My old . . . husband."

They all knew that a fallen woman's definition of a "husband" was different than most decent folks'. Women from boardinghouses would live with a visiting cowboy, or miner, or soldier for a weekend, even a week or two, but no vows were ever exchanged, except for the physical ones.

Over the pounding, Dixie whispered, "He found me."

Other residents, pressed against the door or drawn to the hallway, looked up at Alice as well. Betsy. Star. Lily. She'd told them they would be safe here. If they weren't safe, they had no good reason for risking anger from their former employers and customers by staying here.

"You slut!" exclaimed the voice outside, and the door behind Dixie shook with Quentin Moore's blows. "Get out now, or it'll just go harder on you!"

"Wait here." Alice lifted her skirts and petticoats and ran back up the steps to her room.

Ignoring the memories sitting on her worn bedcover, she lifted the shotgun over her door, then opened the window onto the street. Cold air washed over her as she pointed the shotgun downward.

"Mr. Moore!" she called.

Passersby crossed to the other side of the road with little sign of distress. This sort of activity was common on Market Street.

So why were her hands shaking?

Moore looked upward, his face grizzled and his

eyes bleary. He swore. "You drawing down on me, Church Lady?"

The Promise House had no particular church affiliates; it was open to Catholics, Baptists, and even women with no strong religious beliefs. But few in the community believed that. Their assumption that good must follow a prescribed creed annoyed Alice, but she generally had larger battles.

Like this one. "Dixie does not wish you to call on her anymore," she announced clearly, over the double barrels of the shotgun. "If you must abuse someone, and heaven help you if you continue in this pattern, you must find someone else."

Moore's dull eyes brightened with threat. "You give me back my woman, Church Lady, or that someone else I find to abuse is gonna be you."

Alice tightened her hands on the shotgun, against a shudder of revulsion. "Go away."

But he was starting to bang on the door again. What if he wasn't merely inebriated? What if he'd been sampling some of those horrible drugs from Chinatown? She'd heard stories from the girls about how some of those potions could render a man invulnerable to pain . . . or at least make him believe so.

Their door was only so strong.

"The law should be here any moment," she warned, hoping he would not force her to actually shoot him. But she knew that if he broke the door, she would do just that before she let him hurt Dixie again. "I will gladly press charges."

"Bullshit! The law don't come 'round here unless it's to cause trouble themselves, and you know it." Moore put his shoulder into his next lunge against the door.

Perhaps Alice imagined it, but it felt as if the house shuddered.

Perhaps she should shoot into the air, to attract the attention of someone who might help. Alice's faith in her fellow man had been supported more than once with help from the bartenders or gamblers who frequented this area, those who did not resent her for helping ruin their fun. But most of them were asleep right now.

And if she unloaded one barrel of the shotgun, she would only have one shot left.

"I'm warning you," she called, feeling ineffectual despite her firm belief that she could and would kill the man before she'd allow him to hurt Dixie again.

Then, to her dismay, she saw Dr. Joe Erikson jogging down the street, black bag in hand—and fury in his gypsy eyes.

What could a doctor do against a drunken miner?

Three

As soon as he got the call from the charity hospital—where he told his impoverished patients they could reach him—Joe changed clothes and hopped a trolley car for Market Street. Even if it wasn't Friday yet.

According to the hospital, a woman named Dixie claimed that Rose was ready to have her baby.

They needed a doctor.

Joe knew that often as not, women had babies without a doctor's help. Especially poor women. But he was worried about Rose and how undernourished she'd been before arriving at the Promise House. Just as concerning—she was a black woman. He feared that if she had complications, other doctors might refuse to treat her. Unjust or not, he'd known it to happen.

Besides, he wanted to see Alice again.

He had not, however, expected to see Alice perched in a third-story window, pointing a shotgun downward at a belligerent drunk. Heavens, but she was magnificent.

Too bad he had to run to her rescue instead of pausing to admire her.

"Hello, there," he called, before he reached the

drunk. A miner, Joe saw immediately. He could tell from the kind of clothes—and dirt—the man wore, from the posture and the skin pallor. "Is there a problem?"

"There is if you don't mind your damned business and keep walking," growled the drunk, and slammed his full body weight into the door. The *No Men Allowed* sign tilted.

Joe heard high-pitched yelps from inside.

"I'm Joe Erikson," he said smoothly, to explain how it *was* his business. "I do the doctoring here. I'd hate to have to pick shot out of what's left of your head when Mrs. Prescott gets done with you."

Then he tipped his hat upward. "Mrs. Prescott."

"Dr. Erikson," returned Alice, never wavering in her hold of the shotgun. "Perhaps you should move out of the way."

Shotguns were hardly precision weapons.

"I will if it becomes necessary," Joe promised her, and turned his attention back to the drunk. "So that's my name and my business. What's yours?"

"I'm Quentin Moore, and that damned church lady is keepin' my Dixie away from me. *Dix!*"

Joe tensed tighter every time the man cursed in front of Alice, but learning who this man *was* became a more immediate concern.

"And her leaving you has nothing to do with the broken ribs you gave her a few months back, huh?" Damn, but he wanted to hurt this man. *First, do no harm,* he reminded himself. An ancient doctor named Hippocrates had once said that. Most modern doctors agreed.

"Hey, she was askin' for it! And she and that church lady got worse comin', if they don't—"

Joe tossed his medical bag to the stoop and had the man by one shoulder, arm twisted behind his burly back, before Moore could finish the sentence. "Here's your one chance, Quentin. You leave, you sleep it off, and you never come back. Got it?"

"Hey!" Moore clearly didn't like being bullied in the direction of the jail by someone slightly smaller than him. Not that an elephant wouldn't be slightly smaller than him. "Le'go!"

"If you ever do come back," warned Joe, continuing to bodily steer the man several steps down the boarded sidewalk, "then I'll let Mrs. Prescott shoot you. Deservedly so. And if you survive that—which won't be with any of *my* help—I'll make sure you don't get out of jail for a long, long time. Understand?"

Moore might be drunk, but he must have understood that he looked like a fool in this encounter. Especially in front of all the people he'd woken up on his own, with his shouting.

One minute, he was fighting Joe's grip with confused slowness. The next, he jerked free of Joe's hold, spun, and swung a hammy fist at Joe's head.

From the third-story window of the Promise House, now slightly behind them, Joe thought he heard a scream. He almost let it distract him. Almost.

Instead, he ducked under Moore's blow. As the man lurched past, Joe swung a fist into his gut, then cut him across the chin with his left. Then, while Moore staggered, Joe caught him behind one foot and tripped him to the boardwalk.

A plank or two splintered under the impact.

Joe had never believed that *First, do no harm* applied to self-defense. Or defense of others.

"How did . . . ?" Moore tried to lever himself back up, but between the drink and the blows, he was truly disconcerted now. "How did you . . . ?"

Joe crouched and felt the drunk's pulse, looked into his eyes. Moore didn't seem to be seriously injured. "I spent the first seven years of my life in a place called the Bowery," he said, over Moore's grunts. "I've had some experience fighting people bigger than me. Throw in attending school with the children of miners . . ."

He shrugged. Why *wouldn't* he know how to fight?

"Miners . . . ," muttered Moore. "Erikson! Hey, you any relation to—"

"Time for you to head to jail," announced Joe loudly, before Moore could finish that sentence. Luckily, by then several of Alice's neighbors had been sufficiently roused—and several of them owed Joe for doctoring different wounds or ailments. They took Moore away for him, so that he could go back and tend to the ladies.

The sign that said *No Men Allowed* still hung, crookedly, but Dixie opened the door right up to him, before he could even pick up his bag. Joe loved that.

He loved even more that Alice came running down the stairs as he entered, no longer holding a shotgun. "J— Dr. Erikson, are you all right?"

What he hated was that he couldn't run up the stairs to meet her, to gather her into his arms, to prove with his embrace and his kisses just how all right he was.

Moore's earlier threats twisted like bile in his gut.

"I'm fine, Mrs. Prescott," he assured her. "I'm just glad I got here when I did. Not that you didn't have the situation well under control yourself."

Despite his concern for her, he had to grin. She'd looked so very . . . forceful, holding that shotgun. Forceful and beautiful.

"I didn't want to shoot anybody," Alice confessed.

He didn't want anything but to just stare into her beautiful eyes. "I know."

Then someone upstairs screamed.

They hadn't told her Rose was in labor.

"We didn't want to worry you," said Dixie, while Alice brought in more clean towels. But that didn't ring true.

Rose, catching her breath between contractions, was the one who told them the truth. "And Dix wanted to be the one to telephone Dr. Erikson."

Joe seemed to not even be listening to the conversation as he took Rose's pulse. Alice felt a pang of—was it envy?

"But I didn't get to talk to him," confessed Dixie. "The lady who answered said he wasn't there."

"I wasn't," answered Joe, without looking up from his examination of Rose. Alice noticed how, despite Rose's obvious pain, some of the tightness that stretched across the woman's dark face eased under the doctor's easy confidence.

Alice had never been around childbirth, and her mother had never spoken about it. But in this, at least—trusting Joe—she understood how Rose felt.

"But you're here all the same," said Dixie.

"The hospital telephoned me with your message." Joe looked up, seeing Dixie's confusion. "At my aunt's house, where I stay during the week."

Dixie continued to look confused. Joe opened his

bag, brow furrowed in some kind of discomfort. "I prefer not to give my relatives' names to my patients, even for telephone calls."

Oh. Alice understood what he meant even before Dixie put it more clearly.

"Especially patients who are whores and beggars?" said Dixie.

Joe retrieved some kind of special soap from his doctor's bag and stood to wash his hands in the ceramic basin. "I don't think of my patients that way. But my aunt and uncle are doing me a favor, letting me live with them and their children. I can hardly repay their kindness by encouraging familiarity at all hours with people they don't even know."

"You mean from whores and beggars they don't know."

"Dixie," interrupted Alice. "That's enough. Doesn't poor Rose have enough to worry about—"

Rose's cry, as another contraction wracked her slender frame, seemed to prove Alice's point. Even if it hadn't, the way Joe immediately sank onto the bed beside her, brushing her sweaty hair back with his wrist to protect his clean hands, should have bought him all kinds of forgiveness.

Then Rose had to go and say, "Ac-actually, it . . . it gives me something . . . something else to pay attention to."

Dixie's chin came up. "See? I'm doing Rose a favor."

"Not if you persist in being rude to a man who has been nothing but kind to you. To . . ." Alice's words faltered as Joe's gaze lifted appreciatively to hers. Oh, goodness. Was it horrible of her to be glad Rose's baby had come so early in the week, to be glad that she didn't have to wait until Friday to see this man again?

Alice grasped desperately at her polite words and the normalcy they represented for her. "Kind to all of us."

But Dixie was in a mood. "When we don't hardly deserve it, is that it?"

"I know you're upset over what happened with Moore just now." Joe's tone remained amazingly mild. "But you're jumping to wrongful conclusions, Dixie. I can't speak to the kind of work you've done, not being a woman myself. But I've been a beggar, and there's no shame in what a body needs to do to survive."

For a long moment, the only sound in the room was Rose's panting. Then Dixie said a word that wasn't allowed at the Promise House.

Alice, instead of correcting her, whispered, "You told Mr. Moore you grew up in the Bowery. That's the poorest section of New York, isn't—"

Rose's next cry interrupted her. With his eyes and a sweep of his hand, Joe asked Alice to take his place by the woman's shoulders as he moved to glance impersonally between her knees.

"Won't be long now, Rose," he assured her, as Alice grasped the woman's sweaty hand. "Keep on breathing, deep as you can."

Dixie lingered by the door, seeming more unsettled by the doctor's confession than by the palpable pain in the room. "How'd you go from being a beggar to being a doctor, then?"

Joe said, "Rose is a little busy just now, Dix."

But Rose said, "I want to know, too. For me and my

baby, Doc, if we're ever to have a chance. I want to know how you did it, too."

But it was to Alice that Joe looked, his dark eyes full of questions. The woman she'd once been would never have wanted to hear, would not have wanted to keep company with a young man from the Bowery, no matter how well he'd grown up. Then again, the woman she'd once been would not have been sitting here, wiping Rose's forehead with a cool cloth, doing what little she could to help birth a bastard child.

In that moment, Alice felt only gratitude for all of them—for Rose, for Dixie, and for Joe. Because of people like them, she'd escaped the narrow-mindedness that had imprisoned her youth. So she nodded. She wanted to know, too.

"Two things," said Joe, even as he reached under the sheets, laying a hand on Rose's impossibly round stomach. "One is, I wasn't content to stay there, to just survive. I wanted to do better, just like you ladies at the Promise House do."

Rose all but sobbed her question. "And the second thing?"

"The second thing is, I lucked into meeting up with people who were willing to help me."

Joe's gaze lifted to Alice's again, and she wanted to duck her head to escape the admiration she saw there. But she couldn't move. She was too hungry for his admiration, too amazed and delighted by it, to do anything but stare back.

"Seems to me," said the doctor, "you ladies have found that, too. Someone willing to help you.

"Now, Rose—let's deliver this baby."

Four

First a few stolen kisses, thought Alice, gazing at the handsome doctor's face, peaceful in sleep. She hugged the quilt in her arms closer to herself. *And now we spend the night together.*

It was so very late at night that the noise of the saloons to either side of Promise House had subsided, and the home's residents, all of them used to working night hours, had gone to bed. By middle-class standards, certainly by her mother's, Joe's sleeping here might well be scandalous . . . but most folks understood the exceptions made for doctors.

And the residents of the Promise House were so scandalous already, did it matter what hours they kept?

Perhaps. Gone were the days when Alice worried about what other people thought. The only code of morality she had to keep was her own, and that which she tried to exemplify for the girls.

The fact that Joe was asleep in the rocking chair in Rose's room, with tiny baby Josephine cradled in his protective arms, kept this moment from being anything but pure. She'd fetched the extra quilt for him, but now she hated to risk waking him even for that.

He'd spoken as if he equated her with the people

who'd helped him escape poverty, people he clearly cared for. As if he found Alice and what she did . . . worthy.

Was she? Was she really? She knew that the women who'd taken her in, after Gilbert's desertion left her friendless and alone, had been angels on earth. But her own work . . . could she trust what he saw in her?

Joe's lashes lay dark against his olive skin as he slept. Alice's gaze lingered on his mouth, and when she remembered kissing him, just last Friday, she felt . . . tingles.

If only she'd met Dr. Joe before marrying Gilbert. But of course, before she'd married Gil, she never would have given Joe the time of day—Joe or the Promise House. Or, worse, she might have given the Promise House just enough attention to protest its existence as some kind of slight against proper society.

That's how her mother spoke of ladies of the evening, when she spoke of them at all. With anger.

How very odd, the way a person changed. Between the person she had been, and her first fiancé, and then Gilbert, she now trusted the upper class even less than she'd once trusted the poor. Wealth had twisted and confused her, and she was glad to be rid of it!

Now she could look at Joe Erikson for what he really was. Him and the sleeping baby he'd so recently delivered. Only once during the terrible, wonderful ordeal had Alice realized how close Rose had come to dying—

And that, only because Joe had let her see. In one desperate glance, aching and silent, he'd let her and only her see his concerns.

She'd looked at him and said, "You'll be fine." It was what she'd been telling Rose all along, but this time she meant it for Joe. By the way his dark gaze had lingered on hers, she suspected he knew it.

Then he'd smiled, a smile that sang through her, and he'd gone back to telling Rose the same thing. And sure enough, both baby and mother had survived.

They'd survived thanks to a man so generous, he was willing to do doctoring without taking pay. So competent, he could fix almost any ill. So gentle, he'd been the one who showed Rose how to offer the baby her breast, the one who knew how to fashion a diaper. So strong-willed, he'd somehow gone from a childhood in poverty to being college educated.

A man so handsome, her breathing fell shallow just to look at him, even asleep.

Especially asleep.

Oh, the woman Alice had become could definitely appreciate Joe Erikson . . . now that she was married and no longer available to pursue their obvious attraction.

Her gaze drifted to Rose, also asleep. No matter her agony, Rose had refused to name the baby's father. "He's married," is all she would say—all she would admit to when Alice first welcomed her to the Promise House. Even in the agony of delivering the man's daughter, and in the exhaustion that had come afterward, after Joe had somehow, somehow stopped her bleeding, she would not name him. "I cain't do that to his wife and family. He's married, and he's white, so the baby and I are on our own."

Despite the injustice of this faceless man taking no consequences for his actions, Alice almost admired Rose's determination. Yes, the girl had knowingly lain with a married man, but that had been her decision.

She was living with the results. Sometimes morality seemed strangely fluid, here on Market Street.

Alice lost track of how long she stood there, looking from Joe to baby Josephine to Rose, before she realized what kind of shocking thought she might be forming.

She admired Joe Erikson. She longed to kiss him again—the previous Friday seemed forever, countless aching nights ago. In fact, the longer she watched him, the more she wanted to *more* than kiss him. She wanted it worse than she ever had with her fiancé, who'd not taken liberties, or even with her husband . . . who had.

From the way Joe sometimes kissed her, sometimes looked at her, he might just want the same thing.

Morality *was* strangely fluid, here on Market Street. So . . .

Did being married truly have to stop her?

Joe barely woke when someone lifted baby Josephine from his arms. He sensed no threat to the baby or himself.

Then lips touched his, and he feared he'd been wrong—until his eyes opened to behold Alice, the beauty of Alice in the low light of an oil lamp, filling his vision. He breathed in her scent, her taste, as he fully awoke to wrap his empty arms around her.

This was better than the best of dreams.

"Where's the baby?" he asked sleepily.

"In the basket," she whispered against his lips.

Good enough. With Alice so wonderfully soft and willing in his embrace, he drew her farther into his aching lap—and she came, all of her.

Kissing him.

Heaven.

How long had he wanted her . . . weeks? Months? Maybe since before he'd ever met her, he'd longed to find a woman like this. It wasn't as if Joe had never known a woman before. The sheer number of Cripple Creek ladies looking to show the oldest Erikson boy a good time had been one of several good reasons his adoptive father had moved the family back to Colorado Springs. College life had offered its fair share of temptations as well! But those moments had been flesh and fun.

This woman opening her mouth and her soul to his was *Alice*. The golden hair that spilled over his searching hands and his arms was hers, let down for the night. The warmth and softness of her curving body reflected a warm heart and a tender soul. The passion with which she returned his kisses matched the passion she brought to her cause. And her sense of modesty. . . .

But he found no sense of modesty, tonight. When his thumb brushed the side of her breast, also unbound for sleep, Alice arched against him, pressing herself closer in a silent request for more. Joe kissed from the edge of her mouth to her chin, down the throat that she offered to his hungry mouth, down to the simple frill of her nightgown's collar and downward still, across the curve of her, tasting her softness through the material until, yes. . . .

Her nipple beaded in his mouth, through the nightgown, and she moaned her pleasure as he breathed his need.

Alice?

Suddenly afraid that he'd been tricked in his

sleep—that he was doing this with Dixie, or Star, or one of the other residents—Joe slipped out from under the woman on his lap. He slid her into the chair he'd vacated as he dropped to his weak knees and pushed backward.

Then he felt like a true fool, because the wrapper-clad woman in the chair, her golden hair caressing her shoulders and the darkness of one breast faintly visible through wet white linen, really was Alice.

And now it was too late.

She ducked her head and crossed her hands over the plump temptation of her bosom. "I'm sorry. Joe— I mean, Dr. Erikson—please forgive me . . ."

"Forgive . . . ?" He shook his head. "No!"

The horror in her blue eyes, at that, struck him deep.

"No," he protested, surging forward, capturing her face in his hands. "I mean, there's nothing to forgive. Oh, Alice, I'm so sorry, you just . . . you surprised me . . ."

And since even those words had been a miracle of self-control, he simply kissed her again from where he knelt in front of her.

Heaven, still. Home. Everything he wanted in life . . .

Except for one thing. And since Alice seemed torn now—returning his kisses, but hesitantly, with a catch to her breath—Joe managed to ease back.

It was an important qualification. Any minute his rushing, heated blood would let him fully realize that.

"Um . . ." He had to swallow a few times to regain control of his voice. Words, any words, paled against the need to kiss her more, hold her more, do more. But damn it, words were all they were allowed.

At the moment.

Especially the way she'd now hidden her face in her hands.

"Were you sleepwalking?" he asked, finally.

She shook her head, then peeked up over her fingers. "I'm so sorry."

Sorry? For *that?* He brushed golden hair from her face, trying to convey with his gaze the gratitude and affection he felt, the level of which even his best words would never capture. "Don't be. Please don't be. That had to be the finest few minutes of my life."

"Then why did you stop?"

Joe wasn't *about* to mention the fear that he might have mistaken her for a not-quite-reformed prostitute! That might have been why he'd stopped, but it had little to do with why he hadn't taken up where he'd stopped, as soon as he was sure he was awake. "I wasn't sure it was what you wanted. What either of us really wanted."

"For now," she whispered. "It's what I want for now."

"And for later?" Joe took her hands in his and eased them to her lap, trying not to pay too much attention to the breasts that action revealed or the roundness of her thighs beneath that lap, separated from him by such thin material. "What about babies?"

"I've heard you . . . I've heard you tell the women that there are ways . . ." She shut her eyes against the immodesty of such talk.

"That's not what I mean." And since he'd never been particularly patient with keeping his thoughts to himself, Joe said, "It's just that the happiest times in my life have been with my family, Alice. People who loved me no matter—"

She made an embarrassed sound and pulled her

hands free, pushed herself from the chair, but he caught at her nightgown.

"Please don't leave yet." The words wrenched from him, there on his knees. "Please, Alice. Please hear what I really mean to say, before you leave."

She stilled. For a long, suspended moment of waiting, Joe felt every beat of his heart, every resulting surge of his pulse. Then, as he realized he was holding his breath, she nodded.

He could barely see her ducked face past the golden curtain of her hair, even from the floor. He rose to his feet and offered her the chair. She shook her head—but at least she didn't try to get away.

He stayed standing, too. Belatedly, he slid his hands from her gown to *her* hands, needing to touch her.

Just touching her made him feel strangely complete. Aching and ungentlemanly, but complete all the same.

"I'll listen," she whispered. "I deserve it."

As if he meant to lecture her! "What I meant to say was, I've always been happiest with family. My mother—my first mother—had other babies after me, but none of them lived. Plenty of other children in the Bowery were unwanted, neglected, abandoned. Not me. After she died my papa took me west, despite being sick himself. He figured anything was better for me than that life. He died to give me that chance, Alice, and I spent some time in an orphanage. That's when I learned how precious even that had been. Knowing who my folks were, I mean, knowing that I'd been wanted. Can you understand that?"

She nodded, but said nothing.

"That I could find that kind of acceptance again, as part of such a huge, loving family . . ."

Finally, Alice spoke. "Your adoptive parents had a lot of children?"

Joe nodded. "Three boys, including me, and five girls, including May—they adopted May, too. I've been blessed twice over. So the least I can do to deserve it, the very least, is to make sure I give the same. To make sure that any children I create are just as wanted, just as loved."

She was searching his eyes now, looking for what he meant. He felt like a fool to say it, especially as hungry as he was for her. But. . . .

"I want you, Alice, but not without marrying you first."

Five

Alice could barely breathe. "You're asking me to marry you?"

Joe ducked his head, but the movement took none of the brightness out of his embarrassed grin. "I'm not known for hanging back, Alice, I'll admit that. But . . . I do know you. I've known you for months—your goodness, and your spirit, your strength. Maybe you haven't been paying as close attention . . ."

She had.

"But at the very least," he continued. At some point he'd started looking directly at her again. "At least I want to court you, with the eventual hope of marriage. I want that hope even more than . . ."

Than what she'd shamelessly offered him.

He softly brushed hair away from her jawbone. "Even more."

For the briefest moment, pleasure buoyed Alice higher than she'd felt in some time. Then reality crashed her back into place.

"But I'm already married." The words squeezed out of her, all the harder for their truth. "Oh, Joe, I didn't wait to meet you. I didn't imagine. I was a foolish, spoiled girl, and I married the wrong man, and now . . ."

His gypsy eyes brightened, almost laughed with joy in the faint light of the low oil lamp. "You're sure he's the wrong man, are you?"

Perhaps he wasn't the only one who didn't hold back. Considering how she'd woken him, that ought not come as such a surprise. She felt her face heat, but if he thought she was spirited and strong, how could she look away now? "Surer every day."

His hands squeezed hers. "Then divorce him."

She flinched. It ought not make a difference. The time she'd spent with these women, in this home, should have taught her how little power even the most scandalous words from her youth truly held. But. . . .

"He abandoned you," insisted Joe, jaw setting. He could be dogged, this doctor of hers. "He doesn't deserve you. And you don't—you *don't* love him. Do you?"

"It's not that easy." At the way some of the fire in his eyes wavered, she realized what she'd forgotten to say, and she squeezed Joe's warm hands in return. "And no. I don't love him."

The brightness of his smile justified those words. "I can understand if you're worried about your reputation, Alice. I'm sorry he put you in such a harsh position. But isn't the scandal of a divorce better than the scandal if you didn't get one?"

Slowly, his gaze slid back to the rocking chair.

The memory of his kisses, his touch, his mouth on her breast—and oh, my, her willingness!—heated her face.

Definitely better than that scandal! But . . .

"It's not that, not anymore," said Alice. "Mercy—I run a reform house for fallen women. My own family has practically disowned me. My reputation is already questionable."

"Not among anybody with sense."

A smile pulled at Alice's lips, despite the obstacles ahead of them.

"It's just that, I don't even know where he is," she told him. "My husband, I mean. He might have gone home to St. Louis, but his family doesn't like him very much. For all I know, he's in Europe! And even once I found him, and even if he agreed, divorces take time and money and . . . and . . ."

Since she held his hands, Joe silenced her with a kiss. "One obstacle at a time, all right? Trust in this. Trust in us."

Softened by his kiss and bolstered by his dark eyes, Alice nodded. The very possibility that this could happen, that she could replace both the big, perfect wedding she'd once lost and the hurried, shameful elopement she'd foolishly taken instead, with him, with a simple trip to a simple chapel with this man. . . .

A life. Babies, like the sweet infant curled asleep in her basket by the stove. Was there really still hope?

Joe's smile widened. "I know someone who could help. If you'll let me ask her. She knows the sort of people one hires to find things out, and—"

Despite her need to trust in them, in their hopes, the last two years had taught Alice harsh lessons about money. "But how? How do we pay someone like that? I barely keep this house running on charitable donations, and as fine a doctor as you are, if the rest of your patients pay you as little as we do . . ."

Which was nothing.

Joe took a deep breath. Now he was the one avoiding her gaze, as if embarrassed.

For the first time since he'd pushed back from her, in the rocking chair, Alice felt a twist of true fear. "What? What is it?"

"Nothing bad," he insisted quickly, his quick gaze recapturing hers from beneath a fall of dark, wavy hair. "It's just . . . you've been so honest about everything, your feelings—"

Alice laughed with relief. "Dr. Erikson, I believe you are the one who stole the first kiss."

Maybe.

He grinned back, but with an edge of concern. The danger still wasn't past. "*And* about your situation, and your marriage. And, well . . . I haven't been completely honest with you."

No. A hundred terrible possibilities screamed through her imagination. He was married. Or he had illegitimate children, or a criminal record, or an unmentionable disease. . . .

"Joe," said Alice softly, "you're scaring me."

"I'm rich," he confessed.

The difference between that and the horrors she'd feared was so surprising that Alice just blinked. "What?"

"I try not to let people around here know because . . . well, for one thing, it seems rude." Joe spoke quickly. His usual gregariousness had a nervous edge. "And it could be a bit dangerous, not that I worry about that, but my family does. So I've been circumspect, but . . ."

As the shock lessened—marginally—and she fully grasped his meaning, Alice sensed two distinct reactions deep within her.

The first, to her horror, was a surge of sharp hope. He was rich—and he wanted to marry her. She could live in a fine house again. Reunite with her family. Wear gowns. Attend balls. Employ servants . . . and have a wedding.

A huge wedding, with flowers and silks and satins and an orchestra at the reception.

Her second reaction was to step back from him, away from those horrible, greedy thoughts his confession inspired. She wasn't that Alice anymore. She didn't even *like* that Alice . . . had *never* liked her! She'd thought that Alice was dead.

Who would have guessed that she'd just been lurking, waiting for a man with the kind of bankroll to afford her?

Of course, Joe had no idea how fine a life *she'd* once lived before her family's fall from grace. If he was comparing himself to the people on Market Street, to the women in the Promise House, then even a simple inheritance might seem like wealth.

"What exactly do you mean by rich?" she asked.

Joe tipped his head to one side, clearly surprised by how she'd pulled back from him. But he answered her question seriously. "Very rich."

"You mean . . . uptown rich? A banker?"

Joe shook his head. "I mean Capitol Hill rich. The kind of person that bankers court rich. Invitations from the Sacred Thirty-six rich."

But the Sacred Thirty-six were the high-society mavens of Denver. Like New York's Rockefellers or Morgans or Vanderbilts. He couldn't mean . . . ?

"I'm not originally from Denver," Alice said slowly. "I don't recognize the name Erikson . . ."

"Until ten years ago, we weren't famous for a thing," Joe assured her. "My father's a miner, and he and Grace, my mother, did odd jobs to keep us going.

He wouldn't have let us starve, but some years we would have cut things fairly close if it weren't for my mother's family. She'd been wealthy all along, you see. Her maiden name was Sullivan. Of the Colorado Springs Sullivans."

The Silver-King Sullivans. *That* name, Alice recognized. "Like the Foundation." The one that supported Promise House.

All along, Joe's family had been paying her bills?

Joe nodded. "Not that we took much from them. Jon—my father—he's proud, but he was never stupid. We didn't lack for coal or warm clothes. And whenever Grace was due to have another baby, we stayed with her parents so that she could have a doctor nearby, just in case. But as soon as she and the baby were ready to travel, we always went back to our cabin at Cripple Creek."

"Cripple Creek," repeated Alice. "And he was a miner."

"Still is," said Joe, softly. "But now he runs the mine."

Cripple Creek was the fourth largest city in Colorado. It was also the site of the largest gold strike in the world, ten years earlier. The price of silver might have crashed in '93, but gold. . . .

Joe Erikson was *gold* rich. Mansions not just on Capitol Hill but in St. Louis and New York City and maybe London rich.

And here he stood, in a shadowy, poorly lit room, with a bed-ridden prostitute, her tiny bastard daughter . . . and Alice.

Telling her he wanted to court her.

To marry her.

He was biggest-society-wedding-of-the-decade rich.

She felt suddenly dizzy.

"Alice?" Joe put a hand on her arm, steady and concerned and so very him . . . except he wasn't just the him she'd come to know, the one she'd let steal kisses, the one she'd imagined living a poor-but-honest life with.

He wasn't that man at all.

"I . . . I think you should go," she said.

"Pardon?"

And amidst all her foolish, confusing emotions—hope and horror, excitement and disappointment—that one request, at least, Alice could hold on to.

She lifted her chin, looked him straight in the eye. "Dr. Erikson, I think you should go now."

That hadn't gone the way Joe meant it to. Not that he'd expected Alice to act the way some women might when he confessed to his wealth; she was far too practical, her values far too deep, for that. But. . . .

"Go?" he echoed.

She nodded. She even turned him and pushed him out the door of Rose's room. Then she ducked back in long enough to fetch his medical bag.

Maybe she was angry that he'd kept it a secret.

"I'm sorry I didn't tell you sooner," said Joe—though he did follow the direction of her gentle push, down the stairs and toward the front door. He wasn't such a cad that he would overstay his welcome. But he wasn't such a fool that he wouldn't try to change her mind. "Though I never said I *wasn't* well off, either."

"You aren't well off," said Alice, speaking as low as he did. No need for the home's residents to learn his secret as well. "You're filthy rich."

"Filthy's awfully pejorative, isn't it?"

"You could buy countries."

"Not *nice* countries." When he reached the bottom of

the stairs, Joe turned, stalling, searching. "And I have a lot of brothers and sisters splitting the loot with me."

But they could *all* probably buy countries, small ones, and she clearly knew that. "You need to leave now."

The furrow over her adorable nose—and the set of her chin—it didn't make sense! Joe caught her hands again, smiled his most winning smile. "But, Alice, *why?*"

"Because . . . because I have no respect for rich people." She handed him his coat, before he could answer that. "I don't like them. I don't trust them. I didn't fall in love with someone who was wealthy, I *didn't*, I fell in love with . . ."

"With me," he said, and his heart lurched with the realization of that. "You fell in love with me?"

He'd hoped it, but to hear her say so . . . !

Alice just looked more confused. She shook her head—and opened the front door. "I fell in love with a figment of my imagination, Dr. Erikson. Goodbye."

"But—"

Even as he protested, Joe found himself shoved out onto the front stoop, his black bag in his hands.

The door shut in his face, and he heard the lock turn.

"You fell in love with me!" he shouted.

A slurred voice from the sidewalk, a few steps down, said, "Shaddap. Folks is trying to sleep."

Joe stared at the closed door—at the *No Men Allowed* sign. That hadn't gone the way he'd meant it to at all.

Then, momentarily defeated, he turned and gave the drunk on the sidewalk wide berth as he started the long walk back to his aunt and uncle's home on Capitol Hill.

Six

She didn't want him because he had money?

It was the ultimate irony. For the last ten years of his life, Joe had needed to guard his heart against women who were interested *only* because of his family's wealth. Now, even when he went to the Promise House two days later, for his regular Friday check-in, Dixie sadly informed him that everyone was well that week and he need not come in.

No Men Allowed, indeed.

Disheartened, Joe finished his Friday rounds and caught the train home for a weekend in Colorado Springs. He enjoyed reuniting with his brothers, sisters, and adoptive parents. His mother, Grace, had long ago made their sprawling home warm and welcoming, with pets and flowers and cushions—and very little that was breakable or dangerous.

But as soon as he could, Joe headed down the block to his grandparents' mansion for some information.

It was one thing to hire a private detective. It would be another to find one he could trust, especially as greedy as the newspapers' society pages were for scandal about any of the Sullivans' extended clan.

"Sure and I've employed an upright detective in the past," admitted his grandmother, Bridey Sullivan, after the usual fussing and hugs that went with his return. "But what could you possibly be needing with such a man?"

Trapped in the parlor with her, his grandda holed away in his office where he couldn't help, Joe realized just what a mistake he'd made. He'd always been strong-willed, even wily when he needed it. That's how, as a child, he'd managed to escape an orphanage and find his way to Colorado all by himself. He'd hidden out in this very mansion for several weeks before choosing his new family—and he had, indeed, chosen *them*.

Joe could be determined.

But his determination was nothing against his nouveau riche Irish grandmother's. Bridey Sullivan's hair might be silver, but her flashing green eyes and sharp movements could hardly be termed aged, despite her advancing years.

"Nothing you need to worry about, Nanna," said Joe quickly. "It's a personal matter."

She drew herself up, affronted. "Personal, is it? And what could be so personal that you'd need hide it from your own grandmother? Have I not loved and cared for you as if you were my own boy? Did I not invite the presidents of those high-falutin' universities you applied for to town, just to show you off to them? Was I not the one who threw the ball that introduced you to society? And now it's secrets you're keepin'?"

Joe tried not to laugh—but damned if she didn't manage to make him feel guilty, all the same. "Yes, Nanna, you did all those things for me." Even when he might have preferred she stayed a little less . . . involved.

His younger siblings and cousins were lucky. By the

time they got old enough to enter society, there'd been enough of them to split their grandmother's overbearing focus. Joe, as the first grandchild, had been her own special project.

"But I'm an adult now," he argued.

She put a hand to her chest. "Saints preserve me from such an ungrateful grandchild!"

Now Joe *did* laugh. "Your heart is stronger than mine is, Nanna."

"And no thanks to you!" But, seeing that her theatrics weren't working, Bridey narrowed her eyes. "Personal, you say? Then it's a woman, is it? And about time you considered finding a fitting lady to squire about town. Too many of those debutantes are after you merely for your inheritance, Joey, instead of for your own sweet self. I've seen the way their mothers look at you; they're plotting to win you for their girls, against your very will. Best that you find one soon, if only to protect yourself."

Joe had heard that before, too.

A lot.

"You were going to give me a name, Nanna?" he prompted.

And damned if the old lady didn't fold her arms over her stylishly clothed bosom and smile a dangerous smile. "Private detectives can be hired for more purposes than one, boyo."

"You wouldn't!"

"Go ask your mother or aunts just how far I will or won't go to make sure my own darlings are properly wed," Bridey warned. "Just remember, Joey, that it's for your own good."

He'd heard the stories—and he clearly had no choice. "Yes, Nanna, I've met someone."

Quick as that, his grandmother moved to sit on the sofa beside him and patted his knee, all smiles and encouragement. "Have you now? Is she beautiful, then? From a good family? Are you sure she's not one of those gold diggers who come hunting after you regularlike?"

"That," Joe said wryly, "she is not."

"Good. Then why is it you're needing the services of a detective?"

In for a penny . . . "I want to locate her husband so she can ask him for a divorce."

His grandmother let out a screech of horror that startled him half off the sofa and sent two cats streaking out of the room.

"Jesus, Mary, and Joseph!" ranted Bridey. "What sort of woman have you involved yourself with? And how were you raised, to even consider such a thing? It's the fault of that dirt-mining father of yours, that's what it is, taking you and my Gracie up to that godless town where all manner of sins were for sale, and look at what it's turned you to!"

Both the cook and the downstairs maid appeared in the parlor archway, glanced in to make sure nobody was being murdered, and backed respectfully away.

Bridey, in the meantime, was up and pacing. "You'll do no such thing, Joe Erikson. Not while there's breath in my old body—which won't be for long, should you keep torturing me so! A married woman? Why not simply choose an actress, or a dance-hall girl, or a murderess for that matter!"

Luckily Joe's grandfather, Patrick Sullivan, appeared in the archway. "Joe," he greeted calmly, while his wailing wife sailed past him, her forearm to her forehead.

"Hello, Grandda," said Joe, over the din. While not one to envelop a foundling boy with hugs and cookies and Little Lord Fauntleroy suits, Paddy Sullivan had been just as welcoming in his firm acceptance of Joe, fifteen years earlier. Joe loved them both dearly.

"He's killing me, Paddy!" wailed Bridey. "And that, that is the *good* news. Our Joey has turned to a life of sin and debauchery, and it's dead I'd rather be, dead and in my grave, than see him do it to himself!"

"Debauchery, is it, Joe?" Paddy asked.

Joe didn't have a chance to answer.

"He wants to hire a private detective," said Bridey. "To find some tramp's husband and—"

"Hey!" Now Joe stood. "You can be as dramatic about this as you want, Nanna, but call her a tramp again and I'm not coming back."

That shut her up fast, her eyes wide—and brimming with very real tears. How was it that such clear manipulation could still make him feel so wrong?

Maybe it was because she did love him. She may be smothering, even embarrassing sometimes. But there were far worse crimes than that kind of love.

"Is this so?" asked Paddy, his gray-haired solemnity carrying an authority that none of his wife's melodrama could hope to achieve. "You're sniffing after married women now, are you?"

"Not married *women*," Joe protested. "Just one woman who happens to be married. And barely that. That was a mistake."

His grandfather's gaze deliberately settled on his wife with wry amusement as she slumped, head in hands, onto the settee. "Sometimes," he said, "what feels like a mistake can yet be a blessing."

"This is different," insisted Joe. "A good-for-nothing, no better than a confidence man found her at a weak moment and eloped with her, then deserted her within weeks. He doesn't deserve her."

"And you do?" challenged Paddy.

Not according to her. But Joe meant to change her mind on that account. And in the meantime. . . .

Well, she hadn't *not* given him permission to find Gilbert Prescott for her. Alice deserved a future, damn it. A future free of her scoundrel of a husband.

Even if it was a future free of Joe, too.

"I can only hope so," Joe said.

"Does *he* deserve *her*, you say?" demanded Bridey of her husband. "And what of her deserving *him?*"

Taking pity on her, Joe went to her side, sank into a crouch, and took her hand in his. "Nanna, you know I'm no fool. Alice comes from a good family; her father fell on hard times, but that doesn't change the fact that she's the kind of woman who could have easily turned her nose up at me, and you know why."

Joe wasn't the only person from immigrant stock in this family. Or this room. Just the only one of Italian origin.

"She's never once acted as though I were less than her," he continued. "Not for my parentage or the fact that as far as she knew, I was just a poor doctor. I know it sounds bad, her being married, but she's an incredible woman. She's charitable, and kind, and honest, and I truly do love her."

"And would she be pretty, then?" asked Paddy.

Joe turned from his crouch. "Oh, Grandda, you

have no idea!" Then he saw that his grandfather was teasing him.

"I feared as much." Paddy smiled. He, at least, seemed ready to give Alice a chance.

Bridey, though. . . .

"You say the poor girl was abandoned by her husband?" she asked warily.

Poor girl. That's when Joe knew the old woman might yet come around. "After he stole her away from her family he just left her in a strange city. No money, no connections. But she didn't give up, Nanna. She makes me think of you, that way."

He squeezed her hand, and she smiled.

"And she doesn't even know you've got money?"

"She didn't until this week."

Paddy asked, "And how does this paragon of virtue support herself, Joe?"

"She runs a reform house."

His grandmother clutched at her chest again, though clearly she was having no trouble breathing. Even his grandfather's gaze darkened.

"It's not the best company a lady could keep, Joe," he warned.

That was it. Joe let go of his grandmother's hand and stood. "Fine. You don't want to recommend your private detective to me, I'll risk finding my own. I won't stay here and listen to you cast aspersions on a woman you've never even met." And he headed for the door.

Paddy caught at his arm. "Now, lad, don't be hasty."

But Joe was beyond hasty. "If it makes either of you feel better," he spat, "she doesn't even want to marry me. Not since she found out I have money. Turns out she doesn't trust rich folks."

He glared at them both. "Imagine that."

That, at least, put them in their place.

Joe had almost reached the door before he heard Bridey Sullivan's voice bellow out with indignation, *"And what's so wrong with my grandson, that she canna forgive him a few million dollars?"*

Maybe they would help after all.

"I don't understand what the doc did wrong."

Alice had thought she would be alone in the kitchen, this early in the morning. Surprised by Dixie's comment, she spun around—and dropped her memory book.

"The doctor *didn't* do anything wrong," she said, too quickly, and knelt to gather the loose bits of dried flowers and silver brocade that slipped from the book's worn pages. "But he was here earlier in the week; we need not monopolize his time."

Dixie wasn't that easily distracted. "What's that?"

"Nothing."

"You're not acting like it's nothing."

Dixie had always been forthright, but Alice now saw something different about her. Her outspoken manner seemed guided by more than a desire to poke fun or cause trouble. Instead she almost seemed motivated by . . .

By concern. By a need to do the right thing, even.

Suddenly, and to her relief, Alice felt more as though she was speaking to a potential friend than a Promise House resident.

Not that she knew much more about making or keeping friends than she did about . . . about how to react to a man whose hands and mouth could take her to heaven, a man whose morals and character seemed unimpeachable despite his wealth.

A man who wanted to marry her—and perhaps give her back everything she'd only managed through chance to escape.

The Alice she'd been had been too self-centered and bad-tempered to make any real friends, much less keep them. The Alice she'd become thought back on a series of kind, gracious schoolmates with a sense of loss.

But despite her inexperience, honesty seemed a good way to start. So Alice handed Dixie the book. "It's my memory book. My mother and I once used it to plan the perfect wedding."

Dixie lifted an eyebrow at just what bits she could see sticking out. The brocade. The pressed white rose. "Looks like you meant it to be a fine wedding, all right."

"I did," said Alice—and damned if, even now, a note of pride tried to creep into her voice. "But I had it all wrong. Back then, I thought it had to do with the decorations and the food and the guest list."

Only half listening, Dixie sank into one of the kitchen chairs, opened the book to its first page. Then, with a sense of wonder, to the second. "What's wrong with that?"

"For one thing, I can't even remember my fiancé's face."

"The one who jilted you?"

Mercy. After meeting Joe Erikson, Alice could hardly remember her *husband's* face! While Dixie paged through the book's beautiful, heartless contents, Alice's stomach continued to tighten the knots she'd tied into it when she sent Joe away.

Yes, he was wealthy. But clearly it had not corrupted him, had not turned him into the kind of person her parents had been, her ne'er-do-well husband had been.

She had been.

Joe was the perfect man. One of the two ingredients that, Alice knew too late, was required for the perfect wedding. Unfortunately, the other ingredient was the perfect bride.

She couldn't become that Alice again. She mustn't!

Above them, they heard the tiny, jerking cry of baby Josephine waking up, demanding her breakfast. Everyone enjoyed having a baby in the Promise House, especially Alice.

Alice had grown up thinking of children as little more than one's duty to one's husband, little more than dolls to be dressed and schooled and hopefully shown off—the way she'd been. Every time she held Josie, her eyes welled with tears at the possibilities she'd stolen from herself. That Joe offered to return all those possibilities to her, not knowing what he might turn her into, only twisted the knife.

Reaching the end of the memory book, the kind of awe on her face that might be inspired by beautiful clothing and fairy tales, Dixie asked, "What were you doing with this in the kitchen?"

"I'm going to burn it."

Dixie's hands caught the book to her chest. "No!"

"I've got to! It represents all the wrong things, all the wrong values, and I can't hang on to them anymore. If I have any hope . . ."

But looking at how Dixie held the book, the same way Alice herself often had as she dreamed and planned and wished, Alice had the sinking fear that she would not have gone through with it. Even if she had, what good would it have done?

"But . . . but this is the wedding we all dream of," protested Dixie, and she was right.

Even Alice still dreamed of it. And that's why she had to stay away from Joe.

Then, as if drawn by fate, Star appeared in the kitchen, her wrapper hanging open and baby Josie in her arms. "Dixie," she said, "you remember how to telephone the doc, don't you?"

Immediately both Alice and Dixie were on their feet, surging to the baby's side. They left the book, forgotten, on the table.

"What's wrong with her?" demanded Alice, gathering Josie fearfully into her own arms. Star—who'd proclaimed a dislike for children based on her eleven younger siblings—gladly let the infant go.

"Is she sick?" demanded Dixie, looking over Alice's shouler. "Is Rose?"

"Nope." Relieved of her burden, Star stretched her hands high over her head, a pose that thrust her bosom forward in a manner that left no doubt about her former profession. "She's just gone."

The kitchen fell silent as Dixie and Alice looked at each other.

Finally, as the person in charge, Alice asked, "Gone where?"

Seven

Thank heavens the weather had turned mild.

Alice bundled the baby closer beneath her cape, all the same, as the trolley car slowed to its stop. It wasn't as if Josie's skin was so very dark as to cause a scandal, but blatantly carrying any newborn infant to a senator's house was bound to raise questions.

Besides, Josie had been fussy and sick to her stomach since the ladies at the Promise House had attempted to feed her with milk off a clean rag, after Rose's departure.

The Capitol Hill neighborhood she found herself in was true beauty—lawns kept as well as some palace gardens she'd seen on her tour of Europe. Three- and four-story homes with wide verandahs, sparkling windows, gingerbread latticework, turrets, and gables. High iron fencing around the perimeters, to discourage trespassing or other poor intentions.

Just to test herself, Alice whispered, "I could have this."

As she'd feared, her heart lifted at the idea even before her good sense could push such hope away. If she ended up in a home like this, why *wouldn't* she revert to her old habits, her old self? A drunk's only hope was to stay away from liquor. A flirt's only chance would be to not put herself in a situation that encouraged promiscuity. And Alice. . . .

She had to stay away from wealth, had to remain at the Promise House doing what little good she'd learned to do. Which meant this trip to Senator and Mrs. Barclay's home, the home where Joe had professed to be staying, made only marginal sense. But she needed to resolve this situation between herself and Joe before she could risk seeing him back at the Promise House. She had to bring him the baby.

And it probably wouldn't hurt to remind him of just how unsuited Alice had become for this kind of life . . . just like the once-fine blue travel suit she wore, now faded from too much washing and mending and two years out of fashion besides.

Just to be safe, once she found the address she was looking for, Alice circled to the kitchen entrance . . . despite the friendly sign that read "Welcome" over the front door. The cook let her in, but in mere moments Charisma Barclay herself swept in to collect her.

"What are you doing back here?" Mrs. Barclay demanded, drawing Alice toward a hall. "Please, Mrs. Prescott, come to the parlor where we can visit more comfortably. Missy, would you please take her cloak and fetch us some tea?"

"Tea would be lovely," murmured Alice, half wishing she had the willpower to refuse the treat's temptation.

At the removal of the cloak, Josie awoke with a fussy little hiccup. Mrs. Barclay and Missy, the cook, both stared at the infant for a surprised moment.

It was Mrs. Barclay who recovered first. "Goodness! Is there something you failed to mention to us, Alice?"

But her eyes danced when she asked it, and she

quickly added, "May I call you Alice? You're certainly welcome to call me Charisma; everyone does."

"It's a long story," Alice admitted, as she was ushered to a parlor far too fine for her poor travel suit, her plain-if-neat hair, and her short, work-worn nails. "And I'm afraid it involves your nephew, Joe—though not in any scandalous way, of course!"

Charisma laughed at that. If she noticed how out of place Alice looked in her parlor, she seemed not to mind. "Of course? I'm pleased to hear you think so kindly of my nephew.

"Now sit here," the senator's wife insisted, indicating a velvet settee that looked unfairly soft, "and we'll have a pleasant chat."

Joe was in a foul mood after his rounds at the charity hospital. He was angry at the kind of situations that could crush hard-working, good-intentioned people, although that wasn't unusual. But today he found himself equally frustrated by the situations some of the lazier, less principled people put themselves into, only to cry to him when they reaped the consequences. And then there were a few—diseased men who'd neglected to inform their brides-to-be, prostitutes who sold their own daughters into perversion to pay for their opiate fix—whom Joe would gladly murder himself. But no. He'd had to go and become a doctor.

First, do no harm. Damn it.

He hoped his mood didn't have too much to do with his continued absence from Alice, or another week would turn him from Dr. Erikson to Dr. Jekyll—or worse, Mr. Hyde.

When he ducked into the back entrance of the Barclay house, the cook said, "There's someone here to see you, sir."

Joe hesitated. "Me?"

Missy took his bag from him. "She's in the front parlor with your aunt."

She. Now Joe *was* confused. Was it his grandmother, with surprisingly quick news about the elusive Gilbert Prescott? His mother, visiting Denver and wanting to see him? Perhaps the oldest of his younger sisters was home from college to attend Colorado Springs' Founder's Ball?

But the person waiting for him, sitting across from his Aunt Charisma, was none other than Alice.

His Alice.

Joe stopped in the doorway—for all that he'd longed to see her over the last week, did he want to offer up his heart for more abuse just yet?

It took him only a breath to decide. Yes, he would risk more abuse, if it meant a chance to win her. He'd never been a coward before. What made him think that faced with her fine posture and her golden hair and her serious demeanor as she spoke to his aunt, he would turn coward now?

At least he got to see her again. He got to speak to her.

Charisma saw him first and lifted her smiling face. "Joe! I'm so glad you're here; I insisted that Alice wait for you to drive her home, rather than take the trolley."

He certainly loved his Aunt Charisma. Pleased at her matchmaking, Joe came into the room, kissed her upturned cheek, then turned to Alice.

He wanted to kiss a great deal more than her

cheek, despite her having no respect for rich people. Respect was earned, not given. Once she spent more time with him and his family, saw that they had little in common with the people from her youth, surely she would change her mind.

She had to!

"Mrs. Prescott," he said politely, reaching for her hand.

She gave it. "Dr. Erikson."

He bowed over it. She returned it to her lap, clutched it with its mate.

"To what do I owe this honor?" he asked, while what he really wanted was to kiss her, or touch her, or tease a smile back onto those serious lips.

Alice averted her eyes. "Rose left."

Joe sat. Hard. "Left where? How? She didn't go far, did she? Josie's not old enough to travel."

At that, both Alice and Charisma turned their gazes toward the end of the sofa nearer the fireplace, where sat the basinet that had held all four of Charisma and Will Barclay's children as infants.

Oh. He didn't need to stand, to go look, in order to understand what Rose had done—but he did anyway. He loved babies too much. He had to make sure this one, whom he'd helped draw into life barely a week ago, was all right.

She was fine, her tiny fists clenched beside her head, her eyes screwed shut, her mouth moving slightly in her sleep. Little Josephine was more than all right; she was adorable.

"She'll be hungry when she wakes up," he said softly, fisting a hand to keep himself from touching her, from risking waking her. The way her lips were working, she might be more than hungry—but her mother wasn't there to feed her.

"Missy is warming some milk as we speak," said Charisma, and laughed when he turned to her. "Yes, Dr. Erikson, goat milk. I'm not a complete fool when it comes to babies."

"I am," said Alice simply, unhappily. "We gave her cow's milk this morning, and I think it made her sick. We didn't know any better."

"You didn't hurt her," Joe insisted, returning to his seat. "I think goat milk is better, but many experts believe there's no difference." Or that goat milk was worse, since poor people were more likely to own goats. "You couldn't let her go hungry."

A smile flickered across her face. Then she looked quickly back to her lap, to the small purse she carried. "There's more, Joe—I mean, Doctor."

"We're all friends here," insisted Charisma. "In fact, I believe I'll go see how that bottle is coming."

And like that, Joe's aunt was out of the room, leaving him and Alice behind with nobody but baby Josephine for a chaperone.

"Here." Alice offered him a sheet of paper.

Joe caught her hand, not about to waste this moment of privacy. "Alice, I've wanted to talk to you. I'm sorry for how things went the other morning, at the Promise House. I'm sorry if I insulted you. You've got reasons for your opinions, I'm sure, but—"

"Please." She pulled her hand free of his. "You need to read this."

So he did, reluctant at first. His interest quickly increased.

Deer Mizziz Prescot.

Doc wuz rite. Folks need to want to be better. They need

folks who help them. Doc can help my baby. That's why I name her after him. His folks take in orphans. I am going now. Call my baby orphan and he can take her in. He can aford to do that. I herd when you wuz in my room. She is better with him than me. Thank you deerly. Rose.

Joe sat again. "Oh."

Rose had left her baby with *him?*

"I'm sorry," said Alice.

He had to reread the note a third time, then a fourth, before Alice's words impacted, and he looked back up at Alice. It was a relief to see sympathy in her gaze, instead of last week's rejection. "Sorry for what?"

"If you hadn't been doctoring for us, you wouldn't be in this situation. If I hadn't woken you the other day . . . I'm the reason you confessed. About your money, I mean. Where Rose could hear us."

Oh. That Rose had overheard should worry him more, but the letter drew him back first.

He'd been given a baby? An adorable baby, certainly. And he'd always meant to have lots of children. But . . . damn.

Suddenly he knew how his adoptive father must have felt, when young Joe had decided they were meant for each other.

"For what it's worth," said Alice, "Rose doesn't seem to have told any of the other girls. Even Dixie was asking what she meant about you affording to take Josephine."

A light knock on the doorway from the kitchen indicated that Charisma had returned with the bottle, a flare-bottomed, cut-glass affair with a long tube and a nipple at the end. "All ready," she said. "But now that I think of it, why don't I take the baby to the kitchen, where she'll be warmer?"

Both Joe and Alice said, "You don't have to," at the same time.

"I insist." Joe's aunt put down the bottle long enough to gather little Josephine into her arms. "Although I'm just as glad Will and I stopped at four, there's something soothing about feeding an infant. I appreciate the opportunity."

"Thank you," said Joe, for more reasons than one.

"Alice wanted to know what Josephine's chances would be in an orphanage," said Charisma as she retrieved the bottle.

Joe quickly looked at Alice. An *orphanage?*

Alice refused to look ashamed.

Charisma said, "I explained that sadly, Josie's skin color and her slight weight could hurt her chances for adoption. Was her mother malnourished?"

"Yes," said Joe, a little sharply. "She was. But Josie doesn't need to worry about her chances for adoption. Rose gave her to *me.*"

"Don't be foolish," said Alice. "If people find out they can just leave their children with you, instead of taking responsibility for them, you could find yourself raising dozens of them!"

"Maybe I'll worry about that when I hit the first dozen."

"Perhaps instead," interrupted Charisma, pausing on her way out, "you should worry about your reputation, Joe. More people than not will suspect that the baby is yours, especially if you legally adopt her."

Alice turned on Joe's aunt. "That's absurd! I can vouch that the baby isn't his; so can any of my residents."

"But your word is the only one of those that might carry any weight, Alice. I'm just saying that Joe could find it difficult to court a proper wife, with that kind of scandal hanging over him."

And at that, Charisma left with Josie for the kitchen.

Now they didn't even have the infant as chaperone. But before Joe could truly appreciate that, Alice was on her feet.

Which of course necessitated him rising, too.

"I should go," she said, deliberately not looking at him. "The trolley is quite safe. Don't bother with driving me."

"Because I'm rich, right? Because I have money, you suddenly don't like me, don't trust me, have no respect for me—"

"No!" At least she was kind enough to protest that, even if he'd been parroting back her own characterization. "It's not because of that, Joe. It's complicated. . . ."

"No," he insisted. "It's very simple."

And since they didn't have a chaperone, and he *wasn't* a coward, and he might not get another chance—he kissed her.

To his relief, she didn't slap him.

To his intense relief, she sank into him and kissed back.

Eight

That's all it took—Joe kissing her.

Alice had been determined to say her goodbyes and retreat to her life of doing the right thing, which meant *without him.* But before she knew it, she was sitting beside him in a shiny surrey, being driven home to the Promise House in style.

Worse, she was enjoying it.

"We'll tell the girls it's my uncle's," said Joe. "That won't be a lie."

The clop-clop of the horse's hooves was soothing. The surrey all but glided along, its springs absorbing the rougher parts of the road without subjecting its passengers to them. The seat, beneath them. . . .

Despite her best intentions, Alice let her hand drift to the seat. Velvet, again. She could get used to this kind of luxury—which was her problem.

Most enjoyable, though, was the man beside her. Joe hadn't bothered to change into better than his work clothes, since he was driving her back to Market Street, but even in a mail-order suit he looked good. Dark. Healthy. He handled the reins with easy confidence, alert to her and the horse and street traffic without ever seeming distracted. She found herself watching his hands, wishing. . . .

But that way lay danger. Her lips still tingled from his kiss.

"I have another confession to make," admitted Joe, touching the buggy whip that was attached to the dash, to speed the horse past an uncertain stretch of paving.

"Oh, dear," she said.

"I hired the private detective." He turned to better see her, his gypsy eyes bright in the shadow of his hat. "My grandmother knows of a man who's trustworthy and discreet, and I hired him to find Gilbert Prescott for you. Whether you ask him for a divorce, once he's found, is up to you. I'd recommend it, though. Even if it's not to marry me."

Some of what she'd perceived as simple confidence this afternoon, she realized, was resentment. But she couldn't find it in her to be annoyed, not after this kind of generosity.

"Thank you."

He looked back toward the horse. "I was afraid you would be angry."

"I'm not angry."

"Not all rich people are bad, you know."

That was when she realized just how cruel she'd been to say that the other morning. It just proved her point, though. Even the possibility that she could become wealthy again had turned her selfish and shallow!

"I know they aren't," she said, and braced herself.

As she'd feared, Joe brightened. "Then I can call on you?"

It was what she longed for—and most feared. "You're a good man, Joe. That you have money doesn't change that—perhaps it makes you all the more remarkable! You're friendly, and kind, and you've devoted your life to helping other people . . ."

"Why do I sense that you're about to say 'but'?"

"Not all rich people are bad," she agreed. "But I was, Joe. I am."

"There's not a bad bone in you."

"I'm so very glad you didn't meet me five years ago," she told him, ashamed just to think about it. "Back when my family still had money, I was a terrible person. I didn't care about anybody but myself. I obsessed about fashions and gossip and social standing. I said cruel things about people who weren't as lucky as I, and worse, I felt justified. And why? Because somehow I thought they were lesser than I."

Joe frowned. "You couldn't have been that bad."

"I was worse than that bad. Joe, marrying Gil Prescott was the best thing to happen to me."

Now he looked concerned.

"Marrying him," Alice clarified, touching his arm, "and being deserted by him. That's what led me to my first reform house. *I* was the one who needed a handout then. I needed charity—and people far worse off than I'd been, just weeks earlier, gave it to me. It made me see how much better off I had it than so many women. It forced me to realize that instead of whining about my own petty problems, I could make a difference in the world by focusing on others. Joe, I like who I am now! Do you have any idea how wonderful it is to be able to say that, at last?"

He considered that, splitting his attention between her and the horse's path. They'd left the finer part of Denver well behind, by now. "Are you worried that if we marry, you'll have to give up your work at the Promise House? It's true that you might want to stay home while our children are young, but we can work something out, Alice, I promise. We could even afford a nanny; I'll probably be hiring one for Josie anyway . . ."

"It's not that." Alice hugged herself, wished she knew a better way to tell him all this.

Especially when, perhaps thinking she was chilled, he drew a lap blanket up from behind the seats and draped it over her knees with one hand. What a fine, warm blanket. What a fine, warm man.

"Then what is it? Tell me. We can work it out, don't you see? We can work anything out."

"I don't want to *want* a nanny."

"Then . . . you could stay home?"

"No, I mean—Joe, I don't want to become the woman I was. I learned to like myself only after I left all that behind me, left the gowns and the balls and the carriages and the vacations. If I take it up again, I'm afraid I'll become that woman again, and I can't. Not—not even for you, and I love you, Joe, I do."

His expression brightened, and he ducked to kiss her, but she drew away so that only their knees were touching. He looked hurt, but so be it. He still did not understand.

"I love you too much to risk letting you marry that Alice."

Over the next few moments of silence, as she grew confident he wouldn't try to kiss her again, she sat up. Her elbow brushed his. Their warmth mingled beneath the lap blanket.

To think that if only she could find and divorce Gil, she could have had this all the time. Except that Joe was rich. Except that she would become someone who didn't deserve him.

Joe reined the horse onto Market Street. "You won't become her."

"I might."

"I've watched you. You couldn't forget the Promise House that easily. You couldn't forget the women you've helped, the good you've done."

Did he think she liked telling him her darkest secrets? "I think I could! When you told me you were rich, I immediately thought of what that could mean to me—no more sore back after doing my own laundry or cooking or cleaning, no more chapped hands. Gas lighting—or even electric! Meat at every meal. And . . . and parties! I thought about not having to live on this ugly street, with all these saloons and gambling parlors and dance halls."

"So?"

"So I was being selfish."

Joe rolled his eyes. "You were being human, Alice. You once had all that, and you lost it. What's wrong with wanting it back?"

"Haven't you been listening? What's wrong is the person I was, the person I would become again once I had it."

Joe scowled at her and said, "I love you, too, Alice."

She hadn't realized just how potent those words were—even said as sharply as he said them. Despite the misery of giving him up, they trailed light and hope. False hope, surely, but . . .

But he loved her.

When was the last time anybody had ever said that to her? Her first fiancé had proposed on the reasoning that they were "well suited." Her ne'er-do-well husband had praised her beyond reason, but even he hadn't claimed love.

Had *anybody* ever said that to her? Even her parents?

"Thank you," she whispered, and she wanted to cry.

Because the person he loved was exactly what she risked losing if she went to him.

"Don't thank me yet," he warned. "I love you too much to let you go easily. Even if you did become a different woman after marrying into money—and I still can't believe it—we could just find ways to deal with that. I could control the money."

Alice didn't often descend to sarcasm, but. . . . "There's a tactic sure to keep me from doing every desperate thing I could to trick it out of you."

"Or I could give it all away myself, and we could be poor together."

"Joe, that's ridiculous!"

"It *is* ridiculous, because we may not have to do anything at all. You don't even know if it's going to be a problem. So what I suggest"—and he nodded with his decision—"is some kind of test."

He seemed increasingly cheerful, which somehow worried her.

"What kind of test?" she asked, wary.

"Whoa . . ." To her surprise, they'd arrived in front of the Promise House. Joe draped the reins over the dash and set the surrey's hand brake, then turned to better face her, took her hands in his.

"Next Saturday night is the Founder's Day Ball in Colorado Springs," he said. "Come with me."

There was definitely a downside to a determined man. "You haven't been listening at all, have you?"

"I have, I just don't agree, and that's why I mean to test you. I don't mean for you to just go to the ball with me—I want you to do it in style. I'll have my Aunt Belle buy you something appropriate—you'll like her taste, I promise you. You can take the train to Colorado Springs on Friday, first class, and stay with her and her husband, so that everything is aboveboard and respectable. For the ball, your gown has to be sinfully expensive, complete with jewelry. I'll escort you, in my best evening wear, and you'll have your chance to be the old Alice."

"But I don't *want* to be her anymore!"

"Not even for me?"

"But if I turn back into her, you won't like me anymore."

"In which case we don't get married. But if you stay scared of even risking it, you won't marry me anyway, so where's the risk? At least we will have tried. You can go safely home to the Promise House on Sunday and keep doing good, either way."

But would she? Or would she, after seeing that she'd disgusted Joe, dismiss him as nothing more than a nouveau riche immigrant and set her sights on some other, less discerning gentleman at the ball, simply to keep herself in jewels?

"But if it turns out you *can* handle it," continued Joe, increasingly encouraged. "If I'm right, and you're the same pure, wonderful Alice no matter what you're wearing or where you're dancing, then we can marry. And be happy. And raise baby Josephine and who knows how many others of our own."

"Assuming Gil gives me a divorce," she murmured, her throat tight from resisting the hope that he held out.

Joe said, "I can buy a small country, Alice. Trust me. Gil will give you the divorce. But please. . . ."

Perhaps it was his dark, pleading eyes under the shadow of his black curls. Or perhaps it was the chance he offered, the chance to build their own happy ending.

Or perhaps, whispered her frightened side, it was the offer of a sinfully expensive gown, with jewels, and a first-class train ride to Colorado Springs. But Alice hoped not.

"Yes, Joe," she whispered miserably. "Yes, I'll let you do all that for me. This once."

"We're doing it for me, too," he said, and swung to the street, then came around and helped her down to the sidewalk.

She wanted to kiss him again. She wanted to regain the warmth that she'd had beside him in the buggy, wanted to taste his generous lips, wanted to bury herself in his certainty that everything would be all right.

Instead, before he could bend to take her mouth with his, Alice backed away toward the door. "You should get back to Josie," she said, nervous, and ducked quickly inside.

Past the *No Men Allowed* sign—the sign that provided more than one kind of safety for her and the residents.

Alice sat carefully in the Stanhope's fine parlor, on the evening of the Founder's Day Ball, and felt like a princess . . . and something of a kept woman.

She was marginally encouraged by how uncomfortable, rather than deserving, all of Joe's gifts made her feel.

The first-class train ride to Colorado Springs had been divine—Joe had even sent her to a seamstress on the morning of the trip, for a last-minute fitting into a fashionable new travel suit. Alice had forgotten how much she missed the luxury of having her clothes fitted.

Still, she'd remembered to thank the seamstress. She hadn't been rude to anybody on the train.

Joe had met her at the station and driven her to the Stanhope mansion in a surrey just as fine as his aunt and uncle's. This one, however, was his.

"My Aunt Belle is excited about helping you prepare for tomorrow," he told her. "So I don't get to see you again until the ball. Is that all right?"

"Whatever is most convenient," Alice had said—then took hope in that response, too. The old Alice had never cared about what was convenient to anybody but herself, after all.

Her time with Belle Stanhope, Joe's aunt, proved equally luxurious. Belle had put together everything Alice would need, milk baths and hair treatments to try to rescue her appearance from its last year of domestic labor.

"You simply must let me do this," Belle had insisted, when Alice protested that it was all too much. "Back when I was young, even younger than you, I was terribly plain. You can imagine the teasing I got, named Belle! But I was given help from my very own fairy godmother—someday you'll have to let my sisters and me tell you the story—so this is my chance to return the favor."

Someday, Alice thought, meant if she actually married Joe.

That seemed fair, rather than annoying her, which was also a good sign.

Finally, here she sat. Thus far she hadn't snapped at anybody. Not even when her hair was pulled and tugged and wrapped in rags all night to create the curling gold ringlets that now bounced, upswept, across the back of her head. Not even when she'd had to wield a pumice stone across her elbows and knuckles, to wear away some of the calluses she'd developed over the last year. Not even when the dressmaker had poked her with a pin, hurrying to fit a gown she'd already sewn loosely, with not a day to spare to make it right.

Alice's mother had been fond of quoting the French about how one must suffer for beauty. Well, she'd done it. She'd suffered. But thank heavens she'd suffered in silence, and the results. . . .

Slowly, Alice stood to take another look at herself in the mirror, across the room.

She really was pretty, perhaps even prettier than she'd been at the height of her social youth. Surely it wasn't just this magical dress, or the diamond and sapphire necklace that had been delivered for her. There was more to her face now, more angle, more character. There was even something about her posture. . . .

She smiled at her reflection. Now, if only Joe thought similarly!

As if called by her hopes, a knock sounded at the door. Immediately, as she spun toward it, Alice's heart began to race. Belle was upstairs with her husband, Christopher Stanhope, readying their three sons for bed before they left for the party. Should Alice perhaps answer the door herself?

But of course not. A maid scurried into the foyer, before Alice could even take a step. *Now*, thought Alice, imagining Joe on the other side, wanting to see what he looked like in his evening suit, wanting to see his reaction to her transformation. She imagined entering the ballroom on his arm, and could hardly breathe. *Now!*

But the maid hesitated, staring at her. "Ma'am . . . you're lovely!"

Nine

"Thank you, Maggie," said Joe, stepping into the foyer and turning to look for Alice.

He nearly dropped the flowers he carried.

Oh, my God.

Belle had put her in blue, which Joe himself had suggested, based on Alice's golden hair and blue eyes. But he'd never imagined such a shimmering, tactile blue, nor the sleek sweep of its modern cut. The necklace he'd chosen for her, one he wholly intended to insist that she keep, lapped across the beauty of her neck as if meant for her. Little blue ribbons sparkled in her curled, upswept hair like tiny butterflies among the dewdrops of more tiny jewels. But most of all . . .

With her chin up and her shoulders back, she looked like his Alice at her most powerful.

Except for a tiny worry frown between her eyes.

"Are you feeling all right?" He quickly went to her, leaving the flowers on a table.

Her eyes widened. "You think I look *ill?*"

That made Joe laugh, which seemed to ease her concern.

"I think," he said, "that you're the most beautiful woman I have ever seen. I just take that as quite a responsibility."

In response, Alice slipped her gloved hand into his. "You're up to it, Dr. Erikson," she said—and everything was all right.

"Goodbye, Aunt Belle," he called up the stairs. "Uncle Kit. We'll see you at the ball!"

When he turned back, Alice was staring at him.

"Sorry." In many of the finer homes, that would have been quite the gaffe. "Have I warned you that we're a fairly informal family?"

Alice smiled, her pleasure easily as brilliant as the jewels she wore. He offered his arm. She took it—and Joe felt complete.

Nothing would ruin this night.

Joe had been to plenty of balls in his time, thanks in part to his matchmaking grandmother. He usually enjoyed them, too. But always there'd been that shadow of doubt.

Were the young women who danced with him, laughed with him, and sometimes made inappropriate advances in the cover of a cloak room or a column interested in *him*?

Or were they just interested in his gold-mining money?

Sometimes, when he had politely declined a woman's offer to escort her here or secretly meet her there, she would respond with a hurt that revealed her true intentions. One had called him a bastard, and several more had called him Italian, as if that were quite the slur. And then there was the whispering, when people thought he wouldn't notice. It was all just enough to keep him uncertain.

But with Alice, Joe felt one-hundred-percent confident. She'd kissed him—*loved him!*—before she even knew about the money. True, the money concerned her, but they would work through that. She was at this ball for him, and him alone.

Which made her a delight to squire about.

"This is the *new* Antlers Hotel," he told her, leading her into the ivory, gold, and red lobby of the famous, Italian Renaissance style hotel. "The old one burned down a few years back, and its reincarnation is all the more beautiful for the change."

"It is lovely." Relieved of her blue stole, Alice turned to take in the chandeliers, the high ceilings, as they reached the hotel's grand ballroom. "Certainly as nice as anything I've seen in St. Louis, much less Wyoming."

"And these," said Joe with a touch less enthusiasm, "are my grandparents."

Trust Nanna Bridey to watch the ballroom entrance and to make a beeline toward them the moment they appeared. Joe tensed, remembering how his grandmother had spoken of Alice the previous week.

He needn't have worried.

"Is this her?" exclaimed Bridey Sullivan, her brogue as thick as the peacock feathers that adorned her gown. Joe's grandmother had never quite lost the awe she'd had for pretty doo-da's when she'd grown up poor. Despite her very real desire to measure up to society's standards, she liked pretty things far too much to avoid looking overdressed. "Is this the lass you told us of, Joey? Let me take a look at her!"

"Um, Alice," said Joe, as Bridey held the woman he loved at arm's length, "this is my grandmother, Bridget Sullivan, and her husband, Patrick. Nanna, Grandda, this is Mrs. Alice Prescott."

"How do you do," murmured Alice, clearly unnerved.

At that, Bridey pulled the girl to her bosom and wrapped her arms around her. "You poor dear! For such a beauty to have been so mistreated by the world. Don't you worry about a thing, *Mrs. Prescott.*"

For a moment, Joe feared his Nanna was going to wink slyly, but the wink was only implied.

"My man is on the matter, and he's good at what he does," she assured the younger woman. "Everything will turn out just fine, you'll see."

"Well . . . thank you," said Alice, as Bridey released her.

"Mrs. Prescott," greeted Grandda with an awkward attempt at a bow. "We hope to be seeing more of you."

As soon as he could, Joe extricated Alice from the older Sullivans. "Two down," he said, amused. "More, if you count Belle and Charisma's families. Are you all right?"

Alice looked flustered. "They aren't what I expected."

"I get that a lot," said Joe, and now *he* winked. "It's because I don't look Irish. Are you ready for the really important introduction?"

Alice glanced around the bustling ballroom, clearly nervous. "You see your parents?"

Joe laughed. "If my father is in a room, you see him."

When Alice nodded, he drew her across the room to his very tall, broad-shouldered adoptive father and his smaller mother.

And he tried not to hold his breath.

Until he'd met Alice, Joe hadn't imagined any woman could ever be as beautiful as his mother,

Grace. He'd once vowed to marry no woman who wasn't redheaded like her . . . but as he got older, he realized that her beauty was not so much in her appearance, though she had that, but her character. Grace Sullivan Erikson was kind, loving, gentle . . . everything a woman should be.

Alice was like that, he thought. But with a longer reach, a broader scope in the people she helped. Alice had been through more heartache and been strengthened by it.

"There he is," sounded Jon's deep voice, and the tall, blond man waved. "Joe!"

More of their family's informality, for better or worse.

"Alice," Joe said, "these are my parents, Jon and Grace Erikson. Jon, Grace, this is Mrs. Alice Prescott."

"How do you do," said Alice, and Joe's mother echoed the greeting.

Jon pumped her hand, flashing his most winning smile. "It's a real pleasure to meet you, Miz Prescott. Joe here's told us all kinds of nice things about you. It doesn't seem like he lied, either."

Alice blinked in barely checked surprise at Joe's looming, fair-haired father, and Grace laughed.

"It's a shock at first, I know," his mother said. "Our Joe hardly looks Norwegian, does he?"

Almost immediately, Alice seemed to recover her social graces, smiling at the joke. "So tell me, Mrs. Erikson, how did the two of you meet?"

"She fell for me right off," announced Jon, with a twinkle in his blue eyes—it was an old family joke.

"I fell *on* him, actually," corrected Grace. "I was never a very graceful woman . . ."

While she told Alice the story, Jon drew Joe aside. "She sure is pretty, Joe. Seems real nice, too."

"Really," corrected Joe, half distracted by watching the women, making sure Alice was all right.

"Didn't I just say that?" asked his father, honestly confused, and Joe relaxed. If he wasn't careful, *he* might just turn into the evil prig Alice feared in herself.

"Yes, you did. I'm glad you like her."

"You're the one whose opinion counts," Jon reminded him. "You're the one wants to marry her, right?"

Joe watched the two women he most loved in the world, unable to hold back his smile. "More than ever."

Jon shrugged his broad shoulders. At least now that they were rich, his suits always fit. "We had a visit with your Aunt Charisma this afternoon. Later, maybe you can tell us about this baby you're adopting?"

Joe grinned and nodded. "Yes sir. Maybe Alice and I can tell you together."

He was about to step back toward the women when Jon clamped a powerful hand onto his shoulder. "We're proud of you, Gio. You know that, don't you?"

Joe hesitated, eyes suddenly warm with emotion. Only his father used his old, Italian name nowadays, and that only when he had something private or sentimental to say.

"I'm what you and Grace raised me to be," he managed through his thick throat. "Thank you for that."

His father nodded, now wordless himself, and let him go. Joe took a deep breath, then moved to rescue Alice from his mother. Especially since some unsuspecting soul had given Grace a cup of punch.

"Would you excuse us?" he asked. "Alice and I haven't danced yet." *Ever.*

"It was lovely to meet you," said Alice.

"We'll have plenty of time to chat some more," promised Grace, and wheeled toward her husband—

Who caught the hand with the punch before she could spill it on anybody. Particularly him.

"Shall we?" asked Joe, losing himself yet again in Alice's polished beauty. "Dance, I mean?"

She nodded, and he took her in his arms, and they stepped onto the dance floor into a smooth waltz. This, Joe decided, was what balls were made for. It was a beautiful night, with sweeping music and sparkling chandeliers. He caught a glimpse of his Aunt Charisma with the senator, and of his Aunt Belle— and her ever-present fan—with her British husband, and he loved every one of them, especially tonight. *Everyone* liked Alice, just as he'd hoped.

But the real question was . . .

"Do you like them?" he asked, sweeping her in a graceful circle. "My family?"

The last thing he expected was for Alice to start to cry.

The ache had started upon meeting his grandparents. She'd held it back for as long as she could. But the raw hope in Joe's face, when he asked her about his family, was too much.

Alice began to weep. Worse, she wasn't even sure why—not until Joe led her out a double door and to a quiet bench for some fresh air. All she'd known, until then, was that the kinder his family was, the worse her heart hurt, until now. . . .

Now she understood. "My mother would hate you."

Not surprisingly, Joe stiffened beside her. "What?"

"Not just you—your whole family," she continued miserably, her head bowed, and accepted the handkerchief he handed her. "My mother would think you were beneath me, beneath *us*, no matter how much money you had."

Wealth does not equal breeding, Alice, her mother used to tell her. *You mustn't embarrass us, Alice. You define us by the company you keep.*

No wonder her mother rarely answered Alice's letters, since Alice's elopement and her job at the Promise House. Even those few responses had been brief and perfunctory.

"Well, if that's how she felt," said Joe slowly, "no wonder she raised you to be a bitch."

Now Alice stiffened—and slowly raised her face to see Joe. His dark eyes burned with distaste. At her?

It was just as she'd feared. Now that he'd seen the real Alice, the one she'd been hiding. . . .

Then he said, "But I wasn't asking about your mother. What do *you* think of my family? I believe I deserve an honest answer."

Alice took her time, so that she could give him one. His grandmother dressed like a peacock—in more ways than one—and his grandfather's socks had been mismatched. His father shook her hand like a man's, and his mother seemed to be downright dangerous with a glass of punch. They were loud, and familiar, and almost all of them were, at best, second- or third-generation Americans. Her mother would truly, *truly* hate them, would hate to see Alice with them.

And yet . . .

His grandmother had called her a dear, had given her a hug. His aunts had been nothing but kind to her, far beyond what civility dictated. His parents seemed to accept her as their daughter-in-law already, on their faith in Joe's word alone.

Despite the fact that she worked with prostitutes, or was a married woman seeking divorce, they accepted her.

As much as Alice's mother would hate the Eriksons and the Sullivans, she realized, she would hate Alice even more. But the Eriksons and the Sullivans did not.

"They are kind," she admitted slowly. "Loving. And . . . and they're so forgiving. Joe, your mother says she broke your father's leg, almost *crippled* him, and he fell in love with her anyway."

"I know," he said, seeming confused. "I was there."

"Your grandfather seems to realize just how, well, *extreme* your grandmother is, and he still loves her." Again, Alice wiped her eyes, finally noticing the monogram on her handkerchief. J.E. Joe was taking care of her, even in this. "From what Charisma and Belle have told me, they and their husbands had to resolve some rather extreme issues before marrying, but they're all truly happy, and—"

"Excuse me," interrupted a female voice. Alice jumped, startled and embarrassed to be caught so disheveled.

She was even more startled to see that the young woman who offered her a cup of punch, wearing as stylish a gown as Alice's, had the shiny black hair and almond eyes of the Chinese. At a ball!

"You seem so sad," the girl said, without an accent. "Can I help somehow?"

"You can give us some privacy, to start." But what surprised Alice most was that Joe was the one who said that.

"Joe!" Alice protested, even as the girl backed away. "Don't be rude!"

The girl laughed, hiding her smile behind a hand, and her eyes flashed mischief. "I like her already, Joey."

Joe groaned. "Alice, this is my sister May. May, this is Mrs. Prescott. Will you leave us alone now, please?"

Despite all her childhood training, Alice stared. She somehow managed to form the words, "H-how do you do?"

"I'm well, thank you," said May, with a small bow. Then, rightly interpreting Alice's hesitation, she offered an explanation for her appearance. "I'm adopted. Like Joe."

Alice said, slowly, "I didn't *think* he looked Chinese."

Joe laughed. "Her parents ran a laundry in Cripple Creek, but they died of a fever, maybe three years after we moved up there ourselves."

"I'm so sorry."

"I hardly remember them," said May. "It is a forgotten sadness. I have been very happy with the Eriksons."

"We couldn't pronounce her real name," continued Joe, "and her parents always called her Mei-Mei, so . . ."

"So now I am May Erikson."

"And if people would leave us alone," growled Joe, "maybe I can go on convincing this lady to become *Alice* Erikson?"

"Please excuse my brother," said May. "He is not so terribly obnoxious, once you get to know him."

Joe narrowed his eyes, but May escaped with a delightful laugh before he could exact any worse retribution on her.

"She's very kind," said Alice slowly—and meant it. In fact, she wanted to laugh herself, with relief. She'd outgrown her parents' rigid biases. And thank goodness! If she hadn't, she would never have been able to appreciate the miracle of Joe's family. "They all are. You come from wonderful family, Joe, and I'm honored to have met them."

"Then say you'll marry me," insisted Joe. "What have you got to hold you back now? I mean . . . other than the husband."

Alice laid a hand on his handsome cheek. "Only that I'm not sure I deserve you."

"You aren't the person you used to be, Alice." Joe tipped his cheek against her palm. "None of us are."

"I know that now. You showed me. It's just . . . nobody has *ever* loved me the way your family loves each other. Wholeheartedly. Almost blindly. Oh, Joe, I didn't even know that kind of love existed . . ."

Heaven help her if she wasn't crying again.

Especially when Joe wiped her tears with his thumb, his dark eyes searching hers. "Then say yes, Alice, and let us prove it to you, every day."

"Yes," said Alice, her voice choked. "Yes, yes, yes."

But by then, he was kissing her, and she got to tell him in other ways, in the shadow of the Rocky Mountains and the Antlers Hotel.

Epilogue

June

"You liked the wedding?" asked Joe, as the door closed behind the bellhop, and he drew Alice into his arms. They had a room at Denver's Windsor Hotel, where they would consummate their marriage before moving themselves and baby Josephine into their newly built home by way of a honeymoon.

Alice rested her head on his shoulder, dizzy with happiness. "It was the perfect wedding, Joe. Because I was marrying you."

He kissed her then, passionately, deeply. Then he angled his head and kissed her again, then again. They'd become very good at just standing and kissing—or sitting and kissing—in the last several months. Time seemed to drift away to nothingness while she and Joe kissed. The world became a soft, wonderful place.

But tonight . . . tonight there would be even more.

Mere weeks after he'd been hired, Bridget Sullivan's private detective had returned with shocking news. Not only had he located Gilbert Prescott, but he'd located the man's wife. Rather, his *wives*.

All of them had been deserted after several weeks' marriage . . . two of them before Gilbert ever met

Alice. The man was a bigamist . . . and Alice had never been legally married.

Instead, she'd told Joe sadly, *I'm a fallen woman.*

That doesn't matter, he'd said. *Don't mention this to my mother, but I've fallen once or twice myself.*

Now, as Joe trailed his searing kisses down her jaw, then slowly down her throat, Alice decided he was right. It *didn't* matter. Arching into him, into the incredible way he made her feel, there really was no other man in the world.

"Your parents seemed impressed," he whispered against her chest, over the low collar of her wedding gown.

"My parents are snobs," she said. "They only liked how expensive everything was. But I think my brother and I might become friends. It buttons up the back."

Joe turned her, easy as that, and began to unbutton the many, many pearl fastenings on her silk gown. It *had* been a beautiful wedding, one destined to make all the society pages—and she hardly cared.

Dixie, however—who would be running the Promise House in Alice's absence—had been delighted to be a bridesmaid at such an event. She and the girls had made Alice a whole new memory book.

Alice caught her breath as the cloth across her back parted. The heavy skirt pulled the rest of the gown downward, over her hips with an audible swish, and when Joe drew her close again, she could feel his desire even from behind. When his hands slid up over her corseted front, up to where her suddenly heavy breasts threatened to spill over the top of the undergarment, she moaned her pleasure at his touch.

She loved him so much, she ached with it. But . . .

But she stepped away. "I—I promised the girls I would wear the peignoir that they packed for me."

Gazing at her in the dimmed gaslight, in his shirtsleeves, his black curls tousled, Joe had never looked so much like a gypsy. Or perhaps a pirate, one bent on marauding. "I'm just going to take it off you," he warned, low.

She bit her lower lip, far less shy than she would have thought she'd be. "Good. I'll only be a moment . . ."

Obediently, Joe collapsed onto their bed, a dark-eyed, dark-skinned invitation to ecstasy. Alice was so impatient to get back to him that her fingers fumbled with the latch on her carpetbag. Finally she opened it, ready to lift out the silken negligee that the girls of the Promise House had sworn would double Joe's pleasure in his wedding night. . . .

And she swept a hand to her mouth, to catch back a laugh.

"What?" demanded Joe, sitting up in the middle of the bed.

With a wide smile, Alice lifted out the sign from the front door of the Promise House. *No Men Allowed*.

But the "No" had been crossed out.

Joe laughed, too. "Men? Only one of us, I should hope!"

"Do your job properly, Dr. Erikson, and we'll see," teased Alice—

Only to have him catch her by the wrist and pull her on top of him. Then he rolled, so that she was suddenly underneath him, again in his strong arms.

"The peignoir can wait," he warned, breath hot, eyes hotter, fingers all but burning her. "Just promise to wear it later."

Every bit of her ached for him—so Alice nodded,

and circled him with her arms, and pulled him down onto her. "I promise, Joe. I promise."

They'd been waiting all their lives, after all.

They'd definitely waited long enough.

Silver and Satin

Karen L. King

One

Mary Martha Hamilton had barely entered through the front door of the Boston mansion she'd called home all of her twenty-six years when her younger sister Suzanna raced down the stairs. Suzanna was younger by seven years, but at times it felt twice that or more.

"Oh, good, you're back. You have to start planning the wedding." Suzanna grabbed her arm, almost causing a fatal accident or at least a deep scratch as Mary pulled out her long pearl-studded hat pin.

"What wedding?" asked Mary, her heart skittering in her throat. Had her fiancé's ship, missing for years, finally made port? No, the ship had been lost in a hurricane. The chances of it or her fiancé returning were nil.

"I've bought material for the dresses, but, you know, I'm hopeless with planning an event. I don't even know where to start or what needs to be done. Papa says we must start work right away. He could only get the church for the first Saturday in June."

"Suzanna, I—" Mary tried to interrupt, but her sister was having none of it.

"Other than that, we should have to wait clear until August as Reverend Pritchard is determined to do mission work in the territories this summer. It would be terrible to have the assistant minister, he spits so when he talks. Could you imagine anything worse than being spit upon when reciting marriage vows?"

Had their father finally decided to remarry? He had been paying particular attention to a certain widow friend lately. Suzanna chattered nonstop as if she expected Mary to know what she was talking about. Perhaps she needed reminding that Mary had been absent during recent developments. "I'm glad to see you, too. It's been a long four weeks."

Apparently, Suzanna would not ask about their sister-in-law's difficult confinement or the new addition to their extended family. Mary had been looking forward to sharing her news, but Suzanna had trumped her with these marriage plans.

Mary felt caught out of time. Her head was filled with images of babies and bunting. She could hardly entertain the idea that her family already had a monumental task lined up for her to do when she returned. But the news slowly sank in. They expected her to plan a wedding in less than a month?

Could it be for their brother Nathan, who was engaged but hadn't set a date last Mary knew? But his bride's parents should be in charge of the planning.

"Hurry, you have to see the material for my dress, before the dressmaker starts cutting. I suppose we shall have to contact a florist, and we'll need a cake."

Suzanna circled. Mary secured her hat pin in the band of her large hat and handed it to the maid waiting in the entry hall of their Boston home. She wanted nothing more than a hot bath and a cup of tea, but Suzanna could barely contain her impatience. Mary slipped out of her damp coat; the carriage couldn't keep the torrential spring rains from making everything soggy, including her. "Don't you want to hear about the baby?"

Suzanna made a moue of distaste. "We got your letter. She sounds lovely. I wonder if David hoped for a boy."

Mary supposed if she was as beautiful as her golden-haired and statuesque sister, she might be as excited about a new dress. But Mary was short, round, and brown-haired like a wren. Fashionable dresses with their multitude of flounces rarely flattered her. Besides, she liked babies. She liked cooing to them and rocking them and kissing their dimpled little fingers.

"Papa says you have to help me choose. He says I don't have the sense the good Lord gave a duck. I don't think he'll ever realize I'm fully grown." Suzanna dragged her into the back parlor.

Nobody would, thought Mary, so long as her younger sister darted around like a child playing tag.

Gleaming white satin, mountains of tulle, and yards of lace covered every available surface. Mary drew up short in the doorway, her heart jumping into her throat.

"Won't it be grand? It's like a court dress."

If it wasn't a court dress, then it was a bridal gown. Suzanna was the one getting married? Mary needed to sit down. She'd almost rather Suzanna planned to cross the big pond and be presented to Queen Victoria.

There wasn't any place to sit. Every chair was draped with satin, the tables piled high with rosettes and ribbons. A bridal gown? For her childlike younger sister? Oh, my goodness, now Mary would have to plan a wedding and not her own, not her father's or brother's, but her baby sister's.

For a second Mary wished that Suzanna had made good on her regular threat to run away and live with their Aunt Lydia in England.

"There you are, Mary." Her father peered in and winced at the waterfalls of white. "The house maid said you'd made it home. Nothing has been the same since you've been gone. Dinner has been burned or cold, and no one can find my slippers."

Mary turned around and clung to her father. He gave her a brief embrace, then patted her absently on the head, before shuffling out of the room with an order to direct her sister's choices and get on with planning.

Suzanna danced around waving a handful of fashion plates. "Which one do you think? I like this one, but Papa thinks it is cut too low."

Mary finally managed to find her voice. It was squeaky like a rusty hinge. "Are you engaged?"

"Yes, of course. Didn't you get my letter?"

Mary shook her head. Mail to the countryside was slower and less dependable than mail to the city. "Anyone I know?"

"No. He's very handsome."

Of course he would be handsome. Mary expected no less of her sister. But would he be able to support Suzanna? Would he be understanding when his wife was more interested in attending a party than finding his slippers? "Yes, but what does he do? What is his name? Does Papa approve?"

Suzanna smiled rather like a cat who swallowed the canary. She slowed her skip to a saunter. "Of course, Papa approves. His name is Sterling John Cooper. He says he's from Boston, but nobody remembers him. He does know who is who, though." For half a second

Suzanna looked thoughtful, but the second passed quickly. "He has dark hair and dreamy blue eyes. He's a little old, but he's *an adventurer*." Suzanna did a quick twirl. "I will see the world."

"Are you sure Papa knew what he was agreeing to when he gave his approval?" Mary asked.

While working, their father could be so engrossed in his load manifests and plotting out his merchant ships' voyages that he would not have any idea what he agreed to. He'd been even more absent-minded since his wife's death from a fever five years earlier.

"Yes, of course, Mr. Cooper insisted on asking Papa's permission before he would court me. I told him he didn't need to be so old-fashioned."

Well, that was one plus in his favor. Was her sister not comfortable using her fiancé's given name?

"The dressmaker will arrive any minute now, so will you pick a pattern?" Suzanna shoved the fashion plates under Mary's nose again.

"Whichever one you want I'm sure will be fine." Mary could pull the dressmaker aside and make sure the final version of the wedding dress was modest enough. But what difference did it make? Her sister was getting married. She would be choosing clothes all on her own once she became a married woman.

"I must have a huge ceremony. We Hamiltons have an image to preserve, and Papa agrees. Mr. Cooper thought it should be a little thing with just family, but when I told him that's not how it's done in Boston, he said he'd allow for my greater knowledge in these things. We will have the most splendid affair. I want white horses to pull the carriage to the chapel and pink roses on every pew and candles, millions of candles."

Suzanna detailed her plans for the grandest wedding to ever hit Boston, and Mary wilted at the idea of arranging everything. Suzanna's idea of organizing a special occasion was to state what she wanted and then just expect it to be there when she showed up. And in all the happy plans the groom never figured as more than a shadowy prop. Was her sister marrying because it would be the biggest celebration to hit Boston in a dozen years and as the bride she would be the center of it all?

Finally, Mary was able to get a word in edgewise. "What does Mr. Cooper think of all your plans?"

"I told you, he is letting me plan everything with the wedding."

Great. No help in that quarter, then.

Mary left Suzanna with the dressmaker, but as she was halfway up the stairs to change out of her traveling outfit, a knock sounded on the door. She descended and pulled open the door and found herself face-to-face with a stranger.

An absolutely gorgeous stranger.

His tall hat held in one hand, with his other hand he pushed back a wavy strand of long dark hair that had blown into his face.

He smiled slowly with deep dimples that stopped her breathing. She stood there awestruck. This was the kind of man who made a woman remember she was a woman, and his eyes were so blue she could drown in them.

"Is Miss Hamilton at home?" he asked.

"I am Miss Hamilton."

"I guess I meant the other Miss Hamilton," he said with just a hint of sheepishness.

Oh, no! She was drooling over her sister's fiancé.

Two

Sterling John Cooper rarely wasted time when he had a goal in his sights. However, it occurred to him on his way to preview a house that he ought to ask his soon-to-be bride if she'd like to see her future home. Since the house he intended to purchase was only five streets over from the Hamilton's house, he went to Suzanna's home first.

Now he was standing on the front stoop, nearly on eye level with a curvy little woman who stared at him with an expression of horror on her face. That wasn't the effect he normally had on women.

She was a tiny thing, short enough that he could have wrapped her up in his arms and rested his chin on the top of her head.

Hell's bells, this must be his future sister-in-law. So he wouldn't be resting his chin on her head any time soon. Never, in fact, he thought with a fleeting sense of regret. From the way Suzanna had described her sister, he'd expected a woman much older, much plainer, much less adorable.

"You must be Mr. Cooper." She wiped the look of horror away with a welcoming smile. A neat trick.

He stuck out his hand. "Sterling. You must be Mary."

She invited him in and explained that Suzanna was

with the dressmaker. He followed Mary into the front parlor. She left to tell his fiancée he was here.

Sterling paced the room with its stiff camelback sofa and myriad tables, most skirted and ruffled. Over the fireplace hung a picture of a large sailing ship, reminding him that the Hamiltons had made their fortune in shipping, while he'd scrabbled his out of creeks in California.

Running a successful business as their family had for several generations and through two wars required brains and the kind of connections only an old venerable family had.

Panning for gold required a strong back, luck, and the sense to leave when the gamblers, whores, and confidence men came to relieve the miners of their riches.

He crossed over to look at the painting and the row of ships in bottles displayed on the mantel. Each had a name on a tiny plaque. Replicas of the Hamilton fleet?

"Those are my father's ships," said Mary as she returned to the room.

"I guessed as much. And the painting?"

"My great grandfather's first ship, the *Mary Martha*."

Sterling spun around with amusement. "Are you named after a ship?"

"Actually, the ship was named after my great grandmother, whom I'm also named after." She smiled as if the idea of being named after a ship tickled her.

The idea of naming children for their forebearers pleased him. He had made the right choice to marry into this family steeped with history and traditions. He had come a long way since the days when his cronies had nicknamed him Silver John.

"I'm afraid my sister won't be able to join us for a

bit. She asked me to keep you company." Mary looked
a little perplexed by the idea that she should entertain
her sister's future spouse. "Won't you have a seat? I
have rung for tea."

"You didn't need to do that." Sterling wished he
could call back the words. He could fit in anywhere,
and clearly his gold-lined pockets had bought him acceptance into Boston's venerable elite, but he still
wasn't used to being waited upon or served.

"Oh, but I did," said Mary. "You see, I just returned
from my brother's home near Albany, and I'm quite
famished."

Sterling moved to a wing chair, but took a close
look at his soon-to-be sister-in-law instead. While her
back was ramrod straight like any lady's, her face ra-
diated kindliness. Perhaps her look of horror at the
door was because the last thing she wanted to do was
be polite to unexpected company. In fact, her narrow,
dark brown skirt and fitted jacket might be a traveling
suit. Had she intended to change? Certainly her outfit was a far cry from the bright concoctions of ruffles
and lace Suzanna tended to wear.

"Don't let me keep you if you wished to rest or
needed to change your clothes."

Mary blinked. "Thank you. I don't need to rest. I
probably need to take a walk as I have been sitting in
the carriage all day." Her expression was warm and relaxed. "After I eat that is. Of course, I have been
directed to find my father's missing slippers and make
sure the cook properly prepares dinner. You will stay
and join us, won't you?"

"I was on my way to look over a house I'm going to
buy. I thought Suzanna might want to see it. Would you
like to go in her place? It's not far." He pulled the key

from his pocket and dangled it. "After tea, that is, and I would be honored to dine tonight with your family."

"I should like nothing better," Mary said in such a way that he wasn't sure if she was being polite about the off-hand dinner invitation or seeing his future house.

Sterling finally settled into the chair. He didn't feel an urge to leave, but he was not lingering out of the hope that Suzanna would join them either. Too much time in her company made him impatient. Partly he was sure his annoyance arose because he wanted to get on with the business of making children with her, but mostly because she seemed incredibly young and restless.

Marriage and children would no doubt settle her. Although, he understood too well that restlessness of youth. It had lead him around the world only to realize he really wanted to be back in Boston putting together the home and family he'd always dreamed of belonging to.

Mary sat with her hands folded in her lap, waiting companionably. She was an easy woman to spend time with, unlike her sister, who would have been chattering nonsensically or sulking because he couldn't keep up with her latest revelation about the color of the gown she intended to wear to church. He'd thought she said the pink gown, when she—according to her—distinctly said she was wearing the pink one to the play and the rose one to church, and they sounded like the same color to him.

"Did you have a nice visit in Albany?" he asked.

Mary's face lit up with an inner beauty. "We have a lovely new niece. I went to help my sister-in-law with her two toddlers during her confinement."

Mary's features were very like her sister's, but

softer, gentler with her straight brown hair and doe-like brown eyes. Suzanna's beauty was more flashy, golden curls framing her face and long-lashed sparkling blue eyes.

"You will gain quite an extended family when you join ours," Mary said.

"That's a good thing." One of his main reasons for picking the Hamiltons, beyond their standing in the community, was their extensive family connections, including a member of the nobility in England. That and there was an attractive daughter of marriageable age.

"Do you have any brothers or sisters?" Mary asked.

"No." He usually fended off questions about his background. Supplying answers when he didn't know much beyond his name was difficult.

"You are buying a house here in Boston. Are you planning to live here?" Mary's face was open and earnest. She leaned toward him as she subjected him to the sort of interrogation he'd expected from her father.

"Yes. There's a house not too far from here that will make a nice home for us." It might take him years to get used to having twenty more rooms than he needed, but a Hamilton bride would expect no less.

"Will you be doing a lot of traveling?"

"Not that I know of."

Mary bit her lip. As much as it amused him to be interrogated by a little slip of a woman who was likely younger than him, he tried to answer her honestly. If that's what it took to marry into this long-established family, he was willing to be put to thumbscrews.

"If the house isn't appropriate, I can look for another or have one built." He looked around to see if someone else had said that. No, the words had left his own mouth. He'd already decided the house was right, and barring termites, dry rot, or extensive water damage, he was unlikely to change his mind.

"My sister said you have traveled quite a bit."

"For the last fifteen years." Since he'd left Boston at the age of sixteen. "I'm ready to settle down and start a family and a put together a business." He wanted to build railroads. With his future father-in-law in the shipping industry it seemed like a perfect fit. That and he knew the country; he'd been across most of it.

"Suzanna has the idea you might travel together."

How had she gotten that impression? "I might need to take trips for business, but she certainly won't need to go with me."

Mary's brows furrowed together. "You were born in Boston?"

"I assume so."

Mary looked confused and perturbed.

Sterling took a deep breath. "I was raised in an orphanage down by the wharfs. I was about a year old when I was left on their doorstep. I don't normally talk about it." He rarely thought about it anymore. He hadn't confessed his humble beginnings to Suzanna, and she hadn't inquired. He had the suspicion Mary would insist on the entire story.

All those years of barely enough to eat, the glimpses of carriages going by with real families in them, families like hers, were best left in the past. He'd made up stories to tell himself, that his parents had belonged to one of the high-and-mighty families who didn't notice a dirty urchin like him. He imagined they had died of scarlet fever or in a fire. The truth was if he had come from a family like hers, he never would have been left at an orphanage, even if both his parents had perished.

"So you don't even know your birthday?" She looked flustered and upset.

"No listing in a family Bible that I know of. I generally just mark the day I arrived in the orphanage as the day I change to a new age." He didn't really celebrate it as a birthday, just added on the next year. For all he knew, he might be thirty for another three months, but he'd changed his age last week.

The tea cart arrived, and Mary looked grateful for the reprieve. After he'd taken his tea, no cream, no sugar, and scalding hot, he reminded himself that pouring it into his saucer to cool wasn't acceptable. He'd worked hard on learning the proper manners for polite company. He crossed his ankle on his leg and balanced the cup and saucer on the side of his knee.

She had taken a plate with two tiny sandwiches and a scone, but she repositioned them twice without taking a bite.

"Miss Hamilton, I want to be forthright with you. I expected this kind of questioning from your father, but I gather many of the family responsibilities fall to you. If this is distressing you, we can certainly do it another time."

When she met his gaze, her brown eyes were warm and liquid. Possibly too liquid. He didn't know her well enough to mark the excess moisture as misplaced sympathy for him or worry for her sister.

"If it is only my answers that distress you, I'm sure you can tell your sister to cry off. She puts a lot of store in your opinions."

"Not so much. I don't mean to be such a harridan.

Did my father ask any questions? This all happened so fast."

Sterling shrugged. "I don't waste time once I know what I want, and your father's questions stopped after he learned my bank balance."

She ducked her head down, and he was left staring at the clean line of her center part and the huge bun on the back of her head. Why did she keep her hair in such a simple, unflattering style? Yet, she wasn't wearing a mobcap that would signify she had resigned herself to spinsterhood. She rearranged her food again.

"You know, no matter how many times you move your food around, it's not going to look as if you've eaten any." He touched her arm, wanting to reassure her. An unbidden urge to stroke the length of her prompted him to pull back. "I mean to take good care of your sister."

"Ah, yes, but will my sister take good care of you?" She lifted her brows over her sparkling brown eyes and took a bite of her scone.

He smiled. Perhaps he had passed muster with her. She didn't strike him as a snob who would turn him away for his humble beginnings, but as a woman who was truly concerned for the well-being and happiness of her family. That he would soon be included in that circle of her care spread warmth through his veins. "I can be too frank. I hope you will not hold it against me. Truly, if there is anything you wish to know, I am more than willing to discuss my past or my future with you or your father."

"My father has never quite been himself since my mother died, and I do worry that he does not pay attention to anything beyond his business."

"And you are protective of your sister. She has explained that you very much raised her after your mother passed away." He admired Mary for stepping in to fill her mother's shoes. From the way she'd been described and her family's dependence on her he'd expected a martyred saint, but she was nothing like that.

"I fear I have been too indulgent with her." She pursed her cupid's bow lips as if trying to decide whether or not to say more. Either that or she was puckering up for a kiss.

Sterling shifted, tugged at his pant leg, and nearly spilled his tea.

"I just want her to be happy. I want you both to be happy," she amended.

Her face shined with sincerity. He didn't doubt her. Nor did he believe he had alleviated her concerns, but she had put them aside, perhaps in the interests of civility. Not the usual way of an overly protective surrogate mother.

Spinsters who took over the household for their relatives usually had thin lips, not eminently kissable rosebud lips, didn't they? Weren't they angular and thin, instead of having full curves and satiny skin? Their faces weren't supposed to light up with joy when they talked about family burdens. Just to be sure he hadn't imagined her pleasure when she talked about her family, he said, "Tell me about your new niece."

She put down her scone and brushed crumbs from her fingers. "You can't really want to know about her. Although I confess, I'm bursting at the seams to talk about such a perfect little baby."

"On the contrary, she will soon be my niece, too, and I set a great store by family."

Her face was animated as she talked about the newborn and her siblings. Yes, this was a woman whose whole world revolved around family. She was as foreign to him and his experience as living on the moon, but oh, she made him feel as if he was home.

Mary trailed her finger over the pressed tinwork lining the staircase on what was to be her sister's new house. Suzanna had insisted that Mary would know better whether the house was suitable or not and then gone back to her fashion plates and discussions with the seamstress. Mary had tried to spark her interest with the idea of choosing drapery and such, but Suzanna had waved her off.

The house was lovely, although Mary feared that Suzanna might find the walnut floors and wainscoting too dark. On the ground floor three parlors—or as her Aunt Lydia would describe them, drawing rooms—opened into each other with pocket doors. The kitchen could use a new stove, but it was spacious and well designed. Sterling had mentioned having pipes installed for running water to the upstairs and converting what had been a powder room to a bathroom, which sounded lovely and decadent to Mary and a luxury Suzanna would appreciate.

The dining room was certainly large enough, and there was a perfect breakfast room and enough rooms upstairs to house a growing family.

Just not Mary's.

The clicks of her footsteps down the bare stairs echoed an emptiness she found unexpected. Everyone was getting on with their lives. David's family was growing. Nathan would be starting his soon, and her baby sister Suzanna would be having babies of her own in no time at all. Only Mary was engaged to a man who was presumed dead, and her life had veered off to a side path that was not leading toward the future she expected or wanted.

She loved her father dearly and was proud that she had been the glue that held her family together after her mother's death. She loved being the one her family turned to for advice, for help, to tackle all the matriarchal duties, but she hadn't meant for her own life to be halted. She hadn't meant to lose hope.

"What do you think?" Sterling asked.

"I love it." Mary took a wistful glance around. "Suzanna should be proud to have such a home."

He grinned. "But?"

"She will surely love being able to draw a hot bath without having to lug jugs of water from the kitchen." Not that Suzanna ever did help haul her own hot water. She badgered and sweet-talked the maids until they brought it all for her.

Sterling wrapped his arms over the banister and looked up at her. He was very comfortable in his body and moved with a looseness that surprised her. She couldn't imagine seeing her father or brothers lean so casually on a railing, with a foot propped on a riser between the newel posts. And she should not notice how her sister's fiancé moved or stood or smelled wonderful.

"You will need to employ a very good housekeeper. Do you mean to furnish the house before your wedding?" she asked.

"I hoped Suzanna might take an interest in choosing the furniture and . . . the stove." He looked around a little uncertainly.

Mary heaved a sigh. "The house will need carpets, stair runners, and drapes. The kitchen is lacking pots and pans. Of course, you will need silver and china as well as crockery for the servants. Suzanna should have a few linens in her hope chest, enough to get by for a while." Suzanna would be overwhelmed by the task, so Mary started a mental list of all that would need to be done to make the house habitable.

Mary didn't hope that her sister would interest herself readying her new household. For a girl who had a lot of excess energy, she rarely wasted it on anything constructive.

Mary descended the rest of the stairs, even though she could hardly pass by Sterling without noticing how very near he was to her. He didn't move away; he just watched her progress. She was entirely too conscious of her restrained movements. Her blood felt thick. Had her own fiancé ever looked at her in such a way? Or was it just that Sterling John Cooper had a Midas touch, er look, with women?

He swung around and sat on the third stair and patted the wood beside him. He didn't really expect her to sit on the stairs, did he?

"Don't look so worried. She only needs to purchase the bare necessities and have all the bills sent here." He ran his fingers through his dark hair as if he might be inclined to pull it out. He ended with his elbows resting on his knees. "I have other irons in the fire with business concerns that I cannot neglect right now or I would help."

Mary gave in to temptation, gathered her skirts around her, and sat on the riser below him. She just couldn't sit beside him. The staircase was too narrow, and it would put her in too close a proximity to him. "What business?"

"Railroad."

"Mmm, that is what you do?"

"What I intend to do. I have enough money to last my lifetime, but I should like to build an enterprise to leave my children."

"If I may be so bold, how did you make your fortune?"

"California gold."

"You were a miner?"

"I had a small claim. I sold it when it got hard to follow the vein. Actually, I started in the Colorado Territory working a silver mine with a fellow, so at least I knew what I was doing. But I panned more gold out of the creek than I actually hacked out of my mine."

An orphan, a miner, what made Suzanna conclude he was an adventurer?

Mary leaned forward pulling her knees up, but holding her skirts firmly tucked under her. "There is a lot to be done before the wedding."

"Much of the work will fall to you, won't it?"

"It shall be good practice for my planning my own wedding and household some day."

Sterling was silent a long time. Then he leaned back, resting his elbows on a step above him, as Mary peeked back at him.

"You don't plan to take care of your father's household for the rest of his life?" he asked.

Mary felt inordinately sad that she had been relegated to spinsterhood. "I can look in on him, but I fear my competence has only allowed him to place too much dependence on me, rather than moving on with his life. He is not so old he couldn't remarry."

"And you would like to marry?"

She didn't want him to think she had been totally left on the shelf, although it felt as though she'd been stuffed in a tin, soldered shut, and labeled Old Maid. "I was engaged to a captain in my father's fleet."

"Was?"

"His ship was lost in a hurricane. He was making a rum and sugar run to Barbados. In another year he will be declared dead, but no one believes he's ever coming home."

Sterling put a hand on her shoulder. "I'm so sorry. You must have lost your mother and your captain near the same time."

The heat of his palm spread through her like butter melting into toast. But she felt like a fraud. She had certainly liked her captain, but she was by no means sure that he was the love of her life.

She would have made a good life with him, but she barely remembered his features. The long period of not knowing and the slow death of hope had left her more empty than sad. Mostly she felt guilty that she didn't want to wait until the law declared fact what everyone already knew.

She remembered more the excitement and satisfaction of getting engaged, planning to start a family. She wondered if Suzanna had become so wrapped up in that exhilaration and forgotten she would have to spend the rest of her life with this man behind her. Was Sterling the right man for Suzanna? It sounded as if he wanted the things that her sister found boring, like a family.

He squeezed Mary's shoulder, and she needed to

remind both of them he was engaged to her sister before they crossed an invisible line that loomed before
her like a black cloud bank. "Why did you propose to
my sister?"

He pulled his hand away. It was a horrid question,
and Mary had phrased it badly. Of course he wanted
to marry Suzanna; she was tall and slender and beautiful. She might be flighty and incredibly young, but
men wanted her. Men had always wanted her.

Mary braced herself to apologize for the mean
streak behind her words. Sterling John Cooper would
make any woman a wonderful husband.

"She came from the right family."

I come from the right family, too. Mary realized she had
sailed right through the cloud bank into treacherous
waters. What could be worse than coveting your sister's future spouse?

Three

In spite of her sister Mary's hesitation, Suzanna had reassured Sterling she could see to furnishing the house she had yet to visit. He'd signed the papers the day after he and Mary had walked through the rooms. He'd given Suzanna a key, but not one item of furniture had shown up in the past week.

Not even a rug to make sleeping on the floor a little less drastic. He was too old to sleep on hard wood. He'd bedded down in worse places, but he had enough money to have his own bed, in his own house, damn it.

He stopped by the Hamiltons to see how she was coming with the purchases.

"I have not had the time yet." Suzanna batted her blue eyes at him. "I've had so many fittings. You should see my dress. It is so pretty. Oh, but you can't until the wedding. Everyone will think I'm so beautiful." She twirled around, her butter-and-cream concoction of ruffles and lace swirling into buttermilk, making him dizzy.

"Suzanna."

"Yes, John?" At least she stopped spinning so he could talk to her.

She didn't like his first name and had decided to use

his middle name. He liked it better when she called him Mr. Cooper. John reminded him too much of the life he'd left behind. He gritted his teeth. "We need furniture, and Mary said—"

"I'm so tired of what Mary says. She has been so bossy lately." Suzanna rolled her eyes. "Can't you buy what we need? I am so very busy with planning the wedding."

"What exactly have you done?"

"Since Mary has been in bed with a cold, I have had to go everywhere. I had to go to the confectioners, and I had to go to the florist, and I had to go to the engravers." Suzanna slapped a hand over her mouth. "Oh, goodness, I was supposed to pick up the invitations yesterday, which I had to order all by myself. Mary told me just what to have them say, but still, Nathan could have helped me. He could have picked them up for me, or Papa could have, because I've a lot of dresses to get done. I had no idea weddings were so much work."

"I had to buy a bed today."

"See then, you can do it. Really, it is too much to have me take care of the wedding, get all my dresses for my trousseau made, and furnish the house. That should be your job." She smiled brightly at him. Was her nose just a little too sharp for her face?

He shook his head and folded his arms across his chest. "You said you would take care of furnishing the house. I'm living there with nothing." Not that it was a terrible problem for him, but he didn't think Suzanna would sit on the floor to take tea in an imaginary cup, because he had only his old battered tin cup to use.

Try as he might he couldn't imagine Suzanna's lips ever touching a tin cup. While Mary had happily stood by when one of his old mining friends hailed him on the street. She'd sneezed several times as they walked home, but assured him it was not due to the pungent odor following his former acquaintance, and claimed the experience was worth it to learn that his nickname was Silver John. And then she'd sneezed again.

Suzanna studied him with a hint of uncertainty in her expression. Just the wrong word from him and she would start the waterworks. He hated it when women cried to get what they wanted.

"Fine, I'll take care of buying furniture," he said.

"I would have taken care of it, truly, John. But I was waiting on Mary to help."

Or was she waiting on Mary to do it all for her? "About the servants."

Suzanna bit her lip. "I have never so much as hired a maid."

Neither had he. "Never mind. We'll muddle through getting a staff afterward when we get settled in."

She bounced on her toes, nearly knocking him in the nose. "After we get back from our trip. Where are you taking me on our honeymoon?"

"We're not taking a trip."

"But everyone takes a marriage trip."

Not in his experience. But she was from a different world than he was used to. Had he made a gross misstep in not planning a short trip somewhere? "We can't travel. I am involved in too many business negotiations right now."

He'd been busy poring over contracts and comparing proposed rail routes. He knew he needed to take three times as long as a man raised in industry to understand the legal wording and research costs. Hell, he'd been a teenager before he learned to write his own name. But he had mastered reading and writing and ciphering when others had told him he was too old to learn that.

"But I have the most wonderful traveling suit being made. It has jet buttons and braided trim."

"Suzanna."

She backed away as if he'd slapped her. "But you have been everywhere, and I have never been outside of Boston. We could go to London and stay with my Aunt Lydia. She is a countess, you know. And I could be presented to the queen. I know they have the loveliest balls there."

"I am ready to settle down and start a family, not go to London."

Suzanna dropped her gaze to the couch and straightened a crocheted doily. "I was thinking that perhaps we could hold off on the family, and well, give me a chance to see the world. I know I'm not ready to be a mother."

He'd heard what she said, and it was sinking in like a two ton anchor. "Just how do you propose we hold off on a family?"

Suzanna turned bright red. "I'm sure you know better than I." She dropped her voice to a whisper. "We just wouldn't . . ."

"Sleep together?"

She wadded the doily she'd just straightened in her hands. "Must you be so blunt?"

Blunt be damned. "Not have marital relations?"

She nodded tentatively.

His bride was telling him she didn't want to have sex with him. Not that he had pushed the issue. He'd thought about kissing her, but had managed only a peck on the cheek when they became engaged. She was always bouncing around or twirling. To be truthful, after a few suggestive looks which turned her skittish, he hadn't put much effort into her seduction. If she had gotten the impression that he wasn't interested in that aspect of marriage, he needed to correct it right now.

"No. I want a real marriage and a real wife and children. If you want out, you had better say so now."

She shook her head. "It was just an idea, John. Don't be angry."

"If you're going to call me John, then get it right. Call me Silver John or not at all. Otherwise my name is Sterling." He yanked the parlor door open. Damn, he shouldn't have been left alone with his bride. His bride who didn't want to sleep with him. And what startled him most of all was for a second he had hoped she would call the whole thing off.

Mary dragged herself out of bed, even though her throat was raw and her head felt like a watermelon. She knew she was largely to blame for her condition. She had come home from her brother's house damp and wet and hadn't wanted to change because she preferred to spend time with her sister's fiancé. For which she deserved to be punished with the worst head cold she'd had in years.

She was worried about the wedding. Delegating tasks to Suzanna left her uneasy about whether or not things were getting done. Suzanna had a tendency to gloss over details and ignore the resulting problems. With exactly three weeks to the wedding, they needed to start addressing the invitations and get them mailed.

Suzanna met her halfway up the stairs. "He's a hateful man."

"Who?" asked Mary.

"John, Sterling—I had no idea he didn't like to be called by his middle name. Sterling is such an odd name."

"It's not that odd." A surge of protective instincts swamped Mary. What had Sterling said to upset her sister? On the other hand, what did Sterling have beyond his name and money that he could consider all his own? And Suzanna was rejecting his name, and she'd make short work of his money. "What did he do?"

"He was furious at me. Are you well enough to go out? He's complained because I haven't bought any furniture, but he should take care of that. I can't do everything. But I suppose we shall have to get the drapes and carpets. He only said he'd get furniture."

"He probably wants you to pick out what you want rather than risking choosing things you don't like. And we should order a new stove for the kitchen."

"Why?"

"So it shall be there when you move in."

"No, I meant why do I need a new stove? Oh, never mind, I'm sure you would know. I don't know why he took *you* to see *my* house. And he didn't even ask me about it. I meant to travel. We didn't have to have a house. He's the one who wants to *settle down*; he can pick out the furniture."

Suzanna flounced toward the back drawing room, which had more or less been converted to a dressmaker's lair. Mary winced to see most of the dresses being made were in the girlish pinks and lemon pastels Suzanna favored. As an almost married woman she could have chosen bolder more mature colors for her trousseau.

"He meant for you to see the house and see if you raised any objection to it. But you were too busy with the dressmaker and your wedding gown. And a household is usually considered a woman's province. Why shouldn't he expect you to order the furniture you want?"

"Well, what is he doing all the time?" Suzanna pouted.

Beyond arranging for indoor plumbing for his spoiled bride? Had Mary's indulgence with her younger sister after their mother's death stifled Suzanna's maturity? "Planning railroad routes and the like, I imagine. Why don't you ask him? He seemed very easy to talk with."

"He will be just like Papa, always working, won't he? He says we won't have *time* to travel. He's been to France and Spain and all over America, but he doesn't want to take me anywhere."

Suzanna plopped down in a chair.

"You have the key, we could walk over there and look around your house right now."

Suzanna stuck out her lower lip. "I don't want to. He's probably there."

"Fine." If it was odd that Suzanna wanted to avoid her future husband, who was Mary to comment? "Shall we get started on the invitations, then?" asked Mary.

"I forgot to pick them up."

Mary's head pounded. "You did order them?"

"Yes, I just forgot to pick them up."

Mary turned around and headed for the door. She was half tempted to go back to bed. "I don't suppose the stationery shop is open on Saturday."

"No. I told them exactly what to print on them, just like you told me." Suzanna followed her out into the hallway. She was too eager to reassure. Mary wanted to shake her.

"Where are we going?"

"To your room."

Suzanna ran ahead and held her wedding gown against her front when Mary sedately followed her up the stairs and into her sister's ruffled room. "See, there is only the hem left, and if John were to take me to London, I could wear it to be presented to the queen."

Mary had seen the gorgeous dress more times than she wanted to count. The only area of interest Suzanna exhibited for her wedding was the new clothing. The key to Suzanna's new home hung on her dressing table mirror, next to a daguerreotype of their Aunt Lydia and Uncle Victor.

Suzanna was said to look like their Aunt Lydia, who had been headstrong and had run away to England as a young woman.

Mary moved over to the cedar chest under the window and unlatched the hasp. She had a matching chest in her room. When she lifted the lid a cavernous space greeted her. It was not totally empty, but the contents weren't linens and quilts. The chest held a couple of abandoned embroidery projects and three porcelain dolls and their complete wardrobes.

Mary felt an overwhelming sense of futility. She realized that she had not urged Suzanna to fill her hope chest with the appropriate items, the way her mother had helped her. After their mother's death and her own captain was lost at sea, encouraging her little sister to ready herself for marriage had been too painful to contemplate.

"Well, you have these lovely dolls to give your daughters. I shall give you my linens and quilts. Who knows when I shall ever need them?"

When Mary turned around her sister stood still as a statue, a pose almost never seen with Suzanna.

"I can't take your linens. I know you worked so hard on them."

"I can make new. I'm sorry, darling, I don't think I've helped you prepare for marriage at all." Mary blinked away regret at the thought of all the hours she spent embroidering the edges of pillow slips and sheets with silvery leaves on a satin border.

She leaned over and pulled out a doll. Her sister had never really carried them around, which meant they were all in pristine shape. Mary's childhood dolls had chipped noses, missing fingers, and cracked finishes. She had dragged her *babies* everywhere, and on more than one occasion Suzanna had caused a mishap.

Suzanna had loved giving her dolls new outfits. "Maybe you should keep the dolls, Mary. I'm sure you will want to give them to your daughters. I know I ruined most of yours."

"You were just a baby when I was playing with dolls. I hardly hold you accountable for their nicks and knocks."

Tears filled her sister's eyes. "I . . . I don't want to have children. At least not yet. When I told John we should wait for a while, he was so angry."

Mary wanted to comfort her sister, but this was serious, and the last thing she wanted was to pass her cold to her sister right on the eve of her wedding. "Suzanna, if you want out of the marriage, you must say so right now before things go too far."

Suzanna gave Mary an odd look and put her dress back on the hanger. "That's the same thing he said."

No wonder he had been angry. No man wanted his wife rejecting his attentions and certainly not before the wedding night had even passed. Mary needed to have a serious talk with her little sister about things that she didn't know enough about herself. It would be a serious case of the ignorant leading the innocent. "Suzanna, you probably wounded his pride. Men—"

"I knew you'd take his side." She ran out of the room and down the stairs.

Maybe Mary should try to smooth the waters with Sterling. She could tell him that Suzanna was scared and didn't really have anywhere to turn for reliable information about what to expect. Certainly, Mary couldn't offer any help in that regard.

Since they couldn't work on invitations, she could deliver her hope chest. She summoned a couple of the grooms to carry the cedar chest down to a cart. After she tied on her wide-brimmed straw hat, she grabbed a measuring tape, pencil, and paper. Suzanna wouldn't think to measure the rooms for the carpets and draperies. She tried to find her sister only to learn she'd gone out visiting with Nathan.

Sterling had his shirt off as he wrestled the bed up the stairs. The task would have been much easier with two men, but he hadn't been home when the bed was delivered, and the crate had been left outside.

He'd learned to remove as much of his clothes as possible when panning for gold in California. New clothes, there, had been very dear, and even the Chinese laundry that cleaned and repaired his old ragged clothes hadn't been cheap.

He heard the knock on the door as he flopped the mattress onto the bed. Unwilling to have the weight drag the bedding to the floor and make moot his efforts, he continued shoving and pulling until the thick feather mattress was in place on the wooden frame.

Grabbing his shirt and thrusting his arms in the sleeves, he headed down the stairs. He heard the scrape of a key in the lock. Had Suzanna come to apologize? Tell him she'd changed her mind? He already half decided she was suffering from prewedding jitters.

Which also most likely explained his own growing apprehension about his choice of bride. He was confident he'd chosen the right family. Her male relatives, uncles, father, and brother—the one he'd met—were cordial and offered useful advice and introductions that helped him with his fledgling business.

Her more mature sister epitomized competence. Perhaps too much competence. In her shadow, Suzanna relied too much on Mary. Surely, Suzanna in time and the security of her own household would grow into a full-fledged Hamilton. Wouldn't she?

He had reached the fifth step from the bottom when the front door swung open.

Mary drew to a complete stop; her brown eyes widened as she stared up at him. Bumped from behind, she hastily gathered herself and moved to the side of the entry hall.

"Just take it in the front room for now." Mary said, her voice scratchy. "I'm sorry, when you didn't answer the door right away, I thought you weren't home. I never should have barged in."

"It's all right. I was putting the bed together."

The men carried in a large chest and set it in the center of the floor. She followed them into the empty room and set a paper and pencil down on top of the chest.

Sterling looked out the open door for her sister.

Only a cart with a single horse stood in front of his house. He followed her into the parlor.

Caps in hands, the two men hesitated. Mary turned to them and thanked them and told them to take the cart home; she would walk back. She put her hand on her throat and swallowed.

"Are you sure you should be out so soon after being ill?" Sterling fumbled to get his shirt buttoned.

She turned around and then quickly averted her head and coughed. "I'm fine, although you should keep your distance in case I still carry some contagion." She cleared her throat and raised a measuring tape while studying a corner with keen interest. "I need to get measurements for carpets and drapes."

The two men exchanged looks as if Mary shouldn't be here alone with him, even if he was shortly to be her brother by marriage. She had warned him to keep his distance.

"I'll see her safely home shortly," he said to the two men.

The men cast a last look in Mary's direction, nodded, then made their way out the door.

"Where is Suzanna?" Sterling asked as soon as they were alone.

"She went visiting. That's part of why I came, well, besides to bring over Suzanna's hope chest, that is. I don't think she meant . . . anything earlier." Mary looked a little desperate.

Sterling unbuttoned his pants to tuck in the tails of his now buttoned shirt. Mary took a sharp breath and then coughed in earnest. He headed for the kitchen and returned with a jelly jar filled with water. "I don't think you should be out of bed, yet."

She took the glass jar and drank greedily. When she

lowered the rim, she said, "I wanted to explain that Suzanna is very innocent and I'm not . . ."

"You're not innocent?" He knew she wasn't leading to that, but couldn't resist the opening.

Her cheeks turned rosy in a delightfully charming way, and she dipped her head down. Her large hat obscured her face, so he bent his knees and leaned over to see her wide-eyed expression.

"No, you are teasing me. I have no real experience in this area, and she doesn't really have anywhere to turn for reliable information about what will happen when you two marry."

Sterling waited, his arms folded.

Mary's scratchy voice dropped to a whisper. "You know, in the marriage bed."

"I already figured she's scared." Why was Mary here? How was he supposed to reassure her that her sister would come to enjoy marital relations with him? He would sound unbelievably arrogant and a little too philandering for her innocent lifestyle if he relayed assurances based on past experiences.

"I said from the beginning I wanted a family. Why are you here? You can't fix everything for her."

She coughed. Her expressive brown eyes watered. She was a little hurt, no doubt, by his abruptness. Nor did she look at all well. While she was taking care of everyone else, who took care of her?

He shook his head. "If you never allow her to rely on herself, then she'll never be accountable. I'm making you hot tea. It'll soothe your throat."

He turned and walked back to the kitchen. He'd been forced by his own need to eat to stock food in the larder. He had his old mess kit, minus the two flat dishes, which he made do with.

As he dumped tea leaves into his battered and fire-stained coffeepot and let them steep, he had too much time to think.

The way Mary reacted looking at his bare chest he found so much more interesting than her sister's recoil from the idea of making children. The thought of how much work Suzanna's seduction might require left him cold. In fact, he wished he'd waited to see the older sister before making his offer.

Placing a piece of clean cheese cloth over his single tin cup, he strained the strong tea. He added lemon, honey, and a healthy dollop of whiskey.

Mary was undoubtedly here to smooth the waters and make sure this wedding to her little sister went forward. Not only was she a caretaker, but she was a peacemaker, even when sick.

He'd never been a patient man. His real strength was persistence. He'd made mistakes before by choosing too quickly, but never had one felt as fatal as this one. He didn't want peace between him and Suzanna. He wanted a rift so big it couldn't be mended, but as a gentleman of honor he couldn't withdraw his offer of marriage. He'd made his bed; now he'd have to lie in it.

He tried to remind himself that Suzanna was a beautiful woman, one that any man would be glad to have sharing his sheets. But the woman he'd really like to have lying beside him was totally off limits, forever.

Except she was alone with him, and the only damn stick of furniture in the house was the bed he'd just assembled.

Four

Mary removed her hat and set it on her hope chest. She moved to a corner with her measuring tape. She just wanted to get done and get out of here.

She knew she had been too indulgent with her baby sister. After losing a mother and with their father disappearing inside himself, Suzanna had an unfulfilled and desperate need for attention at a time when all girls felt awkward and unlovable. Mary had been a poor substitute for the mother who had eased Mary's rites of passage as a young woman.

It had been easier to give in to Suzanna's petulant requests, knowing that she suffered a loss perhaps greater than any of the rest of them had borne.

And there was always the danger that Suzanna would make good on her threat to follow in Aunt Lydia's footsteps and run away to England. Their headstrong aunt had done well for herself, but not without mishap.

Mary knew now that she should have demanded more of her sister, but she could hardly correct all the mistakes she'd made in the last five years in the few weeks before the wedding. Now Sterling probably thought it was all her fault that Suzanna was self-absorbed and indolent. He probably thought Mary would make a bad mother. She probably would make a horrid, overly indulgent, overly protective, overly interested in the business of making more children parent, but at least she wanted to try.

She dropped to her knees so she could lay the dressmaker's tape along the baseboard.

"Sit up here, drink your tea, and I'll take the measurements. Just direct me."

He sounded strange. She glanced over her shoulder to where he stood by her hope chest, Suzanna's now. He stared up at the ceiling and held a battered tin cup in his hand. Was he making do with the utensils he'd used as a miner? She really needed to purchase china for him to use.

She stood, and her head swam. Sterling appeared at her elbow, steadying her. He guided her to the hope chest while she protested that she was fine.

He frowned at her, until she climbed on the chest and took a sip from the tin cup. It burned all the way down. "That's not tea."

"Actually, it is, with a few other things thrown in. Drink it."

She looked at him skeptically. "What is in it?"

"Honey and lemon for your throat, whiskey for your cold."

She set the cup down on her hope chest. "I don't drink hard spirits."

He picked it up and put it in her hand. "It's medicinal and only a tiny bit of whiskey." He raised the cup to her lips. "It really is mostly strong tea. Drink or I'll think you're refusing because it's not in a bone china cup and saucer."

He was so close she could see every one of his eyelashes on his blue, blue eyes. She involuntarily leaned toward him.

She obediently took a sip and pulled back. The heat sliding down her throat soothed the ache that had been present for days.

She closed her eyes, fearing that he would see how much she wanted him to move closer and how little she cared what kind of cup he shared with her. Just the thought that his lips had been on that rim.

Heaven help her, she had to stop these thoughts right now. He was to be her brother by marriage, her sister's husband, not hers. Not hers at all.

"I promise it will make you feel better."

She nodded, though she suspected nothing would truly make her heart feel better. "I'm sure you are right. My throat feels better already." The rest of her felt funny, both too hot and too cold and suddenly extra sensitive to the feel of the wood underneath her, the weight of her clothes, and his masculine scent of bay rum and soap.

He backed away rapidly. "What measurements do you need?"

"That length of that wall and the height of the windows." She pointed. "You know, Suzanna has a good heart. I know I have been too lax with her, but she lost so much so young."

"Not so much." He scribbled numbers on the paper. "What else?"

"For now, just the main bedroom."

He gave her a strange look.

"For the carpet. You will want a carpet on the floor, won't you?"

He grabbed the paper and pencil and headed for the staircase. "Stay here."

Mary put her hand to her forehead. Had he guessed the tenor of her wayward thoughts? And she should have known better than to suggest to a foundling that her sister had suffered significant losses in her life. His standard of measure would be so very different from hers.

And she could only admire him that much more since he had triumphed over the circumstances of his childhood and become a warm, decent, and caring man. She couldn't even imagine her father or brothers ever fixing her a tea posset or measuring the walls for her.

Oh, my Lord, she wanted her sister's fiancé for herself.

Sterling made it back inside his new home and leaned his head against the wall. He should just bang it through the paneling. All the while Mary was trying to reassure him that Suzanna was worthy of his affection, he'd wanted to kiss Mary's rosebud lips and explore those hourglass curves of hers. She was so innocent she probably didn't have a clue what he was thinking.

As he was leaving Mary at her home, his bride-to-be arrived, and she looked like a pale pink and white, too frilly and furbelowed, version of her sister.

Mary had asked for the list of people he wanted to invite to the wedding. He wrote down the names and directions of a dozen of his business associates. He was stretching to come up with that many names.

Suzanna had handed it back. "This can't be right. Where are your family members?"

Mary had made a sound of protest, and Sterling realized Suzanna had never bothered to learn he had no family. "I doubt you'd want me to include the other orphans I was raised with."

"You came from an orphanage?" Suzanna screeched as if he'd announced he had the French pox. "Why didn't you tell me?"

"It didn't seem important." He wanted it to be important enough for her to object, but he waited in vain.

"I'm sorry. I'm sure it isn't significant. You just don't behave like an orphan," Suzanna said.

How did an orphan behave? He supposed they didn't amass a fortune and then enter the ranks of Boston society. He shook his head and took his leave.

Now he stood in his empty, unwelcoming house. Would it ever become a home?

He crossed to the lonely chest in his front parlor and opened it. It was full of linens. He pulled out a set of tea towels with neat lavender flowers embroidered down the edge. Had Suzanna made these? Mary said the chest was Suzanna's.

The stitches were neat and even, the pattern soft and elegant. Maybe she had some redeeming qualities after all.

He pulled out a quilt, and below it stowed in tissue was a set of linen sheets. The weave of the fabric was tighter than anything he had ever owned. As he unwrapped the sheets he discovered the generous, satin-faced hems. The stitches in shimmery silver thread mirrored the grape leaf pattern carved in the bed he had assembled this morning. Silver and satin, maybe Suzanna wasn't so wrong for him.

The woman who had sewn these expensive sheets had taken painstaking care, and she had paid a great deal of attention to detail. This was a woman he wanted running his household, raising his children, and standing beside him as he grew old.

Had Suzanna made these linens, or had her sister done the task for her?

Mary stared at the box of wedding announcements with horror. "Suzanna, your name isn't on these."

"I told them exactly like you said. Robert C. Hamilton, Esquire, announces the marriage of his daughter to Sterling John Cooper—"

"His daughter, *your name*. I know I said to put in your name." Or had she? She'd been sicker than a poisoned dog when she insisted Suzanna go to the stationery shop and have the invitations printed, that the task couldn't wait.

Suzanna shrugged. "We'll get them done again."

"We don't have time. You'll have to write in your name."

Suzanna tried one. She wadded it up and threw it away. "It looks awful. I can't fit my name in there."

"How could the printer neglect putting your name on the invitations? Surely they would know better. Didn't they ask?" Mary wished she could call back the words as soon as she voiced them. Not everyone was looking out for her sister or would guide her past an oversight.

Suzanna looked at Mary and teared up. "I'm sorry. I'm not good with details. You know that."

Mary saw where this was headed, that she shouldn't have required her sister to have her own invitations printed, for her own wedding. For once, anger trumped Mary's desire to make everything right for her sister. "This is not my fault. I didn't schedule a mad dash for the altar as if you were in the family way."

"Oh, my goodness." Suzanna shoved back her chair and stood. "That is what people will think, isn't it?"

Suzanna stared at Mary as if she'd sprouted horns. In two seconds she would run off and leave Mary with the monumental task of addressing two hundred invitations. Sterling's assertion that Suzanna needed to be relied upon kept circling in her head. The invitations weren't perfect, but it wasn't Mary's wedding, and they needed to be mailed.

"If you want anyone to show up for your wedding and see your dress, sit down and address those invitations."

Suzanna stared even harder. Mary supposed she might as well grow a tail and horns, too. A few months ago, Mary would have accepted the responsibility for the invitations being wrong, because she hadn't seen to it herself. She would have tried to placate Suzanna and written out the invitations herself out of a protective urge to save Suzanna from any unpleasantness.

But Mary's head spun. There was too much to be done, and she didn't care if anyone showed up at the church for a marriage she didn't want to witness herself, a marriage that could put the final nail in Mary's dreams of a future. Why, oh why, had she fallen for her sister's intended?

Then Suzanna threw herself at the desk and buried her face in her arms. "I don't know what I want. I thought John would take me places."

Mary took a step backward. She couldn't say anything for fear she would encourage her sister to forgo her engagement. But that was what Mary wanted and wasn't necessarily the best thing for Suzanna.

She would have to marry sooner or later, and Mary couldn't think of a better man for her, for any woman, than Sterling. And just because Mary wanted him didn't mean that he wanted her back.

He had asked Suzanna to marry him.

He was a very solicitous man, caring and kind. Suzanna would expect that. She would need the pampering he had offered Mary this afternoon. Normally, Mary didn't need caretaking, she was quite sure she shouldn't like it much when she was well. She was used to taking care of herself.

Mary took another step backward. Ironically, she might be the one who would have to sail to England, because she didn't think she could sit back while her sister married the man Mary wanted and set up house just a few blocks away.

"Why weren't you here to talk sense into me?" Suzanna moaned.

"Because I was helping David and his wife," Mary said cautiously. Did her sister mean to end her engagement? Hope and guilt knotted in Mary's stomach.

"You shouldn't have left me alone. You know, I'm headstrong like Aunt Lydia. I got my heart set on a great big wedding, and he doesn't even have anyone to invite."

A thread that held her emotions in check snapped inside Mary. "Aunt Lydia may have been willful and stubborn, but she at least managed her future. She arranged passage to England and evaded her searchers for months. Except even she had to be shot before she learned common sense. She didn't wait around for her sister to do everything."

Mary clapped a hand over her mouth. She spun

around. She never meant to be so vicious. Not that there had been any real malice in her description of Aunt Lydia's escapade. Her aunt always said she didn't have a bit of sense until she was shot. She had even married the man who shot her, although it was all a great secret to non-family members.

"She didn't have a sister," pointed out Suzanna. "And she certainly didn't have someone like you who is so good at everything."

"I'm not doing the invitations. I have too many other things to do today."

Suzanna lifted her tear-free face from her arms. "I just don't think he loves me."

Mary reached out for the back of a chair, gripping it as if it were a lifeline and she was adrift in stormy seas. "Do you love him?"

The weeks to the wedding had passed quickly. Sterling donned his black tails and silver ascot. The linen sheets with their silver thread and satin hems were on the bed underneath the quilt from the hope chest. He just wished he was anticipating his wedding night with more joy. Instead he had a sick feeling of doom and dread.

He took one last look around the bedroom, making sure everything was ready, before heading for the chapel. He was ready to take the next step in his life. His bride would mature eventually. After all, no one stayed a child forever. Perhaps he could promise to take Suzanna to England after the birth of their first baby. He truly did want her to be happy, even though he hoped only for contentment himself.

He'd been through enough hell in his life that happiness ought to be easily achievable. He just wasn't sure why he felt so empty on the verge of having his dreams of acceptance into one of the acclaimed older families of Boston realized.

Several evenings of the past three weeks, he had dined in the Hamilton household. As a family they were everything he wanted. But more often than not he ended up talking with Mary. Because she was older her interests were wider and more varied than Suzanna's. His bride's favorite topics where clothes and gossip. Since he preferred Mary's high-necked slimmer gowns rather than the monstrous ruffled and hooped skirts Suzanna wore, fashion wasn't a topic he felt comfortable discussing with Suzanna.

And even good-natured gossip sat ill with him. His own past was too riddled with tidbits people would find interesting beyond their worth. The orphanage had turned him out fit for little beyond being a dock worker or a criminal or both. And well, who knew about his parentage. He didn't want to think that any of his past might ever be a part of a conversation over tea, but with Suzanna's penchant for tittle-tattle he feared it would just be a matter of time.

As he scooped up two envelopes from the floor below the brass mail slot, it occurred to him, Suzanna's clothes trunk had not arrived as scheduled last night. He'd hoped to have her things put away when she arrived, but now the task would have to wait.

Mary had made her sister take more responsibility for her things, which was probably why the trunk hadn't shown up yet. Suzanna had probably forgotten to arrange its delivery. Sterling was sorry he'd said anything, because forcing Suzanna to take more responsibility had been hard on both sisters. Then again, he wanted her to know he expected her to be a wife, not a toy or decoration. His bride found him a poor ally when she complained about the amount of work she had to do. He reminded her that it was for her own future, not her sister's, leaving her in a miff.

At least of late her conversation had been broader than her wardrobe or inquiries about his travels. He had answered badly when, out of the blue, she asked him if he loved her.

The truth was he hadn't considered love a prerequisite for marriage. He wanted connections to a respectable family and a woman who was raised in a warm, loving, and giving environment as unlike an orphanage as possible. Suzanna met his requirements on both counts. On top of that she was beautiful, not as curvy and cuddly as her sister, but she turned heads with her spirits as much as her looks.

They'd been riding in his carriage, as Mary had suggested he'd neglected his courtship once Suzanna agreed to his proposal. He reluctantly had to admit that he had let his attentions drop off, as much because of his own commitments to establish his business enterprises and readying the house as anything. However, he meant to be a good husband regardless of his stupid oversight in not considering love as an important ingredient for marriage. But as they drove about the nearby countryside in his open gig, he'd had to make a conscious effort to hold Suzanna's gloved hand.

She'd watched him patiently as he fumbled for an answer that he would come to love her, and she need never fear, that he would always treat her with great respect.

She'd nodded as if the matter was of no great importance and gone on to ask if he was content with the carpets and draperies.

When he said he was well satisfied, she said, "I know you wanted me to do more to choose our things, but Mary helped me inordinately. She has always been so much better than I with practical things."

"You'll learn," Sterling had said gruffly.

Suzanna looked earnestly at him. "I hadn't dared to try when Mary does everything so well. She isn't interested in fashion, so that has always been my province."

The last thing he wanted to do was discuss her sister. "If you try, you will find that most anything you want to do is within your grasp. You are well capable of running your own household." He pledged to himself to be patient. "I wouldn't have asked you to marry me if I thought different."

"Yes, but I always do the wrong thing. I wanted to have the cook prepare more French food while Mary was away, but it was a disaster. Papa complained the whole time. And well, the cook was not so good with the sauces. You have to be able to make all kinds of sauces to cook in a French manner."

Food was food to him. Of course, most of his life he'd eaten anything edible to survive. "Sometimes failures teach you as much as victories."

"I suppose that is very wise, but it is poor comfort to one who always has failures. I find I am very good at winning only when it is the worst possible thing for all involved."

Then she'd launched into the latest description of her newest clothing choices. He'd breathed a sigh of relief that his awkward answer about the depth of his feelings for her had been given little notice. He knew too well he'd dodged a cannon ball. Not too many times in life did a man get away with less than a fervent vow of passionate love for the woman he meant to marry.

Suzanna must have a deep practical streak under that frivolous exterior to let him get away with that lukewarm declaration.

He should have pulled the gig to the side of the road and given her a kiss or two, but the plan struck him more as duty than desire and perhaps not the wisest course given that he had just told her he didn't love her yet.

Did he expect this afternoon's ceremony to alter his emotion? And since when did bills get delivered on Saturday morning?

Mary ran through the house with a growing sense of dread. She'd checked the front parlor, the back parlor, all the bedrooms, and the attic. She'd even checked the vegetable garden as if Suzanna might have suddenly taken an interest in how the carrots grew.

Last night on the eve of the monster wedding, Suzanna's trunks had been in the front entry hall. Mary remembered seeing her tie on her bonnet and breeze out the door, saying, "Don't wait up for me. John has promised to take me for a drive after we unpack my trunks."

Had Suzanna even returned home? That was it; she must have spent the night with her future husband. It was dreadfully depraved and utterly immoral but not unheard of. Couples had been known to get a little ahead of themselves. They had been on several unchaperoned excursions lately, which was acceptable because they were engaged, after all.

Aunt Lydia had lived with her future husband for several weeks before he made an honest woman of her. As long as no one outside of family realized that her sister and Sterling had gotten a little frisky before they should have, no harm was done.

Mary sat down on the steps fighting nausea. In her dreadful anxiety of not being able to find her sister, hope had reared its ugly gargoyle head. She shook herself. No one besides her and the wayward couple needed to know anything untoward had happened if she fetched Suzanna home this instant.

She grabbed her hat and shoved it on her head. She was halfway out the door when her father called out, "Where are you off to, Mary? Shouldn't you be supervising your sister's preparations?"

"I just have to check one last thing at the church, and when I get back I'll help Suzanna dress."

She walked as fast as she could to Sterling's house and pounded on the front door. She was still holding her hat on her head with one hand when he opened the door with the lovely stained glass panels.

Thank goodness he was fully dressed this time. She didn't know if she could have withstood the sight of him half undressed knowing that her sister was in there with him. "Where is she? I have to get her home right away to get into her gown. If we hurry, no one will know she didn't come home last night."

Sterling pulled the door all the way open, revealing the carpet Mary had picked out and a lovely little side table with a jade and black ginger jar under a gilt-framed mirror. "You'd better come in."

She didn't want to go in. She didn't want to see her sister in a state of undress.

"No. Just tell her to come out when she's ready. And for God's sake tell her to hurry."

Sterling reached out and grabbed her upraised arm and tugged her across the threshold. "She's not here."

He shut the door behind her, turned around, and folded his arms across his chest.

"The Cinderella carriage with the two matched white horses to draw it that I had to hire all the way from New York is coming to pick her up in less than an hour. I need to find her."

"You've got a long swim, then."

All the world came to a stop. "What?"

"Suzanna's gone to London, and we won't be getting married after all." Sterling waved an envelope in her face. "She left this for you."

Mary didn't know whether to laugh or cry or both, so she did nothing, standing there staring at Sterling with her hand firmly holding on her hat, which wouldn't blow away now.

"Here, sit down." He pushed her back into one of two chairs flanking the rosewood table.

All her plans, and work, the pink roses Suzanna insisted upon, the towering, tiered cake with sugar bells, the candles that were no doubt being lit as they spoke. That and everyone who was anyone in Boston was invited to this wedding. Her father's reputation would suffer. Sterling's reputation would suffer.

Oh, my goodness, poor Sterling. How devastating to be left at the altar. She couldn't let her flighty sister wound this man. Even if it should kill her, she wouldn't allow her sister to destroy his dreams.

"But, the marriage can't be called off. It's too late. We have to find Suzanna. Her ship won't have left yet, or one of my father's ships can fetch her back."

"Let her go. Even if we could catch her, I'd rather not bring her back and force her to marry me."

"Oh!" Mary stared at him. "I see." She felt tears burning the backs of her lids. He was too kind and too considerate.

"Read your letter."

"Yes, of course." She eyed the envelope with her name on it as if Suzanna's large, curly script might bite her. Slowly opening the envelope, she tried to read. Phrases kept jumping out at her: *wants an alliance with our family . . . has no great affection for me . . . not ready for the responsibility of running my own household, let alone children.* But Mary couldn't string all of the written sentences together to make sense. A horrid thought kept circling in her head. A horrid, awful, magnificent idea kept intruding.

Sterling paced back and forth in the entry hall, heaping on a distraction she couldn't ignore. He looked wonderful in his tails, but then he'd look wonderful in a flannel shirt and denim pants.

He paused, his back to her. "It's a shame to let all your hard work go for naught."

She let the words fall out of her mouth before good sense and rational thought stopped her. "Perhaps you could marry me instead."

Five

Sterling had probably been too rough when he pushed Mary down into the chair. He took the hat that she acted determined to hold on her head. She must not be thinking straight. She was a fixer, a peacemaker; she probably had not thoroughly considered her far-too-tempting offer.

He knew that it was all wrong. To have one sister throw him over and the other pick him up just in time for an already scheduled wedding.

"Would it bother you that much to see all your preparations go to waste?"

She made a sound between a squeak and a moan.

He turned and crouched before her chair. "Mary, your offer is most generous, but I cannot think that you are doing this because it is what you want. Are you again trying to fix everything for everyone else?"

She averted her head and wadded her sister's letter in her curled fingers. "I am so sorry. I didn't want you hurt or embarrassed."

"I've survived much worse things in my life." Actually, he was not nearly as hurt by his intended's defection as he should be. He was relieved.

"I know I am not as pretty as Suzanna, but the invitations went out without a name. A few people would be surprised, but I should imagine they would keep their own counsel."

He wrapped her clenched fists in his own hands. Since she was prettier than her sister, he dismissed her objections as meaningless. "But, Mary, what do you want?"

She looked at him then, her brown eyes dark pools in her pale face. Her hands trembled. "My wants are simple. I've told you before."

She snatched her hands out of his grasp and ducked around him, moving in a walk-run toward the front door. "I will post a notice on the church door. The guests will arrive soon, and I have to tell my father. I am so sorry this has turned out so badly."

He reached around her and held the door. "Mary, wait. We aren't done discussing this."

"We don't have time to talk about it. I understand. I shall make it clear that my sister is the one who has fled for no good reason."

He reached for her waist and slid his arms around her. He'd wanted to hold her like this since the first moment she'd opened the door to him. With her back to him, she stiffened. He released her. "Can you fit in Suzanna's wedding gown?"

"No!"

His heart thumped irregularly. Did she already think better of her offer?

He took a deep breath. "I would be honored if you would marry me, but you deserve better than this hurry-scurry, last-minute substitution for your sister." Hell, she deserved to be asked, to be courted, to be assured of his affection.

"I'll be fine. I have a dress I can wear, unless you'd rather not." She reached for the doorknob again.

"I'd much rather marry you."

"Then I have to get ready." She fled out the door as if the hounds of hell were on her heels.

There was so much he should have said, but suddenly everything felt surreal. He should have offered to inform her father. He should have reassured her that she was the sister he wanted to marry. He should have told her he was more than half in love with her.

Although after the way she reacted when he reached out to hold her, that should more likely frighten and confuse her. She was so constant in her emotions and deeds, the seemingly abrupt transfer of his affection from her sister to her would strike her wrong. She would think him as changeable as the tides. When in truth he had known for a long time he had asked the wrong sister to marry him. But he had gone to considerable lengths to keep that knowledge to himself.

He yanked his fingers through his hair.

Mary flew into the house and ran up the stairs. She felt both giddy and galled at her own audacity. Oh, goodness, she had grabbed at what she wanted with both hands and little consideration for anyone else's feelings.

She would marry Sterling.

Her stomach knotted. She didn't fool herself. His response had been tepid. In the end she hadn't known why he agreed. She didn't want to know. She just wanted it done.

She vowed to herself to be a good wife, the best helpmate ever so he would never regret his acceptance of her offer to stand in for her sister.

His far-too-generous assessment of her reasoning was wrong. She wasn't doing it to make things better for him or anyone else. She had offered herself in her sister's place because she wanted Sterling for herself. She wanted his easy smile and friendly nature. She admired his longing to found a lasting legacy to leave his children. And she wanted him because when he had put his arms around her, she had been singed by a burning pleasure that must surely spring from the fires of hell.

His embrace had startled her so much her only thought at the time was that it was wrong to enjoy his touch. She had wanted to melt into him; instead she thought she should flee.

She peeled back the muslin covering from the wedding gown her mother had worn years ago and cried out. The satin had aged. What had been a gleaming white gown had mellowed into ivory and cream. It was a sign that she was not pure enough in heart to wear white.

She was scheming and evil and about to get her deepest, darkest wish fulfilled.

She told herself not to think and took great care with the dress. The style was not current, with the material flat across the abdomen and the small bustle in the back.

Mary rang for a maid as she stripped her day dress off. She was shaking like a leaf when the maid finally had her corset strings laced and yanked as tight as a hangman's noose. The long row of buttons down the back of the wedding gown was fastened. Now Mary had to tell her father she would be the bride instead of Suzanna.

A sudden wave of dizziness reminded her she could

not move quickly. As tightly as she was laced she could not breathe deeply. She would be miserable before the day was over, but she didn't wish to risk any strain on the old seams of her mother's wedding gown. It would be too just a punishment if she split her seams in front of the extensive guest list Suzanna had insisted upon.

Now that Mary was alone in the last few minutes before marrying Sterling, her reasoning seemed the height of absurdity. That Sterling and she got along well enough and he didn't seem any more fond of Suzanna than he was of her didn't mean he wanted to be married to Mary.

"Mary, what's wrong?" Her father asked.

She released the newel post at the bottom of the stairs.

"Are you wearing your mother's gown? You look lovely, my dear, but I thought Suzanna was the one getting married."

"Suzanna's run away to London."

"Oh, dear." Her father straightened his gloves. "Well, I expected as much. Headstrong, just like Lydia. You don't mean to fool her intended into thinking you're Suzanna, do you?"

"No, I talked to him this morning and offered myself as substitute." Surely, her father would save her from herself and call the whole thing off.

"Ah, well, he is a good fellow, and I shall be glad to welcome him into the family. I daresay, he'll have an easier time of it with you. Shall we go? The carriage is waiting."

Oh, heavens, would no one save her from herself? Perhaps Sterling would have come to his senses and not be at the chapel.

She nearly collapsed as she was handed into the fes-
tooned-with-ribbons-and-roses carriage drawn by the
white horses, which her gown did not match. Black
spots danced before her eyes. Perhaps the maid had
pulled her corset strings too tight. Mary had held on
to the bedpost and urged tighter, tighter, until they
were both exhausted. She bit her lips to restrain an
impulse to giggle.

Sterling watched his bride slowly walk up the center aisle of the church. Mary rested her free hand on
her father's arm and held herself rigidly straight,
stretching for every inch of height she could muster,
no doubt. He'd half feared that Suzanna would have
danced up to the altar.

The unusual cut of Mary's gown emphasized her
hourglass figure, and Sterling swallowed hard. Was
her waist really that tiny? She was beautiful, dignified,
and extraordinarily pale.

She looked as if she was on her way to her funeral,
not her own wedding. Was her distress because she
heard the gasps of guests who had expected to see her
sister?

Sterling shifted his gaze to the nosegay of pink
roses in her trembling hand. His heart pounded heav-
ily. Did she find marrying him a colossal sacrifice?

His worry increased as she chewed her rosebud lip
while her father handed her over. She met his eyes
only briefly during the ceremony as she gave her answers and vows in a shallow, breathy voice unlike her
normal tones. Her gaze remained fixed in the neighborhood of his chin. She swayed, and he reached out
to steady her, putting a hand against the tiny span of

her waist. She shuddered and then continued to tremble.

He couldn't tell if his touch comforted her or not. He wanted to whisper reassurances to her, but he had never heard two hundred people so silent with all their attention trained on them.

The ceremony seemed interminably long as his concern for Mary grew. Why had she suggested this if she hadn't wanted to marry him? But he searched his mind to come back to what she had said. She wanted to be married. He could guess from her enthusiasm over her new niece, she wanted children. Was he just a means to an end? Would any man do, since the man she wanted to marry was long dead?

Then the ceremony was over, and he leaned over to brush a kiss on her mouth. The brief touch of his lips to hers finished too quickly. He supposed he could have taken longer, but he was reminded that he had never kissed Mary before, and she had been startled when he tried to embrace her earlier in the day.

He kept an arm firmly around her tiny waist after the ceremony, although she tried several times to put space between them. But she just didn't feel steady. Her breathing was too shallow and her skin too pale. Standing next to her tiny frame he felt hulking and overpowering. Perhaps, his size scared her.

Finally they moved to an assembly hall where, after they received everyone's well wishes, they sat down to an elaborate dinner. Mary pushed her food around on her plate. He encouraged her to eat, but she shook her head.

"You must eat," he repeated.

Her brown eyes suddenly looked too moist. "Truly, I cannot."

Feeling bewildered that he couldn't ease her tension, he looked around the room. For once the crowd's attention was diverted by the meal instead of focused squarely on him and Mary. "Everything has gone well, wonderfully well."

She nodded and looked miserable.

"You did an amazing job."

"A small ceremony would have been nice."

Less people to witness her substitution for her sister? Less people to know of her sacrifice? Less people to explain to later if she decided to have the marriage annulled?

The only time she looked hopeful during the ceremony was when the minister spoke his bit about *speak now or forever hold your peace,* as if she hoped a savior might leap up and protest her marriage to him.

He leaned close to her. "Are you all right? You look pale."

She dipped her head down. "I never look my best in white."

"It's not the dress."

"I know, it is not quite white."

"The dress is beautiful, and you are beautiful in it."

She bit her lip and mumbled a thank-you that sounded more like a protestation.

Good Lord, he hadn't complimented his bride. She was so tiny and perfectly curved, and he wanted to explore all those curves, yet she looked more miserable than a whipped dog. His thoughts spun in a vicious circle. He wanted her alone, but he didn't want to scare her.

The only thing he was sure of was that she acted as if she had made a mistake. He wanted to lose his formal clothes and sprawl back in his chair with his heels kicked up on the rungs.

Was the dress the one she had intended to wear in her marriage to her captain?

"How much longer does this go on?" he asked.

A guest heard his impatient comment, and the double entendres and nudges started. Sterling resisted the urge to clap his hands over Mary's ears. They weren't so wrong. He, like every bridegroom, wanted his bride alone, naked, and in his arms. How innocent was she?

While everything was muted and toned down from the kind of raucous celebration his California cronies would have thrown for him, his thoughts jumped to the night ahead. He didn't want to scare her, so he would be deliberate and gentle.

Mary took a timid look around the company and said, "There will be dancing after dinner." She looked down at her lap where her hands twisted together. "We can leave whenever you want."

Now, there was encouragement. He'd be damned if he dragged her away from her elaborately prepared reception. He'd just have to exercise patience. And he'd exercise restraint when he got her home. He wanted a lifetime with Mary, and he wouldn't risk ruining their future by being too demanding or impatient or not understanding.

He knew this had all happened too fast for her. Her behavior today was clear as a bell. He would go slow if it killed him. He leaned over and whispered in her ear, "You tell me when it is an appropriate time to take you home."

She swallowed hard. He heard it.

"Don't fret so. Everything is fine."

She cast a quick glance at him and looked even more upset than before. He ran a hand through his hair and leaned back in his chair. He didn't know what to do or say to calm her down, and he'd thought Suzanna was high strung.

Mary was just plain miserable. Guilt that she had trapped Sterling into this marriage swamped her. Her wedding day should be the happiest in her life, and she was just plain sick with worry. Aside from her biggest fear that she had pushed Sterling into a marriage he didn't want, she worried that her father would not eat without her there to urge him to the table. She worried that her sister was in a horrible predicament and worried that her corset was mashing her insides so tight, she'd never be able to conceive a child.

She didn't even want to finish that thought, because every time Sterling touched her she couldn't breathe. Which was half corset and half her reaction to him. The last thing she wanted to do was let Sterling realize how very enamored of him she was. She didn't want him to think she had anything to do with her sister's flight. She didn't want him to think she had planned to step into her sister's shoes. She didn't want him thinking she was a schemer and a manipulator, even if she was.

After dinner was cleared away and the musicians had played for some time, she stretched up on her toes and said, "We could leave now."

Please, let him be ready because she needed out of this dress and her laces loosened. She felt heat creeping up her face.

"You are ready?" Sterling asked.

Ready for what? She nodded, uncertain of what she was agreeing she was ready for. Sterling had his hand at her back, and he guided her toward her father.

"Take good care of my Mary." Her father hugged her and gave her a pat.

"Will you be all right, Papa?"

"I'll be fine, sweetheart. I survived the month you spent at your brother's house, now, didn't I?"

"Yes, and will you send someone to see after Suzanna?"

"She'll be fine with her Aunt Lydia. If anyone can talk on her level, my sister will." Her father shook his head. "Go on, you need to take care of your husband now."

He reached out and shook Sterling's hand. "Welcome to the family, son. Come by for dinner after you two get settled in."

Sterling struck her as the last person in the world who needed caretaking. What had she done, marrying a man who needed little of her strongest skills?

They left the hall she had rented for the reception. The slanting late evening sunlight outside startled her. Even though it had been midday when the ceremony began, Mary felt as if an eon had passed. It should surely be dark. But no, there was plenty of light as they moved through the gauntlet of well-wishers.

Sterling lifted her into the carriage she had hired. He barely had the door shut when he asked again, "Are you all right?"

"I'm fine." She felt heat stealing into her face. She sat up straight as much as she could, trying to ease the pressure of her corset.

"At least now you have color in your face."

Mary felt so flustered she didn't know what to say. She glanced around. Sterling looked so solemn. Had he smiled at all today? Yes, but not when looking at her.

Sterling reached up and loosened the ascot around his neck. "Are you afraid?"

"No. Of course not."

"You've been as jumpy as water drops on a scalding hot griddle all through the ceremony. What is wrong?" He folded his arms across his chest.

Besides her laces being tied so tight she could barely breathe? He might be her husband, but she really wasn't ready to share that with him. Oh, goodness, he was her husband and a man who knew how water behaved on a hot griddle. "I . . . I am afraid I tricked you into marrying me."

He looked at her sideways. "With what trickery? Did you force your sister to write those letters and then make her run away?"

Mary blinked. She had almost forgotten Sterling had known Suzanna ran away before Mary did. And she didn't know what her sister's letter to him had said.

"It's done. Unless you want an annulment, it's for the rest of our lives."

"Do you want an annulment?" she asked, and her voice squeaked unnaturally. That he had even thought of that option told her how little enthusiasm he had for the course they followed.

"And go through that circus again? God no."

Mary felt a small bubble of amusement break free. At least he considered marriage to her ranking above the horror of going through an overblown wedding ceremony.

Sterling smiled at her gently, encouragingly. "I believe I did better than I expected to."

Mary ducked her head, not sure if he meant surviving his wedding day with all the guests or more than that. Besides, she couldn't look at him long because it would adversely affect her breathing.

The carriage pulled up in front of his house, and he wrapped his hands around her waist and lifted her down before she could climb down the step. "You are so tiny."

Tiny? She was short, but too full figured to ever be considered tiny or anything so feminine as dainty. She shook her head as she climbed the stairs to the front stoop.

Sterling spoke to the coachman, tipping him, then dismissing him.

She breathed an abbreviated sigh. Finally, she would be able to loosen her laces—except she didn't have a single stitch of clothes here.

Oh, my goodness! She couldn't get out of the overly tight laces with nothing to wear. She pivoted and slammed into Sterling's chest. "I have to go home."

"Mary, you are home." He wrapped one arm around her and reached behind her to unlock the door.

She heard the door swing open with a sense of impending doom. She couldn't stand the thought of staying trussed up any longer. "I don't have any clothes here. I need just a few things."

"No, you don't. Not tonight." He scooped her up with one arm under her knees and one arm behind her shoulders.

Alarmed, she clutched his shoulders while her head spun from a lack of oxygen. "I can't stay in this dress any longer."

"Good." Sterling kicked the door shut behind him.

Oh! He meant to . . . they would . . . consummate their marriage. Oh, heavens. In all the anxiety of the day she had tried only to get through each minute as it came. She hadn't really thought about the wedding night. Or if she had thought about it, she had dismissed the normal course of events because their marriage was so abnormal. "It's still light out."

"You prefer the dark?" He grinned down at her.

She was mesmerized by his deep dimples and the amusement in his eyes. "Yes, no. I don't know."

He carried her still, but they hadn't moved to the stairs. They would need a bed, wouldn't they? Lord, she didn't even have anything to sleep in. "I'll . . . I'll need a nightgown."

"You can use one of my nightshirts. Can't stand the damn things anyway. Don't know how you keep them down."

She swallowed hard. So they would be sharing a bed, she knew that, had expected that. She could act as if discussing one's sleepwear with a husband was normal. "So what do you sleep in?"

"In the summer, as little as possible."

She felt her face heating up. More than her face.

"So what do you think? Do you like the furniture?"

Mary had to break her gaze away from Sterling's chin and look at the front parlor. The drapes and carpets she had picked out were there. Couches, chairs, and cabinets in rich mahogany wood were cozily grouped around the room. He'd purchased furniture in modern designs replete with carved grape leaves, slender cabriole legs, and whorled feet. Different from her father's home, yet similar enough to soothe her. It was not the empty space she had seen before; it was now a home, her home with Sterling. "It's lovely."

"We can rearrange whenever you want. There's more rooms to be done, but this should get us by for now."

"Are there any servants?"

"Not yet." He headed for the entry hall and the staircase. "Cook starts tomorrow."

She grew anxious. She was alone in the house with Sterling. "I can walk."

He set her down on the bottom step, but kept his hands on her waist. She was not quite on eye level with him and his wry expression. "Sure you want to?"

She nodded jerkily.

"How about I fix you a cup of tea and light the fire under the water tank. That way you can have a nice warm relaxing bath before bed."

He stroked her waist. Warmth might be unneeded, relaxation probably impossible, but losing her corset would be heaven.

Uncertain, she gave a tiny nod. Him seeing her without her corset scared her. He might be disgusted.

He pulled her against him, and she reveled in the strong, secure feeling of his chest. She was both frightened and reassured. His right hand shifted to her nape, and he made a soothing sound. "Don't worry so. Everything will be fine. Go on up. I'll be there in a minute."

He was taking care of her needs, and she should be so much calmer if she was easing him in some way, but how? She climbed the stairs and walked into the bedroom. She gripped the bedpost, trying to breathe deeply enough to stop the black spots from dancing before her eyes.

Anticipation and dread mingled in her squished but empty stomach. What if he didn't want to consummate their marriage? Why was he sending her on ahead alone?

All too soon he was behind her, pulling the drapes closed, blocking the orange glow of a setting sun. It was too early for bed. He lit a lamp beside the bed before moving to the dresser. There he pulled out a white garment. Then he stood in front of her with it held up to her shoulders.

"See, this will be plenty long enough, although you'll have to roll up the sleeves." He draped the nightshirt over the foot of the bed. "I thought you wanted out of that dress."

There was no way she could get that long row of tiny buttons down her back undone. "I need a maid."

"Guess I'm it."

"Oh." A shudder passed through her, and she looked up at him.

Sterling ran his index finger down the side of her face. "Did I tell you how beautiful you looked today in that gown?"

She drew in a sharp breath and nearly choked. She shook her head, not trusting her voice. Tears stung at her eyes, he was so kind. She hadn't looked good today. Her color had been nonexistent or too high. Pale clothing didn't suit her; it made her skin look sallow. With her dark hair, reds, wines, and jade greens suited her best.

He gave her a crooked smile. "No, really. The way

the dress shows your perfect curves, I was stunned when you walked down the aisle."

His tone sounded sincere, but Mary was unused to compliments unless they were about how helpful she was. She bit her lip.

"Don't do that." With the pad of his thumb he touched her bottom lip. Then he stroked across it. "You have the sweetest mouth."

She wanted to believe that comment. She wanted to understand why that brief touch of her lip left her so hungry. She wanted to know why her blood felt thick.

His hands found her waist, and he lifted her onto the bottom stair of the bed steps. Her eyes were level with his nose, and then he kissed her.

For a moment she didn't know how to respond, and this was more intense than the peck he had given her in the church. His lips clung and pressed to hers. Then the tip of his tongue tested the seam of her mouth. Startled and intrigued, she let her jaw loosen. He adjusted the tilt of her head, and the kiss deepened.

A part of her wanted to draw back and say, *oh, is this how it is done,* and a part of her was shocked that Sterling would touch her tongue with his, and the biggest part of her wanted to explore these new worlds.

He lifted her arms and placed them around his neck.

Oh, she was horribly inept. She should have done that without his prompting. She tried to follow his movements and imitate them, but then his body pressed against hers. Shock wave after shock wave traveled through her. He held her tight against him with one hand, and with the other he stroked her side.

His slow caresses gradually lengthened until he slid his hand over her hip to the top of her thigh and back up, slowly up, and up until his hand curled around her breast, while his kiss went on and on.

Mary felt as though she could shatter into a thousand pieces, every part of her tingled so. He slid his hand down and farther down her leg, then back up, this time adding slow circles against the full flesh of her breast. The coolness of air wafted against the back of her neck, and she realized Sterling was methodically releasing the long row of buttons.

Her head swam, and her body rioted with sensations. Only then did she realize she had forgotten to breathe. She pulled back from his kiss, but now it was too late to draw in enough air to hold back the closing darkness. "No . . . o," she moaned as the last tiny circle of light closed into nothingness.

Six

Sterling caught his wife as she went totally limp and slid down his body. Her head lolled back as lifeless as a rag doll's.

Hell's bells. His virginal wife had fainted during his attempt to seduce her.

He laid her down on the bed. What to do? Smelling salts.

He had none.

"Mary." He knelt beside her and shook her.

Nothing happened. He pressed his fingers against her neck. She had a pulse, too fast and too thready, but she hadn't dropped dead on him.

What else should he do? Burn feathers? All right, he'd give her a minute, and if she didn't respond, he'd wipe her face with a cool rag. Then he'd burn feathers. He could rip apart a pillow and get feathers.

Why had she fainted? Had he been moving too fast for her? She'd been participating, slightly, with his guidance. She hadn't protested his increasing intimacies, not until he had her gown half undone and she'd moaned a low "no."

He watched her breathe. Her chest rose and fell ever so slightly and too rapidly. She wore a corset, he'd felt the rigid stays underneath her gown. He'd dealt with them before. Even run into a few women who refused to take them off ever, which made it into a one-time visit for him.

Lordy, she was pale, the skin around her lips bluish. He rolled her to her stomach and finished undoing the buttons and fumbled with the double knots of her corset strings.

Damn she had the strings tighter than a dried rawhide drumstring. He finally got the knots released without resorting to his pocketknife.

She moaned.

He lifted her enough to get the dress down to her waist, and he yanked the strings completely out of the grommets of her corset and pulled the contraption of torture out from under her.

Had the liberties he'd been taking shocked her so badly she passed out?

He figured he'd never dealt with a virgin before. No, no probably about it. The few women in the western territories were either married or making their living on their backs. There had been one Chinese laundry girl who had taken a shine to his looks, but even she had been well versed in the art of seduction.

Mary hadn't protested his advances, but would she? She was in the habit of accommodating others' needs rather than protecting her own well-being.

He had shocked her. Clearly she wasn't ready for the physical side of a marriage she'd suggested only just this morning. He'd been in too much of a hurry to make this marriage permanent when she was still getting used to the idea of promising to spend her life with him.

He grabbed the nightshirt from the end of the bed. If his unbuttoning her gown frightened her, waking without the gown or her corset on would scare her witless. Leaning back against the headboard, he pulled her up to a sitting position. Her body had more rigidity, and she moaned a protest. Good, she was coming around.

He swiftly pulled his nightshirt over her head as he made short work of her chemise. He winced as he saw the angry welts the creases in her undergarment had made on her skin where her corset had been.

"Sterling?"

"Shhh." He grabbed her wrist and pushed it through the sleeve, and she followed suit groggily with the other arm. He pulled the chemise out from underneath his nightshirt and removed his hands. He lifted her up and pushed the dress down below her hips, and the satin slithered to the floor.

She put a hand to her forehead. "What happened?"

"You fainted." He slid out from behind her and yanked down the covers. "Lie down."

Instead, she bolted upright. "I fainted?" She sounded bewildered and alarmed.

"I want you to rest. You've had a trying day." He needed to get out of the room before the idea that he had undressed her and had her in his bed tempted his overheated blood to continue to explore her perfect little body. He backed away from the bed. "I'll get you a fresh cup of tea."

She looked down at nightshirt he had pulled on her and looked up at him, her brown eyes wide and questioning.

He felt like a heel. A molester of innocents, a man who never should have aspired to touch her. Perhaps she had been trying to tell him something when she protested the daylight. Perhaps in her world, relations only occurred hidden in the dark. Good God, he'd swear she'd never been kissed before. "Nothing happened. You fainted."

He wished she didn't look so relieved.

Mary was only glad she hadn't missed anything. What he had been doing had felt so wonderful and wicked and oh, so right. Her knowledge of these matters was sketchy, the role she should play even hazier. She started to say she didn't need tea, but he had left the room.

He must have realized her corset was too tight, because she had been stripped of it. Yet, he'd put her in a nightshirt to preserve her modesty. She'd woken to feel her clothes being tugged off. She had a slight headache, and her shoes were still on her feet. She bent over and struggled to push the buttons through the leather without a buttonhook.

Mary straightened the room, hanging her mother's wedding gown in the wardrobe, and Sterling still hadn't returned. She picked up the cup of tea he had left on the dresser, found it tepid, and drank it anyway. Now that her stomach was no longer squished, she realized she hadn't eaten at all today. She'd never eaten breakfast because she'd been trying to find Suzanna, and well . . . she was hungry.

And where was Sterling?

She sat down in front of the looking glass and removed the pins from her hair. Because she didn't have her brush, she finger combed it and plaited it in a long braid.

She picked up the cup and saucer, and with the

trailing nightshirt held in her other hand, she made her way down the darkened staircase.

Sterling stood in the kitchen, leaning against a wall near the stove. She studied his broad shoulders and his bowed head. Her husband.

A swelling of satisfaction settled under her breastbone. The way he had carried her into the house and his kisses surely meant he wanted to be her husband, perhaps not as much as she wanted him, but enough for their marriage to work. She wanted to move forward and touch him, but shyness held her back.

"Sterling?"

He spun around, a crockery mug held in his hand. "What are you doing out of bed?"

Mary took a step back, gathering the neckline of the nightshirt in her fingers. "I'm not sleepy."

He stared at her.

She forced herself to move forward to the table in spite of the intense heat in her face. She was tired, but too full of an edgy anticipation to sleep, to even lie still. "Actually, I'm a little hungry. Is there bread or perhaps a tin of biscuits?"

"Sit down. I'll fix you some ham and eggs." He thumped his mug on the table.

He had coffee. She could use coffee. "I can do it."

"Sit. You just fainted."

"I forgot to breathe. I'm fine now."

He pointed, and she sat on a straight chair by the solid butcher table in the center of the room. She felt suitably chastised. He opened a door to what must be the larder and emerged with a partial ham and three eggs.

She folded her arms across her chest, hiding the

jiggle in her unrestrained figure. "I'm sorry, my corset was too tight."

"Don't ever wear one again."

She stared at him. She had thought he liked her corseted figure. He had seemed interested in her waist. "I have to, my clothes won't fit without one."

"Buy new. I can afford it."

"I promise I won't ever lace it so tight." Was he angry that she had fainted? She stood up and picked up one of the eggs. "I never eat more than two."

She replaced it in the larder and took a look around to see what shopping she would need to do, but the larder was well stocked. When she returned to the kitchen he had a big slice of ham sizzling in a pan. She covered the remaining ham and returned it to the coolest part of the larder. Grabbing a towel, she leaned over to get the pot that must contain the coffee.

"Will you please sit down?" he said.

"I'm used to taking care of things." She poured the black liquid in her teacup before setting the now empty pot on the stove. "Should I make more coffee?"

"No. Would it be so terrible if you were taken care of for once?" He folded his arms across his chest and looked at her and then looked quickly away as if the wall had suddenly sprouted horns.

If she were her sister, she would expect to be taken care of, but she was Mary, the one who took care of everyone else. That was what everyone valued her for. She sat down and tried to appreciate his efforts to make her comfortable and instead felt robbed of the one thing she was good at.

"Your bath water was too hot, but it should be comfortable by the time you're done eating."

He was very nearly acting as if he was her personal servant, and she couldn't explain why it made her uneasy. He seemed to be studiously avoiding looking at her. Would there be a resumption of his caresses and kisses after she ate, after her bath? She rather felt he was imposing a number of artificial delays.

She searched her mind for suitable subjects of conversation. "I'll put an advertisement in the newspaper for servants as soon as I have clothes to wear."

Sterling rested his hands behind his head and stared up at the ceiling. Mary lay beside him with her back to him. He wasn't sure if she was asleep yet, although they both should have been dreaming hours ago. He vowed he wouldn't touch her until she was settled into the marriage. When she was in the bath he slipped into the room and changed out of his clothes into one of the nightshirts he hated. After that he'd stayed downstairs for a long time, staring at the pages of a book and turning them every now and then.

Mary had padded down the stairs on her bare feet after her bath and peeked in, but he had pretended not to notice her.

He knew he could pull her into his arms, and she would submit. The thought tempted him, but she had fainted. As much as she blamed her corset, part of it had to be shock at what he was doing to her.

He wanted her to want him, to need him, to love him. And how likely was that, he asked himself. He hadn't even hoped for love when he asked Suzanna to marry him. Hadn't hoped for it, because there was no earthly reason he should expect more than duty.

His wealth had bought him a good wife of acceptable family, and he knew to want more was to tempt fate. Even if Mary did think she loved him, one hint of the man he'd been as Silver John would have her despising him forever.

But when he had been kissing her and filling his hands with her full curves he'd tasted a pleasure beyond the physical, beyond earthly desire. Oh, Lord he'd given her his heart.

As he stared at the ceiling he cursed the dreams of his lonely childhood that had bid him to strive for the fancy carriage and the fancy house just to learn the only thing he really wanted was this woman to love him. He knew the cruelest emotion to an orphan was hope.

And she was eager to fill the house with servants so they would never again be alone together.

Mary had spent the week following her marriage with practical matters. Only practical matters, like hiring an upstairs and downstairs maids, a groundskeeper, a scullery maid, and making sure the cook had menus and a schedule to follow. She'd discussed budgets and additional purchases for the household with Sterling, but there had been no more passion. No kisses, no touches, not even so much as an interested look from him.

In fact, he hardly looked at her at all. Well, except the one time he caught her with her hair down and unbraided and he'd stood staring as if mesmerized for a moment or two, but then when she touched his shoulder that night in bed, he'd gotten up and gone downstairs and slept on the floor.

She didn't know what to do. She couldn't make herself over as pretty as Suzanna.

Sterling was as considerate as ever. He treated her much the same as he had treated her when she was to be his sister-in-law. But she felt shut out, shunned, held separate when she should be growing closer to him. She missed her father's absent-minded pats on the head. She missed Suzanna's twirling around the room full of empty chatter. She missed feeling needed.

Her days were empty, and a newly wed woman wasn't expected to entertain visitors, even if her husband spent long hours working. On a whim, she took a trip to the church and asked the minister where one would take an orphan in Boston. Recruiting a friend for companion, she traveled to the orphanage near the docks. Her friend found the squalor of the living conditions too much to bear and was waiting in the carriage.

Children with dirty faces, tattered clothes, and runny noses stared at Mary as she walked through the dormitory where the children were housed four and five to a bed with little regard for age. The little ones surely suffered for space.

A chubby woman with few teeth and a bulbous red nose named Mrs. Crump led Mary through the cramped and sour-smelling building. Mary could understand only about every other word the woman uttered.

"What do they eat?"

"Gruel, for they mornin' meal, round 'bout ten so. Gets a bowl o' soup and a bit o' bread for supper."

"And for dinner?"

"Don't get no dinner, just gruel and soup."

Many of the children didn't look as if they had

more than skin on their bones, and they had the gray look of sailors returning from long voyages without enough fruits and vegetables.

"Do you remember Sterling John Cooper?"

"Ah, little Johnny Cooper, he was a rascally one. Pretty child, could always steal himself silly. People trusted those purty eyes o' his. He stole so much the fences started calling him Silver John."

"He was a thief?" Mary tried to keep her voice neutral.

"Thief and worse. Fair near killed a man, then took off for Spain or some such. 'Spect the law was after him. Why you ask about him?"

Mary needed time to absorb this. Sterling was a good man, an honest man, she'd stake her life on it. "I'm married to him."

The woman put her hand on her chest and reared back. "Lord almighty."

"Are the children schooled?"

"You married Silver John?"

She'd have to wait on answers to settle this woman's curiosity. "Are there any records of his parents?"

"Oh, no, child. None of them what's left here like he was have a mother worth having. No better than she ought to be."

"Are you saying his mother was a . . . prostitute?"

"Well, I ain't saying that for sure, but she weren't no salt of the earth like as not."

"Do you know who she was?"

"No, I might o' had a guess back then, but that was a long time ago."

"You must have been a very young woman then." Mrs. Crump looked pleased.

"Now, do the children have proper schooling?"

The woman shook her head. "Ever now an' again some women come down and try to learn the children, but they are wicked wild. The minister comes and reads the Bible to them twice a week, though. Most of the healthy ones get apprenticed. Silver, now, he ran away from every apprenticeship got for him."

"Destined for better things," said Mary. Did he realize back then? Or was he just fighting to survive this horrid place. "How many people work here?"

"Me an' Mrs. Potter are regular like. There's a few others what come and go. You can leave money for the care o' the children."

There were at least forty children that Mary saw. "Thank you for showing me around, Mrs. Crump."

She left without ceremony and before Mrs. Crump asked again for money that Mary wasn't sure would make it past the liquor cabinet. This place needed more than money. How had Sterling survived a beginning like this?

"You went where?" Sterling shoved back his plate on the dinner table and stood so quickly his chair tumbled backward. Shock and fear coursed madly through his blood. How could she have gone there?

Mary folded her napkin and placed it beside her plate. "I went to the orphanage where you were raised."

Sterling ran his fingers through his hair. His heart was pounding. His Mary had seen that . . . that place? How could she sit down and eat a meal with him after seeing the filth and squalor where he'd lived? "Why would you do that?"

She met his eyes squarely. "I want to improve conditions for the children. Organize a society to reform the orphanage."

He paced down the length of the dining room. He felt cut open, raw, and exposed. "No, stay away from that place. You didn't give them money, did you?"

Desperation clawed at his throat. What did she think of him now? If he had scared her before. . . .

"I didn't think money would make it to the children. I suspect Mrs. Crump is too fond of strong drink."

"Is that wicked woman still there?" Oh, God, what had Mrs. Crump said? Did she tell Mary about the bullwhip she kept in the cupboard?

"The children need better food and education."

"It won't help."

"Sterling, you came from there. How can you just ignore the conditions?"

"I've been trying to put that place behind me my whole life."

She stood and rang the bell for the maid to clear away their plates. "Then you shouldn't have come back to Boston."

Sterling stormed out of the room before he threw a plate. He paced the darkened parlor, but Mary didn't follow him in. He shouldn't have reacted so strongly. He sank down onto the sofa and buried his face in his hands. He was lost. How could he ever gain Mary's admiration if she knew his past?

Truth was, he knew nothing about how to gain her trust. He feared if he touched her, kissed her, he would not be able to stop. And he wouldn't know if she was frightened or repulsed unless she fainted again. He didn't know anything about how to live in this world with a woman who had been sheltered from earthly pleasures.

If he had married Suzanna, he never would have worried about it. He never would have cared if Suzanna loved him.

Mary didn't know what to do. She had angered Sterling, and she hadn't meant to. She just wanted to know and understand him. But now that she had seen the conditions of the orphanage she couldn't turn her back on the orphans.

She was tired of spending her nights in a bed inches from Sterling, yet not touching him. Afraid to touch him. She wanted him to kiss her again, but he didn't. She no longer wanted to torture herself with the idea that she should be tall and slim and blond like her sister.

As she readied herself for bed she told herself it was time to admit failure. She had caught Sterling in a moment when he was vulnerable and persuaded him to enter a marriage he clearly didn't want. At least not with her.

In the morning she would tell him that she wanted a divorce.

She folded back the quilt to the foot of the bed; the summer night was too warm to need it. A slight breeze from the open window served to keep the heat from becoming unbearable.

Mary slid between the sheets she had sewn with loving care. She wondered if Sterling would come to bed at all. He would undress in the dark with his back to her, long after she had climbed up the bed stairs. Then he would be out of the bed before she woke in the morning.

Only as she lay still into the night, she suspected

sleep would elude her. She knew almost as soon as she offered herself as substitute for her sister that it was wrong to ignore everyone else's wishes to steal what she wanted.

And as Sterling must have learned, stealing didn't gain the thief what was really needed. There must have been a point when he turned away from a life of crime and relied on his own hard work to get ahead in life. He must have learned that the things worth having, like love and respect, were gained more often by giving than by taking.

She sighed and turned on her side. She pretended to sleep as Sterling tiptoed into the room. He had removed his shoes in the hallway outside their bedroom. Either he was very considerate, or he really didn't want her to waken.

Mary didn't move and kept her breathing steady and even. He settled into the bed, lying flat on his back, his hands behind his head. She must have dozed at some point because she woke in the darkest part of the night.

She could hear Sterling breathing, regular and deep. She turned to her side and studied his silhouette. He was such an admirable man. The conditions of his youth broke her heart. She wished she could comfort him, take care of the rough and tumble youth who had fought to survive when others were beaten by the deplorable hand they had been dealt.

She, who had lived a soft, pampered life, could only admire the strength of his will that had made him triumph over the harsh reality he had been faced with. She wanted to take care of him, pamper and spoil him, but living in close proximity to him in the last week, she had learned he was uncomfortable with her efforts to take care of him. He was more at ease turning the tables and taking care of her.

She leaned up on an elbow. This would be the last night she spent in bed with him. She would return to her father's home tomorrow. There was no point in staying. She had spent the evening packing her trunks.

She wished he could have given her his heart. A wave of longing and despair swept over her. Tentatively, she reached out and laid her palm on his chest. Her hand encountered warm skin and light springy hair.

Goodness!

Because of the warmth of the night, he must have taken off his nightshirt. She knew he didn't like them, but he had worn one faithfully every night of their marriage. She flattened her hand against his skin, then traced her fingers up the thick line of his collarbone, enjoying the solid warmth and feel of his chest.

What she wouldn't have given if he could love her. But the very thing others valued her for, her caring and compassion, was the trait that made him uncomfortable.

Still, she wished things had been different, but just for a moment, in the darkness she wanted to pretend things were all right, that her husband would allow her to soothe and cherish the child in his heart who had experienced nothing of kindness and love. She leaned over and brushed a kiss on his shoulder closest to her. She started to pull back, but found Sterling had lowered his arm around her. His hand rested between her shoulder blades. Was he awake?

Her heart began to beat frantically. Had his breathing changed? The silence of the night bore down on her as she realized her own breathing had changed, was faster.

He brought his hand to the back of her head and urged her to rest against his shoulder. She felt awkward and uncertain.

"I'm sorry. I didn't know you were awake."

"I'll pretend to be asleep. Don't stop," he said.

His voice was low and sleep-burred, and it stirred her in a way she couldn't explain. She wanted to hear his voice more, to explore its effect on her, and she had no idea what she was doing. Was he awake enough to know it was her? Did she care?

A tug on her scalp made her realize he was loosening her braid.

"You have beautiful hair," he murmured before pressing a kiss to her forehead.

Then he lifted her hand to his mouth and pressed a kiss in her palm and another on the inside of her wrist. With his arm around her back he pulled her tighter against his side. "Mary, are you going to pass out on me?"

"No. Of course not." She wasn't wearing her corset.

"Good. Because I don't think I can pretend to be asleep."

He tilted her chin up and kissed her. His fingers stroked along her neck, and she closed her eyes and held on. His bare skin under her fingers enthralled her, and she explored the delineation of the hard muscles of his back. His body was so different from hers, strong and firm where she was soft and pliable.

He kissed her throat and stroked her back. She savored the feel of him, his weight pressing her into the mattress. His kisses made her blood grow thick, and her bones turned liquid. She waited for him to touch her breasts, yet he seemed maddeningly interested in avoiding what she wanted. She arched up against him wanting . . . wanting . . . more.

She whimpered.

"Are you scared?" he whispered against her throat.

She threaded her fingers in his hair. To be honest, fear was part of the emotional concoction coursing through her mind, but so was the hope that this wouldn't end. Holding his head she found his mouth in the darkness. "A little," she whispered against his lips. "But I trust you."

He nudged her legs apart with his knee and settled his lower body against hers, supplying a pressure that was intriguing and subtly rhythmic as if they were about to engage in some primitive dance.

As she stroked him, exploring the indentation of his spine, she felt a sheen of perspiration coating his back. She pressed her lips to his shoulder, tasting salty skin. And he caressed her in places that hungered for his touch.

His kisses deepened, and she could no longer think, just feel a building thirst that only he could quench. She sensed the same urgency burning in him, heating his skin, roughening his breath and in his low moans. "Mary, I have to light the lamp. I have to see you."

A drop of doubt clouded her roaring senses, but he wasn't waiting for her permission. He'd leaned to the side and lit the lamp on the table beside the bed. He trimmed back the wick until only a soft glow lit the room. Then she realized that he wouldn't want the light if he wanted to pretend she was another woman.

When he turned back to her, his deep blue eyes were dark and heavy-lidded. In no time at all he shoved off his drawers and unbuttoned her night-gown. As he peeled back the material he scattered kisses over her exposed skin. She clenched her eyes shut as the last of her clothing was stripped away.

He stroked her hair and spoke softly to her in a mix of encouragement, commands, and compliments. Sweet nothings, she supposed. Then he was touching her in that most private of places, urging her legs apart. His fingers found a rhythm that made her feel as if she was coming apart. Pressure built, and she clawed at him until she shattered.

She whimpered, and he stroked her and held her and urged her to open her eyes. When she did he pressed forward with a new nudging force at her very center. Then with a tearing thrust he was inside her, part of her, and it felt as if she had been waiting her whole life for this joining to happen.

She held him tight as their hearts beat together. In this moment united with him, she felt love and boundless hope in her heart. And she had been so close to walking away from the marriage, from him and this wonder she had no idea existed before this night.

Sterling couldn't believe it when Mary touched and kissed his chest, but he ran with it. He could do no less. His beautiful wife's response to him was every-thing he could have asked for, everything he dreamed about, and he never wanted this moment to end.

His heart pounded, and he wrapped his hands in her long dark hair. For the first time in his life he felt as if he was home in her arms. She held him tightly as he found heaven.

He brushed a kiss on her nose and cradled her close. He rolled to his back, taking her with him, and pulled the sheet over her lush body. He didn't want to crush her; he didn't want her to grow cold; he didn't want to ever let her go. Yet, as he leaned up to put out the lamp, he saw what he had missed before in his haste to make love to his wife.

He rolled her off of him and swung his feet to the floor.

Her trunks and bandboxes sat beside the door. The lid of one full trunk stood open. He glanced at the dressing table and most of her toiletries and her box of hair ribbons and jewelry were not on the surface.

It could mean only one thing. His chest hurt. If a sledge hammer had been slammed into his chest, it couldn't have hurt worse. "You are abandoning me?"

Seven

That Sterling classified her defection as abandonment made Mary still deep inside. She caught a glimpse of uncertainty in him. Odd, he always seemed secure, sure of himself.

She pushed herself up to a sitting position, against the headboard. Sterling sat on the edge of the bed, leaning forward. He looked defeated.

"I thought you might want a divorce," she said. "I packed to move back to my father's house."

"After what you witnessed, I shouldn't be surprised." He rubbed the heel of his hand against his forehead. "I won't stop you."

The words shocked her. Was this how little she meant to him? How little did he value the pure bliss they'd just shared?

"I don't understand." The words choked her.

He shrugged. "If you want a divorce, I won't stand in your way."

He reached for his drawers and pulled them on. Then he stood up.

Mary grabbed the waistband and pulled him back on the bed. She was almost shocked at her aggressiveness. She wouldn't let him make nothing of what had passed between them. She might have been innocent, but that earth-shattering experience reached into her and touched her soul. That wouldn't have happened unless . . . unless there was more to it than lust and physical gratification. Unless there was love. "I don't think a divorce would be appropriate now."

He didn't look at her. "We'll wait a month or two and make sure there are no consequences."

Consequences? Was that how he described a baby? "I want consequences. I thought you wanted consequences."

"Mary, let go."

"No." Had she erred in not displaying the depth of her feelings for him? She had been so afraid he didn't really want *her*.

Heavens, her strength was taking care of people because she loved them, but she had held back with him for fear he didn't want or need her.

She wrapped her arms around his shoulders. The press of her bare breasts against his back deluged her with residual echoes of the pleasure she had just shared. "I thought you didn't want to be married to me, because you hadn't touched me or kissed me since our wedding night."

"You passed out."

"My corset was too tight."

"I know I scared you. It was all too much for you to take in. I wanted to give you time to get used to me."

Had he been afraid of scaring her with his passion? How could he have thought that when he was so tender and gentle? If she had known all she had to do was convey her willingness to make love, she would have made a move much sooner.

Suddenly she understood. Just as her own doubts had almost lead her to make the worst mistake of her life, he had his own demons. After what had happened to him in the orphanage, could he accept love as his due? Learning to exist in an environment where no one wanted him, no one valued him, no one took care of him, and he had been left, most likely abandoned by his mother, All this must have left him hopeless and distrustful of love. She should have known better.

"I want to talk," she said.

"What is the point?"

"The point is you don't understand me and I'm not sure I understand you." But he needed to know she believed in him, she trusted him, and she loved him. "Tell me about the orphanage."

"Mary, I put that behind me."

"I know that place is a hell hole. I know that you did whatever you needed to do to survive. Only a strong, indomitable spirit like yours could have emerged a decent man. I know that in spite of what Mrs. Crump says there is more to the story of the man you nearly killed."

He winced. "Mary."

"Tell me what happened." She knew she was taking a chance. There might not be an honorable explanation, but she believed there was. A person didn't become honorable overnight. The seeds of goodness had to be there before the transformation. "You don't let me care for you. I want to understand who you are and why you are."

"I beat a man who hurt a girl I knew. Only by the grace of God did he survive. I didn't mean him to. Satisfied?"

"Yes, I knew there would be a good, honorable explanation."

Sterling snorted. "There is no honor in attempting to murder a man."

"You were protecting a female. That is honorable."

"Yeah. She repaid me by finding a protector the next day."

Mary heard the part he didn't say. He'd been abandoned again. She pressed her lips against his shoulder. "Did you love her very much?"

"No, but I thought I did. I was too young to know what love is."

Did he know now? Did he recognize it? Or had his early life so deprived him that he didn't see love when it was right in front of him. "Then you do realize, I love you."

"Mary, you don't have to say that."

"I know, I don't, but I have this enormous honest streak. I thought you were in love with my sister. I thought I more or less tricked you into marrying me. I couldn't bear the idea of being married to a man I loved when he looked at me and saw a mistake."

He finally turned to face her. His forehead was furled in concern. "I was fond of Suzanna, but the glimmers of traits I saw in her paled into nothing but poor imitations of your strengths. I knew I wanted you as my wife, almost the first minute I saw you. But I was engaged to her, and she had done nothing to violate our agreement."

He had been trapped by honor into a proposal he didn't want to carry through with. Mary released her doubts to the winds. All her misconceptions didn't matter anymore. They could make this marriage work. His very tender lovemaking spoke volumes. He did care about her. He did want her, just as she wanted him.

"I felt hopeless as if I could never have what I wanted. I have been holding my feelings for you inside so long I thought it would crush me," she said. She had been trapped, too, by the idea that she could never have the future of her dreams. Too much had happened that made her think it wasn't possible.

"I thought I just wanted to be part of a family like yours. I thought that the most I could hope for was to be part of a family that held together no matter what. Oh, God, Mary, I love you. Please stay, I'll do anything."

"Then you must let me love you."

He touched his forehead to hers. "How could you, when you've seen where I came from."

"How could I not, when I know what a kind, gentle, and honorable man you are? The adversities you must have overcome only strike admiration in me."

"You are deluded," he whispered.

"Deliriously. Even if you are a thief."

He froze. She pulled him down on top of her and pressed her lips to his. She couldn't let him suffer too long. "You stole my heart."

He grinned, his deep dimples charming her and warming her. "I used to beg for bowls of bread and milk. Then I would steal the spoons. I got real good at filching sterling silver. That's how I got my name. I was incorrigible."

"You were terribly bad. There should be terrible consequences," she said in mock seriousness. Then she kissed him. "Could we make some little consequences now?" She reached between them and untied the string on his drawers.

He pushed her hand away and drew the sheet up over her. He smoothed the satin border with silver leaves across her shoulders. "Not now, you'll be sore. You made these sheets, didn't you?"

She nodded with a rueful smile.

"Always taking care of everyone." He shook his head.

"Yes, and you will have to understand that I must take care of those children at the orphanage."

"I know," he said with such pained resignation she grinned.

While cradling his face in her hands, she said, "But I'll always take care of you, if you'll let me." Then she stretched her arms over her head and inched the sheet down with her toes. "But I confess, I really like it when you take care of me."

With the darkening in his lowered eyes, she knew it wouldn't take too much more persuasion to get him to stop worrying about making her sore. He pulled the satin border over her breasts in a way that she had never anticipated in all those months of sewing painfully perfect stitches.

While watching his blue eyes darken, she wriggled her toes, inching the sheet back down. With the wisdom borne of Eve, she knew that this was one area in which he would accept her love. And in time he would come to understand he was safe with her. She would never abandon him. Their toughest battle might be getting him to believe that love was possible for him.

But she believed once again, with love, all things were possible.